To Have Faith

BOOK 3 OF THE
MEN OF THE SPRAWLING A RANCH SERIES

BY

ANNA ALEXANDER

http://annaalexander.net/

Newsletter
http://eepurl.com/Q0tsz

House of Rosenorn
To Have Faith

ISBN:9780990595557
ALL RIGHTS RESERVED

To Have Faith Copyright © 2015 Anna Alexander
Print Edition

Edited by Gwen Hayes. Copy Edit by Eilis Flynn
Cover design by April Rickard with Dewpoint Studios
Cover photography by Kim Killion with Hot Damn Designs

Book publication August 2015

Ben Castillo was every woman's fantasy. More precisely, Faith O'Leary's fantasy. Tall, broad, and oh-so handsome, he had a deep voice, and big hands, and the best part of all – he was just as kinky as the rumors suggested. Even kinkier. When he agreed to help Faith explore her submissive nature, she mistakenly thought her biggest obstacle would be in getting Ben to believe her when she said she wasn't going to walk away after his tutelage was over. Instead she finds herself facing the scorn of their conservative community when it's discovered that their relationship also included time spent with his cute roommate Colby.

Ben was convinced his time with Faith was limited, and she'd move on to someone closer to her own age and settle down once she had her fun. The vicious gossip going around town is a sign for him to walk away from the woman he's come to love, but Colby thinks Ben's a fool, and will do whatever he can to ensure a happy ending. For all of them.

DEDICATION

Para mi familia. Siempre.

Find Anna Online

Website

http://annaalexander.net/

Facebook

www.facebook.com/pages/Anna-Alexander/282170065189471

Twitter

twitter.com/AnnaWriter

Newsletter

http://eepurl.com/Q0tsz

Chapter One

BEN CASTILLO HAD seen a lot of odd things in his forty-two years of life, but the sight outside of the Mission Barber Shop ranked right up there as one of the strangest.

Nestled between the bait and tackle shop and Mindy's Diner, the little one-chair storefront was a hole in the wall open four days a week to help keep the men of Mission well groomed. The ladies of the town felt more at home at Shirley's Cut and Curl across the square, where they indulged in nail treatments and other tortures that women endured to impress their fellas. To avoid being labeled politically incorrect, George O'Leary said women were welcome to sit in his chair if they wanted a quick buzz with the clippers, or a nice close shave. Needless to say, he never had any takers.

Yep, the barber shop specialized in the good, old-fashioned nice and tight haircut for fifteen dollars a head that had you out the door in under twenty minutes, just how Ben liked it. Every six weeks, he'd head into town and stop at the feed store to pick up the ranch's supplies before heading over to the barber's to have his ears lowered. If it wasn't for his four-thirty standing appointment, Barbara Sue at the Bingham feed store would want to talk his ear off for hours about the local town gossip, not that

Ben was one who enjoyed listening to the rag mill. He suspected Barbara Sue had a crush on him and used any excuse to detain him. So as not to encourage her affections, he was careful to keep his speech polite and not too friendly. She was a sweet woman, but a little too vanilla for his tastes.

In his opinion, the entire town of Mission was on the vanilla side. Located almost plunk in the middle of Washington State, Mission was a sleepy little hamlet. An all-American agricultural town and the unofficial capital of gingham and pickup trucks, and where schedules were worked around church socials and football. The last bit of excitement occurred four months prior when Gabriella's ex-husband kidnapped her from the parking lot of The Crescent Moon tavern and beat the crap out of Ben's fellow ranch hand, Jack. Gabriella's boyfriend and brother took after them right quick and were fortunate enough to have her home within two days' time.

With the trial having just wrapped up and the defendants found guilty and sentenced to not enough jail time, in Ben's opinion, the local chitchat had died down and life was returning back to its lazy way.

At least he thought it was.

A group of about six men stood outside the lone window of the barber shop, and he could see another two men inside. For a moment, he thought there might be an emergency, but the men appeared jovial, and there wasn't an ambulance or police vehicle in sight.

"Hey, Travis." He stepped up on the sidewalk and called out to the closest man. "What's going on?"

Travis Maguire glanced at him from over his shoulder and nodded in greeting. "Howdy, Ben. Haven't you heard?"

"Obviously not. Is George all right?"

"Yes and no," he said with a chuckle. "Last weekend,

George was helping us during roundup, like he does every time we're ready to sell off the cattle. Well, ol' George got caught between some heifers and the cattle guard. In the melee, he shattered his ankle."

"Ooo." Ben winced in sympathy. "Sounds painful."

"Looked painful. But you know George, refused medical attention until my dad threatened to withhold his pay. Now George is down at Valley with a few pins in his ankle. Doc said they'll let him go home when he can hobble around on crutches without falling on his ass."

"That's a damn shame," Ben said with a shake of his head. "I don't think I've seen George sit still for longer than two minutes in my life."

"Yeah. I heard he's giving the nurses hell and they're itching to kick him out sooner rather than later."

Ben chuckled and nodded at the crowd. "Then what's all this about here?"

Travis's smile widened. "Faith moved to Yakima about a month ago. She's come home to take care of the shop while her dad's out of commission."

When several seconds of nothing more was said, Ben raised his brow. "That's it? Faith's home?"

The other man laughed while rocking back on his heels. "When was the last time you saw Faith?"

He drew in a breath and looked up at the sky in thought. "Can't say. Been awhile. Probably before she graduated high school and left for the city."

"Shoot, man. That was over ten years ago." He shook his head. "No wonder. Well, let's just say Faith grew up to be a mighty fine-looking woman. Yes, sir. Mighty fine."

A good-looking woman was the reason for this crowd of observers? Seriously? Sure, Mission was a small town, but it wasn't so small that a beautiful woman was considered an anomaly. There were lots, okay, a few pretty girls in town. Young girls, who were jonesing to skip town for greener pastures as soon as they were old enough.

Old enough. If that wasn't a twisted thought. If he was thinking of college-age girls as potential dating material, then maybe Faith's presence was unusual enough to cause a stir.

Ben gestured again to the crowd. "So y'all are just hanging out, staring at the poor girl through the window?"

"Not all of us. Those she's been able to squeeze in for an appointment are still hanging around, and the others are waiting to see if her 4:30 shows or cancels."

"Sorry to disappoint you, then." Ben grinned. "I'm the 4:30."

Travis's smile fell. "You? Aw, hell."

Those close enough to overhear also grumbled their displeasure and stepped to the side as Ben strode to the door with a tip of the hat to those he passed. A bell chimed and blended sweetly with melodic female laughter inside as he pushed open the door. Three more gentlemen lined the wall or sat in the few chairs provided, but it was a flash of red-orange that caught his attention and made his breath catch.

A redhead. Now why didn't he remember Faith was a redhead? Actually, there was very little he could reconcile of the woman laughing at Ned Peterson's corny joke and the girl he remembered.

Of course, he was a good twelve years older than her, so it wasn't as if they had traveled in the same social circles. He did remember her being on the skinny side, with long strawberry-blonde hair and glasses. And drama. He recalled George talking about her being in the school plays and heading off to the city to work in the theater industry doing hair and makeup.

City living certainly had agreed with her, because the cute

little girl had blossomed into a certified, prime cut, gorgeous woman. Faith O'Leary had rounded out in all of the right places, with an hourglass figure accentuated by a brown suede skirt belted around her slim waist. Matching suede boots hugged her calves and drew attention to the bare length of leg under the skirt's short hem.

And that hair. Soft waves of copper that fell just past her shoulders. She had the kind of hair that made a man want to run his fingers through the strands while he held her head and…well, do all sorts of dirty things to that sweet mouth of hers.

Damn. What was it about redheads that made him stop in his tracks and his blood rush from his big head to the littler head? He'd been with many women of all hair colors, but it was always the redheads he remembered long after the sheets had cooled.

Look at him. What a disgrace. Two seconds in her presence and he was already thinking perverted thoughts. He was no better than the horny buggers outside.

As his cheeks heated with shame, he gently closed the door behind him and became aware that all conversation stopped the moment he entered. He looked up and met a gaze so blue the irises of her eyes almost appeared to be neon.

"Good afternoon," she greeted with a soft smile.

"Ma'am," he replied with a tip of his head. His naturally deep voice rasped even more than usual as he added, "I'm Ben. I have an appointment."

The light in her eyes brightened, as did her smile. "Oh, yes. I remember you. Mr. Peterson and I are almost finished. I'd say have a seat, but it's kinda crazy in here today. I'll be just a moment."

"Take your time." He shuffled over to the stand Faith's

father used as a reception desk and leaned on the top with his elbow.

An appointment book lay open near his arm, and he noticed the long list of names in the ledger. The poor girl had been working nonstop since ten that morning with not even a break for lunch. Friday's schedule was shaping up to be just as busy, with every slot filled.

"All done, Mr. Peterson," Faith said and removed the cape from around Ned's neck. "Don't go too far. I need to brush you off."

"Is that what she calls it?" Jorge Garcia snickered under his breath by Ben's side.

The peanut gallery whispered amongst themselves as Faith took a fat sable brush and whisked the tiny hairs off Ned's neck and shoulders. Her movements were quick and professional, but by the way the men leered, one would have thought she was doing a striptease.

"There you go." She set the brush down and reached for a broom resting against the opposite wall.

"Thanks, Faith." Ned stood and reached for his wallet. "What do I owe you?"

"Same as my dad charges. Fifteen dollars."

"Oh, you're worth more than fifteen, honey. Your dad isn't half as entertaining as you are. And you have a gentle hand with those clippers." He pulled out a ten and a twenty-dollar bill from his wallet and held them out to her.

She waved his offering away. "That's too much. My dad would die if he knew you gave me such a generous tip."

"Are you planning on telling him?" The older man chuckled.

"No." Her answering laughter danced over Ben's skin like the glide of a feather. "But you'll say something in your monthly poker games. I've known you too long, Mr. Peterson. You two love to give each other a hard time."

"It's so much fun." He pushed the bills against her palm. "Take it. You're a good kid."

With a shake of her head, she accepted the money. "Thank you, sir."

Ben sucked in a breath and bit the inside of his cheek. The muscles in his arm jerked with the need to swipe his hand over his face as he strove to maintain a neutral expression. It wasn't the girl's fault he got off on hearing women addressing others with labels of respect.

Shit. He had to get a grip on his libido. Sure, it had been a while since he had some serious playtime with a woman, but he wasn't that hard up. Okay. Maybe he was. It had been a long, long time since he'd made the trek across the mountains to his favorite club in the city, but at his age, the trip for a bit of kink just seemed so...so incredibly sad. He was too old for a casual fling, and too set in his ways to settle for a relationship where he felt as if he had to hide the man he was inside. It was a decision he had come to terms with years ago, and the arrival of a beautiful woman wasn't going to send him on a hormone-fueled rampage like an animal. He had more self-control than that.

"Excuse me. Ben?"

The sound of his name on her lips was like a bolt of electricity, and he jumped where he stood. Nice control there, buddy. "Yes?"

"You're my last appointment of the day. If you don't mind waiting a few more minutes, let me schedule the gentlemen waiting outside for appointments, and then we can begin."

"Sure." He paused to clear his suddenly tight throat. "No problem."

Her smile widened. "Thanks. I'll be quick."

While Faith went outside to take care of the crew of admirers, Ben took a moment to snap out of the cloud of arousal. The allure was dark and mysterious while at the same time ripe with potential danger.

He did a double take as he noticed the trio in the shop hadn't moved from their perches. "Were you fellas waiting on something?"

Jorge smiled with a nod as the others followed suit. "Yup."

A rolling sensation in his belly warned him against asking for any more details, but he was compelled to say, "I hope y'all are treating Faith with the respect due to a lady."

"Shoot, Ben." Jorge slapped his hat on his knee. "We're just having a little fun. The girl knows we're harmless."

"That may be. But she's here to help out her father. Not become fodder for your dirty, old-man fantasies."

"Old man." Jorge sniffed. "You're not that much younger than me, Castillo."

"And yet I'm not leering at her like an immature schoolboy."

"Now that's the magic word right there." Jorge elbowed his crony, Teddy Martinez, who snickered. "Yet."

Ben pursed his lips, refusing to argue with the man who clearly thought he was doing nothing wrong. Jorge's boys-will-be-boys mentality wasn't going to change instantly over a few words of warning. The best course of action was to lead by example and make sure Faith was able to close up shop without any unwanted attention.

Not that he thought any of the men would be out to cause the girl harm. But after what happened with Gabriella and her ass of an ex-husband, all of the men on the Sprawling A Ranch were hypersensitive when it came to the safety of women.

"Whew," Faith said as she entered the shop with the appointment book clutched to her chest. "You'd think these men hadn't had haircuts in forever. Thank you for waiting, Ben. Here, let me hang up your coat and hat."

"Sure." He shrugged out of his denim jacket and handed her his Stetson, then crossed the few feet to the barber's chair.

"Oh, go ahead and sit by the sink first," Faith said.

"The sink?" He glanced to where she gestured and blinked in confusion as he stared at the low-slung sink attached to the wall. How long had that been there?

"Yes. The sink." She smiled and whipped open a maroon cape. "So I can shampoo your hair."

"Shampoo?" he repeated as if he were a parrot with a learning disability.

She giggled, but in no way did the sound resemble anything child-like. "Yes. Shampoo. I need to shampoo your hair. Or as you may say, I need to wash your hair."

"Oh." He shifted his weight and glanced back at the sink, noticing that the chair in front of it had a release on the side to lower the back. "George usually just squirts some water on my head and we're good to go."

The cutest little frown appeared on her forehead. "So I've heard. Well, I like to give my customers the full treatment. Have a seat. I promise, you'll enjoy it," she said with a wink.

And that there was the problem. He was afraid he'd enjoy it a little too much.

To protest any further would probably stir up a bigger fuss than he intended, so he ignored the chuckles from the other men and took the offered seat.

"Don't you all have somewhere else to be?" he asked.

"Not at the moment," Daniel Gomez answered. "Besides, we like hearing Faith's stories of being in the theater."

"I wasn't *in* the theater," Faith corrected as she draped the cape over Ben's chest and secured the plastic around his neck. "I worked *for* the theater. There is a difference."

Ben scowled at the looky-loos as Faith turned to rummage on the shelf behind him. As if those farmers had any interest in the theater. They wouldn't know the difference between intermission and a curtain call.

"Just lie back and relax," Faith said as she lowered the back of the chair.

Well hell. He sighed and closed his eyes.

At least his brain sent the signal to close his eyes, but his eyelids weren't listening. Nope, his gaze shot right to Faith's silk-covered breasts hovering just a few inches from his nose. A roar started in his ears that could have been the sound of the water rushing through the hose as she adjusted the temperature of the stream, but he knew it was his blood pounding through his veins to settle below his belt.

"How's that?" she asked as a warm spray of water cascaded over his head. "Too hot?"

"Nope," he rasped. "It's fine."

As she leaned forward to begin washing his hair, her blouse gaped open, revealing the luscious curve of her breasts encased in a lacy white bra. Restraining a groan, he averted his gaze and spotted the three goobers watching Faith shimmy.

Those dirty old bastards—oh… Faith sank her hands into his hair and began to manipulate her fingers in deep circles. *That's nice.*

His eyes closed as he bit back a moan, falling under the sensual spell of digging fingertips and the light scrape of her nails against his scalp. The shampoo she used smelled clean, fresh, not like some of that overly floral stuff geared toward women. Underneath the fragrance was Faith's sweet scent. From working so hard all day, she had developed a sexy musky fragrance of womanly perspiration that made him think of tangled sheets and screaming orgasms.

Damn. For all of the times he'd played in a dungeon, and all of the kinky shit he'd seen and done, never before had he grown so hard so fast. Not only that, but the desire that swept over him didn't carry the pounding urge to claim and conquer, plunge and pillage. No, this was a warm layer of sensuality that caressed and teased. Soothed and tempted with a gentle suction that slowly pulled him into a cozy cavern he could gladly hibernate in for days.

Something soft and warm brushed his cheek, and he struggled to lift his eyelids. Faith's breasts bobbed alluringly above him. All he'd need to do was turn his head a fraction of an inch, open his mouth, and that pretty little nipple beading against her blouse would be between his lips.

Criminy. He dug his fingers into his thighs and fought to restrain his raging libido. The poor girl was just doing her job. The last thing she needed was to have a randy middle-aged man as her last customer of the day.

Thank God, he almost shouted as she started the water and rinsed the soap from his hair. Another second of her massage and he'd be ready to cum in his jeans, and he hadn't done that since he was a teenager.

The moment she shut off the water, he started to sit up.

"Not yet," she said and pushed on his shoulders. "We're not done yet."

"Wha-huh?" he asked so articulately.

"We're not done." She smiled. "You know. Lather, rinse, repeat."

Fuck it all to hell. With a clenched jaw, and his fingers threatening to carve permanent impressions into his legs, he endured another go-round of Faith's devilish touch while trying not to fixate on all of the ways he could have her bound and begging for his possession.

He had learned long ago that small-town girls weren't quite cut out for the type of bed sports he liked to play. Oh, a few talked a good game, but the moment the flat of his hand came down on their rounded backside, they'd holler "uncle" and call the whole thing off.

He didn't blame them for the change of heart. In his opinion, there were two types of women in Mission: Those who were of the knees locked together, save themselves for marriage, blush at the slightest suggestive comment kind, and those who flirted with any man who owned a vehicle and had the means to take them away to what they thought was a "better" life.

Of course, there were the few women that didn't fit into either category, but Ben had yet to find one who was his match both in the bedroom and out. And it wasn't as if he could be obvious in his search either. Mission was as small town and conservative as they came.

But Faith. Oh...

Faith looked like one of those liquor-filled chocolates. Sweet and innocent on the outside but filled with sin on the inside.

Or maybe he just wished she was filled with sin. If she was, he'd feel a little bit better about spinning his twisted fantasies, but not by much. George was a regular at church, and would probably flay Ben to the bone if he knew Ben was picturing his little girl dressed in a corset with a rope binding her hands together.

"Now we'll just finish up with the conditioner, and you'll be ready for your cut," she said.

Sweet baby Jesus.

When she was finally, *finally*, done rubbing his head, he sat up, slightly sweaty and with his vision blurring in and out.

"How are you feeling?" she asked as she toweled the water from his hair.

"Fine," he rasped. In the mirror's reflection, he saw a dazed-looking man with a slash of red across his cheeks. "That was, uh, different."

"Huh-hm." Jorge hummed from his chair.

Damn, he forgot they had an audience. Good thing he had the cape to cover his erection and hide the way his knees shook as he stumbled the three feet to the chair. He fell into the seat a little harder than he preferred, but at least he didn't fall on his ass.

Faith fluttered around him, toweling off her hands and gathering her clippers and a comb. "You come in pretty regularly, right, Ben? So am I just giving you a trim, or are you looking for something different?"

"Trim will do." He cleared his throat and blinked hard to dissipate the last of the lust swirling in his brain. "Nothing fancy. Nice and tight will do just fine."

Fuck. He winced as the chortles erupted from the men. He was so going to hell.

With the mirror before him, he had a prime view of the red flush rushing up his neck and enflaming his cheeks. He pressed his lips together and willed the butterflies in his gut to still. If he tried to correct himself now, he was only going to embarrass himself further.

Faith said nothing in response. Her beautiful smile never faltered, but a wicked gleam did flash in her eyes as she ran her fingers through his hair. "You have great hair. I could play with these thick strands all day."

Jorge's chuckles turned into a choked gasp as Ben fought a smile. Yep. Hell was most certainly in his future. Apparently, the powers that be felt today was the day to test him.

"I heard your dad's in the hospital. How's he doing?" he asked, hoping the mention of her father would get all of their minds out of the gutter.

"You know my dad. He thinks he's indestructible, but it looks like he'll need some sort of physical therapy to minimize the limp he's going to have and take the pressure off his hips." She flicked on the clippers and his skin vibrated as she rested the moving blades against the comb she laid on his scalp. "I've told him he doesn't need to work so hard at the Maguires' ranch. They have enough hands as it is, but ever since their son was killed in action, he feels that, as Scott's godfather, he needs to be there and fill the hole of his presence. Provide some entertainment. I don't mean he needs to stop helping out, but he doesn't need to do so much of the physical labor."

"Your father is a good man, Faith," Teddy chimed in and folded his arms over his chest and shifted in his seat. "But stubborn as all get out. You tell him he can't and he'll work that much harder to prove he can."

"I know." She chuckled and leaned closer to her work. "I'll just have to use my daughterly charm and get him to see things my way."

As the men joined her in laughter, Ben released the smile he could no longer hide and sat back and watched Faith in the mirror as she worked the clippers with deft flicks of her wrists.

Passion bled from her every motion. From the way she laughed, to how she answered her enthralled audience as they asked her about her adventures touring with a theater company. Again, Ben couldn't help but imagine what all of that passion would look like, feel like, beneath him. Kneeling at his feet.

Before he knew it, Faith set the clippers and comb down on the counter and was reaching for the Velcro clasp of the cape. He quickly folded his hands over his groin before she whisked the cape away and shook the black hairs to the floor.

"Let me sweep up real quick. I don't want your boots to slip in the hair. It's slipperier than you'd think."

"No problem." He turned away from the men and concentrated on willing down his erection before he had to stand.

The brush of sable against the back of his neck made his eyes fly open with a drawn breath. Faith flicked the soft bristles with quick little movements over his skin.

"Close your eyes," she whispered near his ear and a shiver tripped down his spine.

She ran the brush over his forehead, down his nose, and over his cheeks. He folded his fingers into a fist to stop himself from latching on to her wrist and dragging that brush to other parts of his body that ached for her attention.

"I think that's it," she murmured.

When he opened his eyes, he met her soft and sexy blue gaze as her lower lip jutted out in a little pout. She ran her thumb in a line above his brow, and his breath hitched.

How long did they stay that way, staring into each other's eyes as electricity arced between them? Minutes? Mere seconds?

When his lungs threatened to burst from holding his breath, she stepped back. "All finished. You're as handsome as ever."

It wasn't the first time he'd been complimented on his looks, but it pleased him to know she found him attractive. Fat lot of good that was going to do him.

He mumbled a thanks and stood, reaching into his back pocket for his wallet and retrieving all of the bills inside. He held them out to her, not bothering to look at what was in his hand. "This is all I've got."

Her smile widened, and she took two tens and gave him back the rest. "This is plenty."

She turned and crossed to the reception desk as he collected his coat and shrugged it on before setting his hat back on his head.

"Why don't you start locking up? I'll walk you to your car," he offered. No way was he going to leave her alone with her admirers.

"I can walk you to your car, Faith," Jorge piped up, followed by the others.

"Oh, that's sweet, but I don't want to keep you all longer than necessary. Besides, it doesn't take me that long to close up."

"Take as long as you need. I'm in no rush."

"Neither am I," Jorge said.

"Me neither," Teddy began and was interrupted by the ringing of his phone. He looked down at the display and swore. "Shoot. Deborah's bunco game has been over for twenty minutes. Forgot I was supposed to pick her up." He jumped to his feet and tipped his hat to them all. "It was good catching up with you, Faith. I'll be in for that shave later in the week."

"See you then, Mr. Martinez." She waved and began picking up the damp towels and wiping down her station. "If you fellas insist, let me toss these into the hamper and I'll be just a few minutes."

Ben nodded, and as soon as she disappeared into the backroom, he turned his stony gaze at Jorge and Daniel.

"Don't give me that look, Castillo." Daniel stood and copied Ben's stance. "We're just enjoying the pretty girl's company. But I saw the way you were looking at her." He shook his head. "You should be ashamed of yourself. You're old enough to be her father."

"I am not." Uncle, maybe, but definitely not father. "And I wasn't looking at her with anything other than polite interest. She's lived quite the life."

By the way Daniel's lip curled, Ben guessed he wasn't buying his line.

"Okay, fellas. Let me get my bag." She slipped on a tan-colored trench coat she'd brought with her from the back room and belted it around her waist. Then she gathered her purse and a blue banker's bag. "All set."

Ben ushered the others out of the shop before him and waited by her side as she locked the door. "I'm parked in the diner's parking lot just over there."

She led the way, and Ben frowned as he realized that if not for the men, she might have been walking alone with her entire day's take tucked under her arm. It wasn't as if Mission was a hotbed of crime, but to do so just wasn't safe.

He sidled a little closer and made sure his body was between the bag and the view of any passing bystander.

"This is me," she said and stopped beside a small SUV. She opened the driver's side door and tossed her bags into the passenger's seat. "Thanks for walking me out."

"Our pleasure," Daniel said and took the hand she held out. Instead of shaking her hand like a gentleman, he pulled her into a hug, releasing her the moment the older man met Ben's disapproving glare. He stepped back quickly. "Have a good night, darling."

"Take care, Faith." Jorge behaved a bit more respectfully and shook her offered hand.

When she turned toward Ben, his heart rate kicked up. "Will I see you again in six weeks, Ben?"

He stared at her hand, debating the intelligence of feeling her palm against his. *Fuck it.* One handshake wasn't going to bring him to his knees.

The moment their hands met, sparks raced up his arm and that swirl of need formed in his belly. He wanted to feel more of her soft flesh. Taste her skin. Hear her sweet voice lower to a throaty moan.

He should tell her no. He should say he had other plans that were going to delay his routine and he'd wait until her father returned.

"Yep. You'll see me."

Her fingers tightened around his, and she smiled in that way women do when they get what they've been longing for but would never ask for themselves.

"Good. See you then." She stepped back to climb into her car. A moment later she was waving at them through the window and driving off into the sunset.

As her taillights faded into the distance, Ben sighed.

It was official. His ticket to hell was punched, and he was boarding the train.

Chapter Two

"OKAY, CAL. YOU'RE all set." Faith whipped the cape off the flirty farmhand's shoulders and tossed it into the nearby hamper. "That'll be fifteen dollars."

"I've got a better offer." He straightened to his full six-two height and brushed the hair off his arms then settled his fingers around his belt buckle. "How about fifteen dollars and dinner with me tonight?" He wiggled his brows as if they would sway her decision to his favor.

"Oh…sorry, Cal. I already have plans tonight." Which she didn't, but he didn't need to know that.

He slid to the right, blocking her way as she moved to wipe down her station. "Tomorrow then, or this Saturday. Baby, I'm willing to fit you in my schedule."

Well. Wasn't she a lucky girl.

Cal Brotherton wasn't the first client to ask her out as some men misinterpreted her friendliness as flirtation, especially once she inhabited their personal space.

Had she ever been tempted to say yes to a client before? A few times. Was she tempted now? No.

Now, Cal was a good-looking man with a thick set of blond waves and a dimpled chin, but he was too much into his self-proclaimed prowess with the female sex. Just because he drove a '78 Corvette and owned his own home did not make him God's gift to women.

And if you asked her, he was too stuck in the past and his glory days on the high school football team. Peaking at eighteen was not an attractive trait, in her opinion. But the biggest reason for her refusal was that Cal was not the man whose hot and steamy presence in her dreams kept her up at night.

No. That man was due to walk through the door any minute, and she needed to get Cal and his you're-supposed-to-fall-at-my-feet smile on his way.

She raised her brows and blinked in what she hoped was surprised innocence. "Are you asking me out on a date, Cal?"

"Of course." He snorted with laughter. "What else did you think I meant by dinner?"

The question was what did *he* think it meant, and instinct warned her she already had a good idea. "I thought you wanted to have dinner as friends. But I can't go on a date with you. I'm…seeing someone."

"You are? Since when? Johnny Travers said you were single."

"What? I barely know Johnny. What would make him say that? And to you?"

"John's my friend. He told me his girlfriend Emily is friends with Teddy Martinez's daughter Elena who heard him talking to her mother about how you were single, and they both thought it was crazy that some man hadn't snatched you up, married, and bred you already."

Ah. Now she understood.

So in small-town speak, the Mission grapevine was in full effect and the general population still believed it was 1950 and women were only fit to be wives and mothers. And her father had wondered why she'd been so eager to head out to greener pastures when she graduated from high school.

"Yeah. Well." How best to tell him thanks but no effing way without losing his business? She turned up the wattage on her smile. "It's a new relationship, but I really like him and hope he may be 'the one.'" She crossed her fingers on both hands and raised them to frame her face.

"Well, shoot, Faith." He looped his thumbs in his belt loops. "Do I even have a shot?"

"Sorry. I'm a one-man woman. I guess the stars weren't aligned for us." Her gaze flicked to the clock. 4:25. She had to get him out of there. Now. "But I'm flattered you asked. Again, that will be fifteen dollars."

With her hand on his shoulder, she guided him to the door. At this point, she couldn't have cared less if he paid her, she just needed him gone.

"Here you go." He handed her a couple of bills, then set his baseball cap over his freshly cut hair. "If it doesn't work out with this guy, give me a call. Okay, babe?"

"Sure." She flashed him a plastic smile. "You got it."

"All right." He leaned down and brushed a kiss to her cheek. "Later."

"Right. Later." She practically sprained her eyeballs as she tried to resist rolling them. "Thanks. Have a good night."

The second the door closed behind him, she was off to her station to run a brush through her hair and apply a fresh layer of tinted lip gloss. Reaching into her bra, she adjusted her boobs until she had the perfect cleavage, then smoothed the bright blue T-shirt over her belly. Did she have time to powder her nose?

The bell over the door rang and she looked up, gasping as she caught sight of his reflection in the mirror. She spun around and had to hold on to the edge of the counter to keep from melting into a puddle on the floor.

Ben Castillo. Dear lord, was he good looking.

The man wasn't just tall, dark, and handsome. He was sex on a stick. No, he was sex on a stick dipped in caramel, then chocolate and rolled in sprinkles.

When she was younger, she had been aware of the young man who was the embodiment of every cowboy, bad-boy fantasy a girl of thirteen could have when exposed to too much cable television and romance novels. But he was so much older than she was, and of course, never paid any mind to the young girl with braces and pigtails who tried so hard to find a reason to stop by the barber shop during his appointments.

But that was then and now, well, she wasn't a little girl anymore. The moment he had walked into the shop six weeks earlier, all of those old fantasies had slammed into her like a runaway train and were a thousand times naughtier. Poor Ned Peterson never knew just how close he had come to getting a Mohawk that afternoon.

The crush she had carried as a girl for the older boy with dark wavy hair and a gaze that made her believe he was hungry for that illusive, intangible something had now morphed into a near obsession to find out if the rumors she had heard, but had been too young to understand at the time, were true.

Please let them be true.

"Good afternoon, Faith," he rumbled in his deep bass.

Holy cow. His voice alone could make her orgasm. She locked her knees and hoped drool wasn't dripping down her chin. "Good afternoon, Ben. It's nice to see you again."

He nodded and his gaze searched the room. "George is still out of commission, then?"

"It's tax season and he's been doing a lot of traveling, so I volunteered to help him out a day or two a week to take the stress off his leg." Making certain one of those days was Ben's day.

"He sure does get around."

"Those few months of extra work help supplement his income for the year. And he loves talking to his neighbors, which is the entire county."

"Yep, George is a popular guy," he agreed with a small grin then glanced around the room again. "Are we alone then?"

"My last client just left. So it's just you and me."

A frown creased his brow. "Is that safe? I don't think I like the idea of you here on your own. Especially when you're locking up and carrying the cash drop."

"It's not the best situation, but it's not as if we have the money to pay for security or an armored car pickup. And I'm careful."

The frown didn't ease. "I'll follow you to the bank tonight after you close up. I know that's not gonna help for the future, but I'd feel better knowing you're somewhat safe tonight."

Honey, you can follow me every night.

"Thank you. I appreciate your concern," she said instead. "Why don't you take off your coat and have a seat by the sink?"

He paused with his jacket hanging off one shoulder. Before she had a chance to ask him if there was something wrong, he finished removing his coat. "Right. The sink," he said with trepidation.

"Don't you like having someone else shampoo your hair? Most people find it to be quite decadent."

"I bet they do," he murmured and hung his coat and hat on the peg by the door.

Oh my word.

She swallowed a giggle and bit her lip. The man's shoulders were so wide, how did he fit through the doorway? He was muscles packed on muscles, but not in that competitive bodybuilder way that tended to creep her out, but in a tough, manly man's way that made her want to drape herself over his broad back and feel the play of his muscles against her body.

Get a grip. You are not a teenager. You are a grown woman who has been intimate with many—okay, a few—men. Be sophisticated, not obnoxious.

Right. Be cool.

To hide the telltale tremor of her hands, she busied herself by readying a few towels and the cape. As he took his seat at the sink, she stole a moment to drink in the spicy scent of his aftershave. He was so tall that even while seated, his head reached her at shoulder level with only a few scant inches parting them. For 4:30 in the afternoon, his cheeks were surprisingly smooth.

Had he shaved, just for her? The possibility that he might have gone to the extra effort before meeting with her ignited a tendril of delight that was like being dipped in a vat of champagne with all of those sweet bubbles.

On the other hand, there was the possibility he had a date right after his appointment and the smooth cheeks were for some other woman. Oh man, that would suck.

"So. How's your day?" She fastened the cape around his neck and hoped the tremor in her voice was only in her imagination. "Planning on relaxing later, or do you have to rush right back to work?"

Smooth. Very smooth.

"It's been busy. Mr. Rivera sold the thousand acres bordering the A to Trey a few weeks ago, so we've been out there moving fence line and planting seed. And birthing season isn't too far off, but you don't want to hear about boring ranch work."

Maybe not, but she loved the sound of his voice, and he didn't answer her question. "Does that mean I have to hurry so you can head back to work?"

His dark gaze met hers as she lowered the back of his chair and guided his neck into the curve of the sink. "No. I don't have to hurry back."

"Oh. Good." She licked at her dry lips and felt another flare of excitement as his eyes tracked the movement. "Why don't you close your eyes and relax."

With a small grunt, Ben closed his eyes but tension held his shoulders stiff, almost as if he were holding his breath.

Faith held the hose to the bottom of the sink and adjusted the temperature of the water. It took only seconds to find the desired temperature, but she held back and gazed at his handsome face.

Dark brows framed his eyes and those long lashes only men seemed to have and women paid through the nose to obtain. He had high cheekbones and a nice square jaw, but it was his firm lips that held her attention and dared her to lean down and press a kiss to the line to see if they'd soften with her touch.

Actually, she wanted to do a whole lot more than press her lips to his. Like smother him with her breasts, or climb into his lap and grind against the ridge of manhood she couldn't help but notice made his jeans fit oh so tightly. Oh yeah, another rumor amongst the women of Mission was that Ben's stature wasn't the only thing large about him.

Yeah, maybe she needed to turn the water to cold and hose herself down. At this rate she'd be lucky to hold the clippers steady, let alone give him a decent haircut.

With a shake of her head, she concentrated on wetting his hair without losing control of the hose, then set about running her fingers through his thick locks and massaging his scalp. She loved his hair. It was so lush and dark with a touch of gray at the temples that gave him a distinguished look, at least from the neck up. The rest of his body was way more rough and tumble, ride 'em hard, than polished and professional.

"How does that feel? Nice?" she asked, loving the way his lips parted and his head lolled in her hands as if he turned into putty.

"Real nice." His eyes opened a bit to peer up at her. "Your father never washed my hair. In fact, I didn't even realize this sink existed until the last time I was here."

"Yeah, my dad is a minimalist when it comes to indulging his customers. My philosophy is treat the customers extra special, and they'll come back every time."

"Judging by the heard of customers I've heard you've had come through the door every week, you're succeeding."

"Well, I think part of that was plain ol' curiosity. I see my dad all of the time, but it's not like I hang out in Mission. And this town does thrive on the local gossip."

He grunted again, whether in agreement or differing opinion she wasn't certain, nor did it matter as he fell under the power of her touch. But as much as she wanted to linger over massaging his head, he might start to suspect the shampoo was more of an excuse to get her hands on him than to make his hair clean.

After a good rinse and a repeat, she placed a towel over his hair and sopped up the excess water. "Let's get you settled in the chair now."

"All right."

He swayed a bit as he stood and made his way to the chair without incident. He wouldn't have been the first man to stumble after one of her bone-melting shampoos.

She gathered the clippers and a comb. "Nice and tight, right?"

He sputtered with a laugh. "Right," he replied with a quirk of his lips.

They both jumped as she flicked on the clippers with a loud *clack*. She clenched her teeth against a grin as the vibration ran up her arm and the weight of the little machine in her hand reminded her of an oversized vibrator. Just what she needed to help get her mind off of sex. Not.

"So." Perhaps a little small talk would keep her on track. "Melody Webber called me last week all excited because her brother Mark and his fiancée decided to go to Vegas in a few weeks and elope instead of having their wedding out here. Melody is quite the fashionista, and to dress up in Sin City is her idea of heaven."

Ben chuckled. "Mark might regret that plan when they get down there and he has to keep an eye on his bride *and* his baby sister."

"I'm sure you'll be willing to help him out."

"I'm not going."

She paused mid-clip. "You're not? How come?"

"Someone has to feed the cattle. Adam and I volunteered to stay behind."

"Well, that was very nice of you."

"Adam doesn't like to fly, and he can't run the ranch on his own, even for a few days." He shrugged. "Besides, I don't mind. They all deserve to have some time off and have a little fun. I'm sure they'll bring back plenty of photos."

"I know it will be a lovely wedding, even for Las Vegas." She bit her lip and snuck a glance at his reflection as she said, "I can't remember if you're married or not." Snort. Such a lie. "Are you?"

His brows jumped. "Nope. Never been."

"Ever been close?"

"Nope."

"Why not?"

His gaze dropped to the floor. "I figured if I ever was to get married, I was only gonna do it once, so the girl better be the right one. Never found the girl who fit me."

"I can understand that. But I'm sure you haven't been lacking for women who want to fit you. What about your current girlfriend?" Was her snooping subtle enough?

The corner of his lips ticked up, and when his gaze met hers in the mirror, a light danced in the brown depths. "I don't have a girlfriend. Haven't had one in a long time."

Yes. "Seriously? I don't believe that. A handsome man like you must have his phone ringing off the hook. You have a lot to offer a woman, Ben."

"You think so?"

"I know so." She dug her fingers into his hair and trailed them around his ear to caress his neck. "You're strong, kind, loyal, and as I said before, handsomer than a man has any right to be."

"How do you know I'm all of those things?" he asked with an amused quirk of the brow.

"My dad talks about you some. And Barbara Sue at the feed store adores you, amongst many others. People like you, Ben. Word gets around."

Beneath the cape his shoulders tensed. "What else have you heard about me?"

"Oh, a little of this, a little of that." With a sly smile, she sauntered around the chair and began to trim the hair over his ears. "All of it *very* intriguing."

His response was a low rumbling grunt, but she sensed a shift in demeanor. She noted a slight softening of his posture as his knees fell open a bit and a contemplative expression stole over his features.

Her fingers tightened around the comb as a flurry of nerves swirled up from her belly to tickle her tonsils. Could he hear the frantic beat of her heart? Had she shown her hand too fast?

Seducing men was never one of her strong suits. In the beauty industry, appearance was important. And in the entertainment world it was *everything*.

While she made sure her hair was styled and her makeup applied to best flatter her features, she was well aware she was not supermodel beautiful and more on the goofy side than sophisticated. All too often men passed her over for the size-two model or the show's top billed actress. The competition was exhausting.

Ugh. The fact that she even thought of attracting a man's attention as a competition was enough to make her ambivalent about the entire dating scene. But she was human, after all. She wanted to belong to someone. Share their day, and their bed. The few men she had gone out with were nice enough, but that was the problem. They were nice. They lacked aggression, and she wanted aggressive. Not asshole, but aggressive. She wanted, needed, someone to crave her, hold her as if he never wanted to let her go.

While she was dating, she often felt as if the lives her previous boyfriends led would be no different whether she was a part of it or not. What she wanted was a man who hungered for her. When she walked into a room, she wanted a man who would be ravenous to take her and extract every ounce of pleasure her body could provide. A little over the top? Maybe. But this was her wish, after all. And for some reason, she suspected Ben Castillo was that kind of man.

If she didn't turn into a major dork and scare him off.

"I don't see a ring on your finger, Faith," he finally said just as she was about to think she'd either gone too far, or not far enough. "Are you stringing your boyfriend along before you say yes?"

"First of all, I don't string anyone along. And second, I don't have a boyfriend."

"Now that I don't believe. You have most of the single men of Mission, and some of the married ones too, lined up outside this shop, hoping you look their way. I know there must be at least ten more men you have on speed dial waiting to heed your beck and call."

"You're crazy. I've never had men lined up outside my door."

"What about the last time I was here? It was standing room only."

"That was just people wanting to know about my dad," she said with a wave. She set her equipment on the counter and reached for the closure on the cape. "Don't go anywhere until I sweep up first."

"Sweetness, those men couldn't have cared less about your dad. They were here to watch the way your breasts shimmy when you wash someone's hair."

Was that the first move? A statement like that crossed the line. Well, at least touched the line. To hear him talk about her breasts in his low rumble made the muscles of her thighs clench and her skin tingle. She dropped the cape in the hamper and turned to find him staring at her with desire in his dark gaze.

Her throat tightened as she forced the words out. "Were you watching my breasts, Ben?"

His Adam's apple bobbed with a hard swallow as he kept her gaze. "It's kind of hard not to when they're hovering right over my nose."

"Do you like them?" she whispered and pulled her shoulders

back to lift her breasts another enticing inch.

If gazes had teeth, his would have been taking a bite out of her breasts as he stared at her chest and the nipples that were pebbled so hard, they felt as if they were trying to burst through the lace of her bra.

The line of his lips firmed as a muscle leapt in his jaw. His fingers curled over the arms of the chair before he gave his head a little shake. "Little girl, you don't know what you're doing."

"What do you think I'm doing? And I'm not a little girl. I'm thirty. I've been around the block a few times."

"Have you?" He rose to his feet, all six-foot-four of him, and towered over her. The little shop shrunk even more around them as he filled every corner with his sex appeal. "I think you're trying to entice an older, stronger man to have his way with you."

So he had been picking up on her vibe.

If he had appeared angry or disinterested in any way, she'd lie and tell him he was imagining things. But if that light in his eyes was what she hoped it was, now was not the time to back down. "As I said before, I find you very intriguing."

His brow furrowed. "What do you want, Faith?"

Ooo. Her gut tightened. That's it. Just cut right to the chase.

She drew in a breath, hoping to hell she didn't pass out from the nerves, and voiced her secret wish. "I want you to teach me what you know."

He stilled and then cocked his head to the side. "Know about what?" he asked slowly.

"About being a submissive."

He sucked a breath in through his teeth and rocked back on his heels. "What makes you say that? What have you heard?"

She licked at her lips. "That cattle aren't the only thing you rope. That you're a Dom."

Chapter Three

B EN'S KNEES THREATENED to buckle, and for a second, he was tempted to fall back into the chair in order to catch his breath.

There she was. Little Faith O'Leary. Standing before him in her pretty blue shirt and black mini-skirt, asking him to teach her how to be submissive. This had to be a dream.

But damn him, he wanted this to be real. He wanted her to be his. He wanted her on her knees with her mouth parted, ready to take his cock down her throat.

Fuck him to hell and back. What was he thinking? Faith deserved more than to be treated with such objectification. She deserved to be romanced, to be laid on a mattress with soft music, candlelight, and have sweet nothings whispered in her ear. With him, she'd get a hardwood floor, the bite of leather around her wrists, and filthy commands growled against her breasts.

Now that wasn't to say a little down and dirty was a bad thing. Sure, he'd met his fair share of women who craved the darker passions like him, but Faith wasn't one of them. She was too pure to be depraved.

But didn't she make a tempting morsel, offering herself up

to the devil with her big blue eyes, full pouty lips, and those pretty nipples straining against the fabric of her shirt, practically begging him to latch on and make her cry out in pleasure.

No. No. No. He blinked hard against the rush of desire that hardened his muscles and then some. He wouldn't take what she thought she was willing to give.

As he opened his mouth to tell her she was misinformed about whatever gossip the rumor mill had churned out, her shoulders slumped, and a tinge of pink raced up her neck as her lips trembled in what looked like embarrassment.

Silly girl. If there was one thing he was certain of, it was that a woman should never be embarrassed to ask for more, especially when it came to their sexuality. It was a struggle he heard many of his female friends in the BDSM community deliberate over and over again. For centuries women had been fighting the ideology that if they were meek in the bedroom, they were prudes, but if they demanded sexual fulfillment, they were whores. What the world needed to understand was they were human beings who deserved satisfaction just like their fellow men.

Faith had every right to take control of her sexuality. He just didn't think he was the best person to guide her on her journey.

He swiped his hand over his face and sighed. "I'm more of a top than a Dom."

A soft gasp parted her lips and the sparkle returned to her eyes. "Will you explain the difference?"

He sighed again and felt his throat grow tight. Where to begin?

"Every person is different," he said. "Dom and sub. For me, I like to be in control. I like to manipulate my partner's body and pleasure to my liking, but I don't have the need to break a sub down to their essence. I don't need control over every little thing, and I don't need a slave. I like to play. That's about it," he finished with a lift of his shoulders.

"I want to play too. Or at least experience being under someone's control like that."

Good lord, she was making it mighty hard to refuse her request.

"Why?" he asked in a voice he didn't think could sound any more raw. "Why do you want to submit to me?"

Her gaze darted around the room, and he watched as her mind worked on an answer for several seconds. Collecting and voicing one's most intimate desires was not an easy task, especially to do so on the spot. He was willing to give her all of the time she needed.

"I don't know why, exactly. Or where this desire comes from," she began as she swayed on her feet. She ran a trembling hand through her hair and licked her lower lip. "I just know I want more. I want passion. I want to be held down and pushed to endure more than I thought I could stand. I want a man to tell me he wants me, how he wants me, and how I make him feel. With the few men I have been intimate with, I find myself wanting to scream at them to be rougher, to get a little nasty. But when I do, they look at me as if I'm dirty or weird." Concern wrinkled her brow. "I'm not weird, am I? I just want to let go. To feel. I'm hoping you're the one who can help me fly."

The rest of the room faded away until there was only this beautiful woman standing before him and baring her soul. It was, hands down, the sexiest thing he had ever witnessed in his life.

The honesty of her words, the passion, was like a drug he inhaled deep into his lungs and felt seep into his heated bloodstream. His fingers tingled, desperate to pull her against his body as his cock hardened to painful levels behind the fly of his jeans, ready to sink into her depths and deliver on every one of her wishes.

If only it were that easy.

"Faith. You deserve everything you want, and more. But I don't think I'm the man who can give it to you."

"Why not?"

"Well, I'm a lot older than you are. If word got out that we were seeing one another, it might be uncomfortable."

"For whom? Millicent Younger and Stephanie Dodson both married men who were twice their age and the town survived. Besides, you're not that much older than me. And that just means you have more experience."

She did have him there. "What's in it for me? I spend my time training you to be a good submissive, and then what? You'll take that knowledge and use it on some other man?"

"Oh." Her lashes fluttered and she placed her hand on her hip as she shifted her weight from one leg to the other. "I hadn't thought about that. Well, I don't really have an answer, except to say my wish for you to train me isn't because I want to use you. I like you, Ben. I've known you forever, and you're a good man. I trust you. If we were to, I don't know what to call it, embark on this adventure, maybe it will turn into something more. Maybe it won't. But whatever you teach me, I know I'll be grateful."

Did she not realize how much she was tempting the beast? The woman was making it harder and harder to say no.

"I'm a demanding SOB, Faith. I would never set out to harm you physically or emotionally, but you will experience highs and lows I'm guessing you never imagined. I will push you, I will strip you bare and take from you what *I* want. I'll leave bruises on your skin. Marks of my possession. I will ask you to do things you may think are degrading. Will I take away your choice to say no? Of course not, but I won't let you be a coward and run from your fears. What you are asking for is not something as mundane as dating. While we are together, your body and your pleasure will belong to me."

Tears filled her eyes and a tremble shook her that turned into a full-on shake. "That's exactly what I want," she said in a voice so full of need and want, he was about ready to shed a tear with her.

His fingers curled into his palms, the joints aching as he restrained the urge to grab her as a cloud of longing fogged his thinking.

One more out. He'd give her one more chance to back down. If she still wanted him to show her the way, he was going to take what he wanted and not give a damn about who, where, why, or what. She'd have her chance to walk away.

He took one step toward her. Then another. She held her ground, tilting her chin up to maintain eye contact as he invaded her personal space. Her breathing deepened as the rise and fall of her chest caused her breasts to brush his shirt with each inhale.

"Are you on birth control?"

She blinked in surprise then nodded. "Yes, sir."

Sweet mother of mercy, she knew just how to get to him. "What kind?"

"I have a shot every three months."

"Good. You see, there is a reason I haven't played in a while, Faith. I'm a greedy bastard. I want to take a woman every way you can imagine, and even some you can't. But it's gotta be with a woman I can trust. I'm done with condoms. When I fuck you, *if* I fuck you, it's gotta be bare. Nothing between us. But in order to do that, I need to make sure you're clean. I require a blood test and a clean bill of health from your doctor that also confirms you're on birth control. Without that, I won't even consider what you're asking."

Judging by the way the color drained from her cheeks and her eyes widened, he crossed the line.

Well, he figured if he was gonna push her, he'd push her hard. A girl would have to be pretty serious in her desires to go through the potentially embarrassing act of being tested for STDs and have her doctor write up a letter of recommendation. Whoever the doctor was, they were bound to catch on right away as to why a person would need such a letter. However, nothing said put up or shut up like being tested for a venereal disease.

Now the bit about why he wanted to forgo condoms was a bit of a stretch. It was true, they were an annoying necessity, and in the past he always insisted on wearing one, even with a doc's okay that his partner was clean, but at his age, if he was going to play, he wanted all or nothing. He wanted to mark his woman with not only the bite of his fingernails and teeth, but his sweat and cum as well. Cover her in his scent so she never doubted who controlled her pleasure.

To be possessed so completely might not be what Faith had in mind. At the moment, it was all he was willing to offer.

Faith's lashes fluttered as her body jerked as if she just regained consciousness. She swallowed hard. "What about you? Will I get a doctor's note confirming you're clean too?"

Holy hell. Did that mean she was seriously considering following through?

He barely managed to murmur, "Of course. It would only be fair."

She nodded. "Then I agree."

This time his knees did buckle, but he locked them in place before he fell on his ass.

An image flashed in his mind of Faith, naked, her red hair

falling in soft waves to cover her breasts, and in her hand was a ripe, juicy apple she held out to him in offering. Him. A man who had fasted for years and was ravenous for a bite of the sweet fruit.

He was so starved, in fact, he had to turn away and wipe the back of his hand against the corner of his mouth before he embarrassed himself any further.

So. The little girl wanted to play. Hell, then maybe the gentlemanly thing to do was to give her a little taste of what was to come before holding her to her agreement.

You sick bastard.

Yep. That was him.

The click of his boots as he marched across the tile floor to the shop's door beat in tandem to the panting of Faith's breath. The solid slide of the deadbolt in the lock made her posture snap straight. Her eyes widened as he lowered the window blind, giving them privacy from anyone who might pass by.

"Are we starting now?" she asked with a little squeak.

"Let's just call this an audition." He gave her his most wicked smile. "Scared yet?"

"Yes." She laughed. "But in a good way."

He'd see about that.

Drawing a breath in through his nose, he focused on slowing his racing heart and lassoing his boiling passion under control. He wanted to shake her up, not terrify the woman.

With a slow, deliberate slide of his hand, he made a great show of reaching for his throbbing erection trapped in his jeans and shifted the position of his shaft. Faith's eyes tracked the movement, and her lips parted with a sigh.

Yep. She was gonna be a firecracker, all right.

"Lift up your skirt," he said with a voice so low, it rumbled in his chest like gravel in a cement truck. "Show me what you've got on under there."

There was a fine tremor in her hands as she grasped the hem of her skirt and pulled the fabric up and over her hips, revealing the triangle of her black panties.

Click. Click. With each snap of his boots on the tile floor as he stepped closer, her shaking grew as he circled her like a panther teasing its prey. Without him having to give the instruction, she kept her gaze fixed forward like a good sub, but he noticed the muscles in her neck flex as if she were tempted to move her head to keep him in her sights.

He stopped in front of her, leaving scant inches between them. "Take off your panties."

Her breath came faster as she bent and slipped her underwear down her legs.

"Give them to me."

The fabric was warm against his palm as he curled his fingers into the damp cloth. He fastened his gaze on the little strip of red hair framing the lips of her sex and inhaled, drawing the musky scent of her desire into his lungs as a surge of power infused his muscles.

It had been so long since he had felt this drunk with power, so god-like with his ability to make this beautiful creature bow to his command. The rush was a drug, altering his mind until his only thought, his only need, was to make her scream under the onslaught of her orgasm.

He tucked her panties into his back pocket and nodded at the barber's chair. "Sit down. Put your feet on the seat near your butt. Spread your thighs real wide."

A fleeting look of shock flew across her face before she stepped to the chair and fell down hard onto the cushion. She leaned back and lifted her feet and set them next to her backside. The heels of her shoes dug little indentations into the upholstery.

"Look at you," he said as he stood behind the chair and gazed at her lewd reflection. He stepped on the pump, raising the chair until it was tall enough for him to bend slightly and reach around to grip the arms of the chair. Leaning forward, he murmured in her ear. "And here I thought you were a good girl, Faith. But you're nothing but a dirty little slut. Aren't you?"

"Yes, sir."

It took everything within him not to sink his teeth into the vulnerable length of her neck and growl with pleasure. "Take your fingers and open the lips of your pussy. Show me what you're giving me."

A weak moan escaped her lips as she moved her hands between her splayed thighs and rimmed the lips of her sex with the tip of her finger. In the light, her labia gleamed with her desire, her cream seeping out in preparation for his possession.

"That's pretty. You have a pretty pussy, Faith. I like it very much," he rumbled. "Slide your finger inside. I want to hear how wet you are."

"Oh, God," she moaned and slipped her finger into her sheath, working the digit in and out in a slow glide.

"Fuck, that's hot. Do your fingers feel good inside you?"

Her gaze jumped to his and her mouth worked up and down for a second before she stuttered, "Y—yes."

"You paused." He narrowed his gaze. "Why? Don't you like your fingers in your pussy?"

"I do. But—" she broke off and bit her lip.

"Tell me," he breathed into her ear. "Say the words."

"I'd—I'd like it more if it was your cock."

Fuck. He drew in a deep breath through his nose as his fingers tightened around the chrome and padding in a grip so punishing, he almost snapped the arms off the chair.

"Say it again. Tell me what you want, Faith."

The blue of her eyes shimmered with hunger as her fingers moved faster. "I want your cock. I want it inside me, hard and fast. I want your cock, and your fingers, and your tongue. I want it all."

He swallowed a groan and his dick felt ready to burst. She was going to kill him, and he hadn't even touched her yet.

"You'll have all of me and more, sweetness, including that orgasm you're on the verge of reaching." He stepped back and straightened to his full height. "But not tonight. Stop and show me how wet you've made your fingers."

With a strangled cry, she pulled her hand away from her shiny pussy and melted in the chair.

One would have thought he had fucked her hard, judging by the way she sat back with her limbs akimbo and sweat plastering her hair to her face as her chest heaved. Hell, even he didn't look so unaffected, with his cheeks flushed a rosy pink and his eyes wild with desire. Their reflection in the mirror was one of pure sex and debauchery. A scene he thought he would never be part of again.

If Faith wanted to be his submissive, done. Whatever she wanted, whatever she needed, he'd be the one to provide. Including her torture.

"The next time you come, it's gonna be while you're pinned beneath my body with me balls deep in your pussy. You do not come without my permission. Do you understand?"

"Yes, sir."

He reached out and latched onto her wrist, drawing her wet fingers to his mouth. It was insane to test his control in such a way, but he had to taste her. Had to consume her into his being so when he left that night, he'd carry her flavor on his tongue and know the entire event hadn't been a figment of his perverted imagination.

She tasted like honey fresh from the hive, savory and sticky sweet. He could only imagine how much better she'd taste by drinking straight from the source.

As he licked and nibbled on her fingers, Faith writhed and moaned in her seat, staring up at him as if he were the center of her universe. How hadn't any other man picked up on her need for kink? She was made to give and receive pleasure, and any man would be a lucky bastard to have her in his bed. Fortunately, he was going to be that lucky bastard, at least for as long as Faith would have him.

She'd learn her strengths. She'd learn her limits, and then she'd be ready for the man whom she could marry. Someone closer to her age who would be worthy to be the father of her children and provider for her family. Definitely not someone like him, whose own father was a drunk who skipped town when Ben was ten, and whose only experience with child rearing was raising himself and a couple thousand head of cattle.

Man, just the thought of his crappy childhood was more than effective to bring his mood down and gave him the strength to rein in his hungers. He had given her a task to complete in order to be his submissive. To jump the gun on their arrangement would damage his authority.

With a last flick of his tongue against her palm, he released her wrist. "Finish cleaning up and close up the shop. I'll wait for you outside and follow you to the bank. You get me that doctor's note and test results, and I'll give you further instructions. Are we clear?"

"Absolutely." As he shifted to turn, she reached behind her to latch on to the front of his shirt. "Ben. Thank you."

The gratitude in her eyes reached out and punched him in the gut. "Don't thank me yet, little girl. Just wait until I make you scream."

A wide smile curled her lips as she chuckled. "I'm looking forward to it."

You and me both, sweetness. You and me both.

Chapter Four

"**Y**OU'RE NOT GOING to pass out. You're not going to pass out. You're not going to pass out," Faith muttered and turned off the ignition of her car before she wiped her palms on her skirt. Of course, she'd have a better chance of staying conscious if she got control of her breathing. All of this chanting was making her light-headed.

In the two weeks since she'd last seen Ben, she'd been on an emotional roller coaster of nerves and excitement that she swore was turning her into a basket case. On the night he had flipped her ravenous slut switch, she had cried all the way home and for the next three hours straight thereafter.

Her tears hadn't been ones of sadness. Oh, no. The crying jag had been due to finally, *finally*, finding a man who saw who she was, acknowledged what she needed, and gave it to her wrapped up in a cowboy hat and a growling command.

With only the sound of his voice and the intensity of his stare, Ben had had her wound so tight, she had been ready to come with only the heat of his breath on her neck. Funny how having someone take away her control had made her feel both fractured yet settled at the same time.

And she knew she hadn't been the only one affected during

their encounter. For a moment there she had thought Ben was going to burst right out of his skin. All of the muscles in his arms had flexed and pulsed, and his features had tightened into a mask of primal need that had been the most erotic sight she had ever seen. To know he was ready to unleash all of that power on her...ah, she was almost desperate enough to shove her hands into a pair of boxing gloves and bind them behind her back to keep from touching herself. She had never been a slave to her sex organs, but the moment he said not to touch, that was all she had wanted to do. Now she was at the point where the slightest brush against her skin made her ready to scream and she'd swear anyone within a ten-foot radius could smell her arousal. It was almost embarrassing.

But not as embarrassing as it would be for her to faint the moment she stepped into his house. She had to pull herself together. Ben was a master. Used to dealing with women who probably had tons more experience and sophistication than she did. At the end of the night, she wanted to put all of those women to shame.

But first she had to get her ass out of the car.

The chirping of crickets and the bleat of a bullfrog were the only sounds echoing across the wide expanse of the Sprawling A Ranch. Except for where she stood in the golden glow cast by the front porch light, all was dark. The bunkhouse Ben shared with his roommate Colby was separated from the main buildings of the ranch by a stand of cedar trees. In the distance, she could make out an odd light or two of a barn or utility shed, but other than that, they could have been the only two people in the world. As it was, she knew they were about the only two at the ranch, with everyone else in Las Vegas for Mark and Gabriella's wedding. Adam was supposed to be helping Ben keep the ranch running in its owner's absence, but where he was at the moment,

Faith didn't know.

The notion was not lost on her that agreeing to meet a man way out in the middle of nowhere and allowing him to do who knows what with her was probably not the smartest move. And if it had been anyone but Ben making the request, she would have said no way. But she trusted him. More important, her father trusted Ben as well and had always spoken highly of him. Of course, her father would probably drop dead of a heart attack if he knew his daughter was meeting one of his most respected customers for kinky sex.

Funny, if this had been an ordinary date, she would have proudly told her father all about the man who captured her affections, but this was not a date, and she'd do best to remember that little detail. Otherwise, she might give in to the silly fantasy that she was already in love with Ben Castillo.

Sure, their arrangement might blossom into something a little more pedestrian like a normal boy/girl relationship, although the thought of Ben being likened to a boy was so laughable it hurt. She had to keep her perspective. Baby steps. Starting with step one. Knock on the door.

Right. Nothing was going to happen by standing on the man's front porch all night long.

She rapped her knuckles against the solid wood door and tried to focus on keeping her breath slow and steady. In. Out. In. Out.

The door swung open.

Her lungs froze.

Holy hell, was he gorgeous.

And so tall. And wide. He wore a green flannel shirt that he left unbuttoned to expose a wide stripe of his naked torso. The dips and valleys of his rippled abdomen and the dusting of hair on his chest enticed her fingers to come and play. There were so many muscles, and getting a peek at all of that flesh made her mouth dry and a shiver run down her back. The top button of his jeans was undone and his feet were bare, as if he were ready to get naked at any moment.

"Come on in." He gestured with an outstretched hand and stepped aside for her to enter. "Did you find the place okay?"

"Yes, I did. You gave good directions."

"Good. Good," he said with a nod. "Can I get you anything? Glass of water? Shot of whiskey?"

As if she could hold a glass without sloshing all over herself.

"No. I'm good. Thank you," she replied with a giggle tickling at her lips. She hadn't expected him to pounce on her the second he opened the door, but the polite offer of refreshments threw her for an unexpected loop.

You have got to calm down. Remember, sophisticated woman. Not backwoods hick.

Right. Easier said than done.

To distract her from her bout of nerves, she stepped deeper into the man cave.

A giant sectional facing a flat-screen TV blocked the entire front window. A set of stairs was on her left and before her was a short hallway to the kitchen. The room was clean, minimalist, without very many clues as to who the inhabitants of the house were, except for a trio of guitars resting on some stands in the corner, a floor-to-ceiling shelf of movies on DVD, and an assortment of video games and consoles stacked on the floor by the television.

"Are you a gamer?" she asked, nodding at the tower of video-game cases and controllers.

"Nah. All that belongs to Colby. I'll play every once in a while, but he likes those story games, and if you slow him down, he gets all twitchy."

"I've dated a few guys like that," she said with a laugh that promptly died as his smile faded and he stepped toward her with a predatory light in his eyes. The games were about to begin.

He held out his hand. "May I have your list?"

She reached into her purse and withdrew a set of papers. The ends fluttered as she handed them over with a nervous shudder.

"You can set your bag by the door. Then stand in the center of the room," he directed, then turned his gaze onto the papers.

Earlier that week he had sent her a list of varying practices she might be willing to engage in. Not a detail had been missed, as it listed everything from blindfolds to impact play. Some of the items she had to look up, which was quite an eye-opening experience. Blood play was exactly what it sounded like, and nauseated her just thinking about it. She had circled that as a definite "no" right off the bat. After looking at such a long list, she worried he might find her to be too vanilla and not ready to embark on the journey she asked him to take her on.

Once she placed her bag where he indicated, she took her position in the middle of the living room. With her legs slightly parted and her back straight, she clenched her fists against her thighs to keep them from trembling.

Ben circled her as he read down the list. Around and around he strode, not saying a word or making a sound beyond an occasional grunt or murmur. With each rotation, her breath came faster and faster until her head felt as if it were about to float away.

"So," he finally said. "You're a sugar kink girl."

"Is that bad?"

"There is no bad in kink, unless it involves animals and children. As long as you're honest in your desires and find someone who is like-minded, it's all good."

His gentle smile lessened a little of her anxiety. "What is 'sugar kink'?"

"It's just like it sounds. It means you like it nice and sweet."

Well, when he phrased it like that, it didn't sound so mundane.

He set the papers on the coffee table then held his arms open. "Come here, Faith."

With knees as shaky as a newborn colt's, she wobbled over to him and fell into his embrace. His arms were so warm and strong, she melted against him, burying her face into his chest and inhaling his manly scent. But even in the comforting shelter of his arms, her trembling grew into full-on shakes that made her teeth chatter.

"Are you that scared?" His bass rumbled under her ear as his big hands smoothed up and down her back.

"More nervous than scared." She hugged him tight around the waist. "I don't want to disappoint you."

"Ah, sweetness. I told you, as long as you're honest with me, I won't be disappointed. Don't forget, this goes both ways. I'm just as nervous as you. From what I've gathered, you've been wanting this for a long time. That's a lot of pressure to put on a man who wants to give you everything you need."

"You're doing a pretty good job of it so far." She tilted her head up to look into his dark eyes and laid her hand on his cheek. "Thank you, Ben."

"Don't thank me yet, darling." He turned his head to kiss the inside of her palm, sending sparks down her arms and to all of her feminine places. Soon he was going to have those lips all over her, and she couldn't wait. "Have you picked out a safe word?"

"How about 'shampoo'? Since you seem to like it when I wash your hair."

"I bet every man likes it when you get your hands on their head. The big and the small one." He chuckled and set her away from him. " 'Shampoo' it is. Now, take off your clothes. Start with your blouse, then your skirt. Show me what I get to play with tonight."

A sense of calm fell over her as his eyes glittered with hunger. Oh, she was still as jittery as ever, but now her shaking was caused by pure excitement and not anxiety that he would somehow find her lacking. Ben Castillo wanted *her*. And she was going to give him everything.

One by one, she slid the buttons of her blouse open then shrugged the caramel-colored silk from her shoulders. She folded the garment into a neat square and set it on the coffee table next to her list of desires, followed by her skirt. When she straightened, she was confronted with a horny male whose gaze feasted on every exposed inch of her body. The look on Ben's face was worth every penny of the two hundred dollars she had spent on new lingerie.

"You approve?" she asked and snaked her hands over her belly to cup her breasts.

"I think that's obvious," he replied as he reached for the thick bulge in his jeans and squeezed.

Finally, a man who wasn't afraid to be a little vulgar. To see a man in the prime of his virility be so blatantly sexual did it for her. Made her wet and achy and willing to fall on her knees in anticipation of what he was going to do next.

"The game is on now, Faith." He strode closer. "You will not speak unless asked a question. Unless it's your safe word, or you're in pain, the only sounds I want to hear from your lips are your cries of pleasure. You will call me 'sir,' or 'Ben.' Do you understand?"

"Yes, Ben."

He closed his eyes on a breath. "Do you know how hard it makes me hearing you say my name? How crazy I'll become when you scream my name when you come? I'm going to consume you, little girl."

God, she hoped so.

"Turn around. Place your hands on the mantel and close your eyes."

Here we go.

Beneath her palms, the wooden mantel was cool to the touch and just the right width to grip with her thumbs and fingers as she waited for Ben to make his next move. Perspiration gathered along her hairline and upper lips as she strained to listen to her surroundings.

"*Ack-ug!*" she swallowed a shout as his hand landed on her shoulder without warning.

"I got you, sweetness." His laugh buzzed her ear as he swept her hair off her neck. "You are so beautiful. Your skin is so creamy."

With both hands, he smoothed his rough palms down her arms to her wrists then back up again. Over and over, the steady glide traveled from her arms, across her shoulders and down her back. She so badly wanted to open her eyes and watch his big hands against her skin, but she bit her lip and kept them squeezed shut, determined not to fail his first set of instructions.

A gasp burst past her lips as he unclasped her bra and the cool air hit her puckered nipples. The rasp of the straps of her bra sliding down her arms made her shudder as Ben lifted one of her hands, then the other off the mantel, divesting her of the garment.

Those magic hands returned to trail down her belly, his fingers dipping into her belly button and toying with the edge of her panties before skimming down each thigh and back up again.

"Jesus." With his thumb he crushed the crotch of her panties, pushing them into her slit. "You're already wet. That is so sexy."

Wet? She'd been wet all week. What she felt now gathering between her thighs was a deluge. Well, maybe a deluge was an exaggeration, but she had never before been so wet. Her body was ready for his possession. More than ready. It was as if she was made for his touch alone and her girlie parts were screaming, "For the love of God, fuck me already!"

He peeled her panties down her legs and assisted her in stepping out of them. Would he keep these too? She had wondered if he had spent the week using the panties he had kept to jerk off with. Knowing he had possession of something that had been in such intimate contact with her body was another rush to add to the long list of ways Ben had kept her aroused since the last time he had touched her.

The rasp of a zipper caught her attention. A second later came the rustle of denim.

He was getting naked!

Bam! The shakes started back up as anticipation kicked up her adrenaline like a match set to tinder.

Heat exploded up her back as his hands settled over hers on the mantle and he pressed against her. The hot length of his cock fit into the channel of her spine, and she couldn't help but grind back in a silent plea for more.

"Now this is nice," he murmured then gently bit into the juncture of her neck. "You feel so good in my arms, Faith."

Touch me, she wanted to scream, but she bit her tongue and wiggled in his embrace.

"You want more, sweetness? Is that what you're trying to tell me?" The weight lifted off her hands.

He brushed the inside of her arm with his fingertips followed by a light glance circling her belly button. Another light caress ran down her thigh while he palmed her hip with his left hand. No touch lingered for longer than a second, constantly moving and teasing as she held back her moans.

"Ah!" she cried out as he popped her on the butt with the flat of his hand.

"You're holding back. Remember, your passion belongs to me. I earn your moans. I earn every tear. Give them to me."

"Please, Ben. Please," she pleaded. Her knees trembled so badly, she wasn't sure how she was even standing.

"I *am* pleasing you." He cupped both of her breasts in his big hands. "Your wet pussy and these stiff nipples tell me I'm pleasing you."

"Oh, yes," she hissed as her head fell back to loll against his chest.

But he didn't stop there. He bent his knees and thrust, splitting the lips of her pussy with his hard erection and stroking the length back and forth.

Between kisses and licks along her neck and shoulders, Ben growled against her skin as the knob of his cock struck her clit over and over again, pushing her closer to the edge of oblivion to where she knew she'd shatter where she stood.

"Ben," she panted. "*Ooo*. Oh God, Ben."

"Are you that close already? Me too, darlin'. But I'm not done with you yet." And just like that, he was gone, taking all of his warmth with him. "Open your eyes and turn around."

If only her limbs would obey. All of the joints in her fingers ached as she pried them from the mantle. She felt as graceful as a flamingo on ice skates as she turned toward Ben, blinking hard to clear her vision from having her eyes shut so tight for so long.

As the spots cleared, Ben's shape came into focus. All six-foot-four-inch naked bit of him.

"Oh. My. God," she groaned, then a burst of laughter ripped from her lips. She braced her hands on her knees as she doubled over in near hysterics.

This wasn't happening. She had to be dreaming. Had. To. Be. The man was a god, and the source of his power was standing straight and proud, right there from the juncture of his hips.

Her mother taught her it wasn't polite to stare, but even her very religious mother would have swallowed a curse and been struck dumb by the sight of Ben's erection. Some women thought men's penises were ugly, but Faith had always been fascinated by the variety of size, shape, and color. Sure, some men may not have the most attractive of appendages, but others had truly beautiful cocks, and Ben's long, thick rod was mouthwateringly delicious.

"What's so funny?" he asked as he wrapped his hand around the beefy shaft and stroked up and down. "Do you not like my cock?"

"Are you crazy? You are... I can't even form the words. Oh my God," she groaned and clenched her hands into fists to keep from pouncing on him. "You have no idea. I want to throw myself at your feet and stroke you. Lick you and suck you. Gobble you whole. Feel you come all over me. Holy heck."

Yep, she had lost her mind.

Ben smiled and let go of his cock, allowing it to swing in all of its tumescent glory as he approached her. "You sure do know how to make a man feel good about himself."

"Don't be coy. You know you're gorgeous."

His smile widened. "Thank you. Now turn to the side and bend over."

She dropped into position then gasped as his hand landed on her ass with a hard smack, followed by a second blow on her other butt cheek.

"That's for speaking out of turn after you already answered my question. Do it again, and I'll give you a more thorough lesson. Now straighten up and hold out your hands."

Faith didn't dare rub at her hot backside like she wanted and dutifully held out her hands. The deviant side of her toyed with the idea of breaking the rules just to find out how he'd punish her, but he had only established a few rules to start with. To break one on purpose would be childish. Besides, he might do something really horrid in retaliation, like prevent her from orgasming.

He crossed to the coat rack by the front door and collected a belt she hadn't noticed hanging from one of the hooks. She felt her eyes bulge as her heart slammed into her ribs.

"Deep breaths, Faith." He laughed. "Deep breaths. I'm not gonna throw you into the deep end."

She almost responded that she trusted him, but held her tongue and watched with bated breath as he wound the leather around her wrists, looping the ends through the belt buckle twice.

"Is that too tight?" he asked and tugged on the end.

"No, sir." In fact, it felt perfect. Snug, yet loose enough that she knew with a few jerks, she could be free in a matter of moments.

Ben hummed his approval. "Soon, I'll have you bound and on your knees with my cock between your lips. But not tonight. I have different hungers tonight."

Pulling on the belt, he guided her around to the back of the couch.

"Step closer and lean over. I hope you're as limber as you look."

What? Okay. This was new.

The frame of the couch bit into her pelvis as she bent and crawled over the top. Ben grasped her right leg at the knee and lifted, resting her inner thigh across the top of the cushion. She dug her elbows into the couch for purchase as he did the same to the left, leaving her pussy vulnerable to whatever he desired.

Sweat immediately broke out over her skin as embarrassment heated her cheeks. In this position, there was no hiding her response as her sex was held wide open to his gaze.

"Comfortable?" he asked as he massaged the areas where her hips met her thighs.

Depended on the perspective. Physically, the position stretched muscles she hadn't used in a while. Mentally, she had never felt so exposed, so primal, so *naughty* as she did, with the cool air lapping at the lips of her sex.

"I'm...okay," she answered as honestly as possible. She could pass out at any moment, but for the most part, she was unharmed.

"You have no idea how beautiful you look spread open for me. How absolutely sexy, and depraved, and wonderful."

Exposed, vulnerable, and slutty were other adjectives he could probably add to the list. But for the life of her, she couldn't find anything wrong with that.

He smoothed his big hands up and down her legs and over her back in a touch that was both gentle and maddening. Over and over, he caressed her skin until she was ready to scream. Finally he ran his thumbs down the crack of her ass and parted the lips of her sex. The hot puff of his breath against her labia made her tense with anticipation.

Please, please, please.

"Ben," she cried when he finally touched her pussy with the flat of his tongue.

At her cry, he turned ravenous, licking and slurping at her

wet pussy like he was starved.

"You taste so fucking good. Like a juicy peach," he growled then thrust a thick finger into her clutching sheath. A second finger soon joined to scissor inside her, stretching her muscles.

She bit into the couch cushion in an attempt to try to muffle her screams. Not that there was anyone around who could hear her anyway, but she still had that impulse to temper her reactions. Men may claim to want a tigress in the bedroom, but in her experience, it was all talk. As soon as she tried to voice her pleasure, they pulled back. For once, she just wanted to let go, and even though Ben said she was allowed to revel in her sexuality, her mind was afraid to believe.

"Stop," he barked. His open palm landed on her butt in a solid crack that brought her head up with a surprised jerk. "You're holding back. Don't you dare hide your responses from me. Don't you like my mouth on you?"

"Yes," she choked out as tears filled her eyes. "I love it."

"Maybe I need to give you something to really scream about."

He eased both of his thumbs into her sheath and took her clit between his teeth and sucked hard. The tiny bit of pain followed by the incredible sense of fullness had her shouting into the cushion as her hips thrashed helplessly in his hold as the torturous sucking went on and on.

The edge was so close, she could feel the mist of release bathing her face, so of course the bastard pulled away before the mother of all orgasms consumed her.

The loss of his touch was soon eased as the blunt head of his cock swirled against the opening of her pussy. "Is this what you want, little girl? Is this what you've been begging for?"

"Yes, yes." *A thousand times yes.*

"Who owns this pussy?"

"You do, Ben."

"Damn straight."

And with that, he forced the tip of his cock into her sheath, pushing and pushing and pushing. Oh, God, there was more pushing as he fed his pulsating dick into her hungry pussy. The stretch burned so good, and with the top of the frame of the couch digging into her pelvis, she swore she could feel his bulbous head slide up into her belly.

"God damn, woman," Ben groaned behind her. His fingers dug into her gyrating hips. "I've never—Fuck. I've never—shit. So good."

The withdrawal was just as delicious as he stroked all of her hidden nerve endings.

"One more, baby. One more thrust, and you'll have all of me."

Was he serious? There was *more*?

"Oh my God." Her moan turned into a scream as he lunged, filling her to capacity. His ball sac slapped against her clit as he began to stroke in and out.

"That's my girl." Ben laughed, leaning over to slide his hands between her chest and the couch cushions, plucking her nipples as he set a punishing pace. The couch rocked and skittered across the hardwood floor with each thrust.

She wished she could see him. Watch as his body glistened with the sweat she felt along her back, and see his face as he plundered her willing body. Was he as mindless with lust as she? Had the beast inside him taken over like it did within her, focused only on the coiling heat in her belly and the throb of her womb as she cried out for more.

Time stood still as Ben took her to the brink over and over again. The moment her pussy fluttered, he'd withdraw all of the way out, stroking his ridged length between her ass cheeks.

When her bucking slowed, he'd drive home again, pounding away in long, measured strokes until she was ready to shatter.

"You're killing me," she groaned. Her screams now registered an octave lower as her vocal chords burned. Sweat and tears covered her face, making her hair stick to her skin in long strands that obscured her vision.

Ben's sadistic laugh made her fingers dig deeper into the cushions under her cheek. "You can take more, darlin'. You'll see."

His grip on her hip tightened as his thumb stretched across her butt cheek to probe at the exposed hole of her ass. Using sweat and the cream pouring out of her pussy as lubricant, he popped his thumb into her ass to the first digit.

With his other hand, he reached beneath her and began to strum at her clit as if she were one of the guitars in the corner.

A cramp began in her belly and radiated out as her pussy clamped down on his cock.

"Ben," she cried out in warning.

"I've got you, sweetness. Come for me." Fire spread from her clit to her heart. "Squeeze me tight and milk my cock. I'm going to fill you so full of my cum. Do it now!"

The lights went out and someone screamed. It was probably her, although she could have sworn it was a deep bass that rumbled up her back. The only thing she was certain of at that moment was that she died.

Yep. She was dead. Her heart exploded, her lungs, although frozen, were on fire, and darkness had stolen her vision as electricity shot out of all of her pores. It wouldn't surprise her one bit if she turned to ash right there in Ben's arms.

Right on the heels of rapture beat the heavy trod of discontent. No one had ever turned her inside out before, and she would bet her life that no one ever would again. But instead of rejoicing in the satisfaction of obtaining pure glory, she was sad.

As her body twitched in a mass of sweat and cum she only had one thought. A thought so degrading, she was ashamed to even acknowledge its existence, but it would not let her escape the truth.

Ben had delivered her the world, but she was afraid it wasn't enough.

She wanted more.

Chapter Five

FIRE BURNED IN Ben's lungs as he struggled as if surfacing from a hundred-yard dive without scuba gear. The muscles in his thighs twitched as his hips continued to flex, reveling in the clasp of Faith's body. It was official. He was never wearing condoms again.

If it were possible, he'd gladly stay buried deep inside Faith as aftershocks rippled through her, drawing out their pleasure. Damn. The foundation of his world had been demolished, and if his brain weren't so scrambled, he'd suspect it had nothing to do with sex and everything to do with the woman shaking beneath him.

Watching her, listening to the sounds she made as she embraced her sexuality was what made being a Dom so satisfying. It was he who provided her with a safe environment to soar, and soar she did.

It killed him to pull away, but Faith needed him to guide her back down to earth, not crush her under his body weight. He gritted his teeth and pushed up, withdrawing from her sheath in a long, slow glide that tempted him to plow back inside.

Marks of his possession decorated her skin in the form of pink handprints where he had held her hips in place. Rivulets of his cum spilled from her reddened sex, igniting another bout of arousal to stir in his belly. Soon, soon, he'd have her bound to his bed and rub his seed into her skin as if it were lotion, but now his priority was getting her comfortable and holding her in his arms.

It was times like these when he wished he was at The Cavern in one of their playrooms. The club housed not only showers and supplies, but also had hired stewards on hand to help with aftercare. What he wouldn't give for another pair of hands to help get him and Faith up the stairs. At that moment, his limbs felt as strong as a stalk of alfalfa, and his knees shook so badly, he'd laugh at his weakness if he wasn't so completely wiped out.

"Faith, sweetness. Talk to me." His throat burned as if he had swallowed shards of glass, and his voice sounded just as smooth. He carefully lifted her right leg and guided her foot to the floor, eliciting a groan from Faith that interrupted her mewling cries. Her left leg he treated just as gently, then he massaged her hip flexors. "Try to stand for me so I can pick you up."

She shook like a dilapidated barn in a tornado, but she managed to slide off the back of the couch and into his arms. With the sweat and tears covering her body and making her slippery in his hold, he was tempted to lay her out on the living room. But not only would she be more comfortable in his bed, he wanted to see her red hair spilled across his pillow. He wanted to do a lot of things when it came to her hair, but he'd start slow.

"That's my girl," he murmured, monitoring the tone of her sobs.

It wasn't unusual for a person to fall apart after a scene. The adrenaline, the nerves, the release all combined into a powerful cocktail capable of shaking a person to their core. When allowed to give in to the fantasy, it was so easy to fall into the chasm of overindulgence, and a thousand times more difficult to crawl back out into reality.

So far, Faith's tears were pitched more toward the cathartic than those of pain, but he was still mindful to treat her with kid gloves as he carried her up the narrow staircase and to his room. The bedspread was already pulled back for him to set her on the cool sheets.

"I'm gonna step away for just a minute and get us some towels. Do not go anywhere. Don't even sit up. I don't want you to fall."

He hated leaving her on her own for even a second, but the bathroom was down the hall. He wished he had pots like they had at the club where hot, moist towels were always available, but he didn't have a crock pot. To ask Greta for hers was just asking to be questioned on why he'd need one.

Quickly, he gathered his supplies of towels, soaking a few in hot water and placing them in a plastic tub for transport. He rushed back into the bedroom, finding Faith exactly where he left her. Only now, her cries had dwindled to a few hiccups and wet sobs, but the sound, along with the look of sadness in her eyes, stabbed him in the gut.

"I'm here, darlin'. It's all right." He sat by her side and went to work, wiping her face clean before moving down to her chest. "Focus on your breathing. If you're not careful, you're gonna hyperventilate. Come on. Do it with me. Breathe in slow. Breathe out."

Instead of slowing, her sobs began to increase and her head tossed back and forth on the pillow.

"Focus on my voice, Faith. Talk to me. What has you so upset?" He continued to bathe her stomach, switching to a fresh towel as he went to work on her legs. "Are you hurt? Are your muscles sore? Tell me where, and I'll make it better."

A twisted chuckle mixed in with her cries. "I hurt here." She laid a hand on her sternum.

"No wonder with all of this crying. Breathe with me and the pinch will ease."

"No." She tapped on her chest. "*Here.*" She rolled to her side, and if he wasn't in her way, he bet she'd curl into a ball.

The whites of her eyes were laced with red, making the blue of her irises look electrified as she stared up at him in self-recrimination. "Am I a bad person?" she whispered.

Ah. The last of his energy disappeared, leaving him drained and swaying in his seat. The hurt she felt was deep on the inside. Mental rather than physical.

The towel in his hand hit the container with a wet *plop*. He lay down beside her, drawing her into his arms and into his heat.

"Why would you think you're a bad person, Faith?"

"Because," she stuttered. "Because—I—I—" She buried her face into his chest.

"Because you liked what we did?"

"No." Before he could sputter with incredulity, she continued. "Because I *loved* what we did."

"Well, I hope you loved it. I worked really hard on giving you what you needed."

"That's what I'm talking about. It was more than anything I could have imagined. But…"

But…what? What!

"You can tell me anything." He stroked a line from the back of her head to the base of her spine as she fell silent. Long, soothing caresses to help her open up and trust him. "That's what I'm here for, Faith. To share those parts of yourself you think no one will understand. I'm willing to listen."

"You're the first man who has ever said that to me." This time, her chuckle didn't sound so tortured. Her arms curled around his waist. "That was the most animalistic, erotic moment of my life. I have never felt so ravished. At times it was so good, it was painful. But even as you thrust so hard it hurt, and as I burned inside until I felt like I melted, I couldn't help to think that I...I wanted...more." She lifted her tormented gaze to his, and he felt his heart skip a beat. "I'm a slut, Ben. I'm just a horny, depraved, hussy who wants to be fucked all of the time," she ended on a sob and tried to burrow deeper against his chest.

Part of him wanted to laugh at her melodramatics, but her hormones were fluctuating at such an extreme rate, he wasn't sure she even knew what she was saying. However, it was obvious that her distress was real, and that was not a laughing matter.

"You're not a slut, Faith. Or a hussy. Depraved, maybe. But above all, you are not a bad person. You are a woman who enjoys sex, and as long as you're not putting yourself into dangerous situations, there is nothing wrong with that. And I'm not just saying that because I'm the one you're getting kinky with. You are a good person. That's why everyone likes you."

"But if they find out, they won't like me anymore. Will they?"

Ooo. His gut flinched as if she nailed him with an upper cut. "Sorry, sweetness. I'd love to tell you that you have nothing to worry about, but you may be right about that. Society is still pretty fucked up about what is and isn't acceptable. I can be congratulated for shooting a ten-point buck who had done nothing but mind its own business, but if I want to get a little freaky with another consenting adult in my own home, the world as we know it will come to an end. Now, not everyone will be closed minded, but there will be those who won't understand and will try to make you feel bad about yourself. It's unfortunate, but it's the truth."

"Is that why you stopped dating local girls? Because word was getting around you're kinky and people were being mean to you?"

"No." He laughed and gathered her closer, shifting her leg to drape over his thighs. "I stopped dating local girls because none of them captured my attention. But when I was dating, yeah, I had to be careful about who I was with and knowing their limits. Some girls were into kink. Others might have said they were, but when given just the slightest taste, they closed up. As I got older, I got better at being able to read people and learned who to trust. The list is short."

"I'm starting to understand that. Not that I was planning on, you know, telling anyone about anything, but I'm so confused." The corner of her lips lifted into a little smile. "Thank you for talking with me. Most guys aren't into talking or cuddling. This is nice."

"Aftercare is my favorite part."

"Is that what this is called?"

He hummed the affirmative and rested his cheek against the top of her hair, enjoying the softness of a warm and willing woman nestled in his bed. It had been so long since he enjoyed a woman's curves, had her scent in his nose and perfuming his sheets. Things had been so crazy at the ranch over the last few years, he had forgotten he might need to take a moment for himself every so often.

"Why aren't you married?"

"Why are you so chatty?" He stared down at her with one eye open. "You should be asleep by now. Or at least drowsy. I gave you my best, girl."

"Is your marital status a taboo subject?"

"Not really. Just not something I talk about. Why do you ask? Are you looking to fill the position?"

"No." Her lashes fluttered as she looked away. With her middle finger, she began to draw little circles in the smattering of hair that covered his chest. "I was just curious. You're quite the catch. Handsome, kind, sexy, you can talk about feelings without being weird about it, and you like to snuggle. Makes me wonder."

"The answer is simple. I hadn't met—" *you*.

Where did *that* come from?

There were lots of reasons why he never married, finding the right girl being chief among them. But Faith wasn't that girl. She was young, still finding her place in the world. She wouldn't be interested in settling down with an old guy like him whose idea of fancy was using silverware at a barbecue.

"The right girl," he finished.

"Do you think you ever will?"

"Maybe. Don't know. I'm kind of set in my ways. What about you? When are you gonna settle down and marry?"

Her eyes narrowed in a glare and she pouted, acknowledging the deft change of focus on the topic. She trailed her fingers down his belly and drew those teasing little circles down the length of his hardening shaft. "I don't know. It's going to be hard to find a man who can accept my unleashed passion you're encouraging me to embrace. I think you've created a monster."

"Down, girl." He caught her around the wrist and brought her hand up to place a kiss on her palm. Her skin was so soft, he couldn't resist placing another kiss higher up her arm, then higher still, licking a line along her collar bone and up her neck.

When he reached the corner of her mouth, he paused, drawing back to gaze at her face. Any trace of makeup she had worn was long gone. Her eyes were red and swollen and her hair hung in sections against her cheek. She looked exhausted.

And so damn beautiful.

The moment his lips touched hers, she sighed and opened for him, yet he didn't immediately take what she offered so sweetly. No, he savored the softness of her lips, the way she melted into him and her little puffs of breath. And when the temptation grew too great, he flicked his tongue to stroke the inside of her inner lip before diving in for a greater taste.

Slow, languid, the gentle taking of her mouth was just as sweet, just as heated as the earlier passion he had taken her with. But instead of feeling as if he had been struck with a bolt of lightning like before, a sensation of warm honey stole over him.

Faith ran her hand down his belly, and grasped the root of his cock. The selfish man he was enjoyed the pressure of her grip for several delicious strokes before the gentleman within him pulled her hand away.

"If you keep that up, I'll be driven to take you," he murmured against her lips.

"That's the idea," she murmured back.

"Sorry, sweetness, no more sex tonight. I took you hard, and you will be sore in the morning. I don't want to make it worse."

"But I liked it."

Damn. She was cute when she pouted. Lucky for her, he was an honorable man.

"I liked it too." He kissed the tip of her nose. "And I'm going to do it again. Just not tonight. Now lie down. Rest."

"You say that as if I'm staying here tonight."

"You are."

"I am?" she asked, clearly surprised.

"Of course. I told you, aftercare is my favorite part. I'm not letting you leave my side until dawn."

"That gives me lots of time to change your mind about having another go-round."

"I'm tempted to let you try."

With a wicked smile, she licked a path down his chest to his beaded nipple.

Faith was right. He had created a monster.

Chapter Six

"**M**Y EYES! OH my God, my eyes," Adam shouted.

Ben whipped around from his post at the stove and shifted his grip on the wooden spoon in his hand into a makeshift weapon. Once his gaze landed on Adam and he realized the younger man was just fine, he blew out a breath and relaxed.

For a moment he'd been afraid that Adam had done the impossible and poked his eyes out, but instead he had fallen prey to the dastardly bastard that was a yellow onion.

Tears streamed down Adam's face as he glared accusingly at Ben. "I'm blind, man. You've caused me to go blind."

"I did nothing. You're the asshat who forgot to rinse the halves under cold water before you started slicing into them. Don't panic. You'll live. Look." He gestured to the Australian shepherd snoozing in her bed in the corner of the kitchen. "Even Daisy knows you're not in danger. Go rinse your face. It'll help," he ended on a laugh.

"It's not funny. I'd like to see you try to cut these things without crying, Mr. Tough Guy." He stomped to the sink and threw the water on cold and stuck his face under the spray. "Fuck, that's icy."

Ben shook his head. The kid did have quite the flair for the dramatics. Guess it came naturally when you were the baby of a family of six.

Picking up the task from where Adam had left off, Ben quickly diced through the last onion. "Who taught you how to cut vegetables? All of the pieces are uneven. They won't cook at the same rate."

"Sorry, Master Chef," Adam said through the wad of paper towels he had bunched to his face. "I don't cook anything but toast and soup from a can,"

"Then why did you offer to help cook?"

His blond eyebrows shot up as if to say "duh." "I didn't want you to get all of the credit."

Ben grunted. "Then you get to keep helping. How does the oil look? Is it hot enough or too hot?"

Adam took a peek into the giant pot. "Looks yellowish."

"Great." He restrained an eye roll. "Dump the onions in the pot. And when I say dump, I mean *put* them in the pot, not literally dump them. Otherwise you'll be sprayed with hot oil and make a mess."

"I got it, Obi-wan. I'm not an idiot." Even as he grumbled, his expression turned to one of suspicion as he carefully added the onions to the pot and eased a sigh of relief when all of the pieces made it in without incident.

"Good job. Now add the rest of the peppers. You can turn the burner down too. Not too much, just a little."

It took Adam a second to find the right dial, but once he eased it down, he looked over at Ben with a huge smile. "Hey, look at that. I'm cooking."

"Not yet. Here." He handed him a wooden spoon. "Start stirring and then you're cooking."

"Awesome."

Together, the two men worked at getting the rest of supper finished. Okay, they did cheat a little with store-bought corn bread and salad from a bag, but Ben was able to find Greta's fancy bowls and serving plates to make the meal look nice. And of course, they made sure to clean up after themselves with each step. Greta's kitchen was her domain. A place she took great pride in. If she came home to a dirty kitchen, she'd likely tear them a new asshole, and with all of those pregnancy hormones running through her system, she was likely to maim first and ask questions later.

Adam lifted the lid off the pot, releasing a spice and tomato scented cloud into the air. "Fuck, man. This looks so good. I say, let's take the whole thing back to my place and let the others fend for themselves."

"I'll let them know you said that," Ben said as he ripped the top off the case of beer and added another set of bottles into the chest of ice he had placed on the floor.

"Hot, hot, hot," Adam sputtered around the spoonful of chili he swiped. "But it's good. You know, it kinda reminds me of the chili they serve at The Crescent."

"It should. It's the same recipe."

"How in the hell do you know how to make The Crescent's chili?"

"I learned more than how to dodge flying beer bottles and chucking out the riffraff when I worked there in my youth."

And it paid to make friends with the kitchen staff with the offer to help prep when you were making less than a living wage. At nineteen, his entire diet consisted of what he pilfered while working as a bouncer at the local watering hole. To this day, he couldn't eat a French fry at a leisurely pace. The knee-jerk reaction to inhale his food before being spotted hit him every time he saw a fried potato.

"What is that glorious smell?" Greta asked as she stood in the doorway with her purse in hand and overcoat still on. "And what are you two doing in my kitchen?"

"Welcome back," Adam shouted and swept the small woman into a bear hug, mindful of the growing bump of her belly. "You guys made good time."

Trey entered the room behind her and slid his arm around his wife's waist. "When you have a pregnant woman threatening to pee in your beloved truck, it motivates you to break the speed limit just a little bit."

"Speaking of." Greta thrust her purse at her husband. "Don't say anything exciting until I get back."

"Wouldn't think of it, magpie." As soon as she was out of earshot, Trey nodded to the cooler. "Is there beer in there?"

"Yep," Ben answered.

"Hallelujah." Trey crossed to the counter and scooped up an icy-cold one. "Two and a half hours on the plane and two more in the car from the airport with stops every thirty miles for a potty break. It's sure good to be home."

"Did the rest of the fellas head to their place?" Ben asked.

"Yeah. They were going to unload their stuff and try to convince Giovanni's to deliver pizza out here."

Ben nodded at Adam. "Text the guys and tell them soup's on. We'll be up and ready in a few minutes. So how is the happy couple?"

"Good," Trey answered after taking a healthy swig from the bottle. "Winging their way to Hawaii as we speak."

Adam groaned with a shiver. "Trapped on an airplane over all that water? No thanks."

"If it meant a week on the beach with Gabriella in a bikini?" Ben asked.

The younger man's brows rose for a moment before he

shook his head. "Tempting, but nope. You will never get me on a plane."

Greta returned with a relieved sigh. "So much better. Okay. What is all this about?"

"Ben and I figured you'd all be hungry and tired by the time you returned, so we cooked y'all dinner," Adam announced proudly.

"Aw." Tears filled her eyes. "That is so sweet. Thank you."

Adam's smile widened as she threw herself into his arms. "No problem, Mrs. A. It's my pleasure."

She released the young man and turned toward Ben to give him an equally enthusiastic hug. "This was your idea, wasn't it?" she whispered in his ear.

"Let the kid have his moment. Now go sit and I'll fix you a plate."

"This is such a wonderful surprise." She sniffed and waddled to her chair at the head of the kitchen table that was big enough to seat twelve. "My word, I can't stop crying. I can't wait until I don't feel so weepy all of the time. Anyway, it looks delicious."

Trey slapped Ben on the back. "Thanks for doing this, Ben. Greta had already started planning what I could whip together for dinner based on my skill set. Or lack thereof. This takes some of the pressure off."

"Adam said it before. It's our pleasure. Grab a bowl and tell us about the trip. How was the wedding?"

Soon the kitchen was full of weary travelers as Jack, Rafe, and Colby arrived to load up on grub and tell stories of their time in Sin City.

In the photos they shared, the bride looked gorgeous and the groom beamed as if he'd won the jackpot. Ben never knew Mark had so many teeth, the man was smiling so widely. Actually, everyone in the photos wore huge grins when they weren't mugging for the camera. Every picture showed a group of friends, happy. Laughing. Enjoying life.

Sitting at the table, Ben sat back and drank in the noise of friends laughing, reminiscing, and it reminded him of when he had first come to work at the A. When Trey's father had dragged him out of The Crescent Moon and given him a home, he was able to redirect his life toward the good and no longer scramble for table scraps. These people were his family, and it did Ben's heart good to see them together and laughing again.

He closed his eyes and drew in a breath, willing the moisture in his eyes to dry. Greta's mood swings must be contagious. They had to be.

When the huge pot of chili was scraped clean and only crumbs remained on the platter of corn bread, the men sent Greta off to bed and between the five of them made quick work of the cleanup.

Adam, Jack, and Rafe set off toward the house they shared west of the horse barn, while Ben and Colby headed toward their house to the north.

For the last three years, Colby had lived as his roommate in the two-bedroom home, and they got along like two pups from the same litter. Newcomers to town often mistook them for brothers, which didn't bother either of them none. They were both quiet, kept the place relatively tidy, and always gave each other plenty of notice if visitors of the female variety were coming over. Not that that happened very often.

They were so well matched that Ben knew Colby's moods and sensed his friend's mind was occupied. He had been extra quiet during dinner—not that he was a huge talker anyway—but every once in a while, Ben noticed a faraway look in his eyes that meant he was ruminating on something.

"Truth, Colby. What did you really think of Las Vegas?"

Colby shrugged then kicked a golf ball–sized rock farther down the road. "It was all right. Loud. Flashy. Tons of people. It was cool for Vegas, but I wouldn't want to live there. I think the three days we were there were plenty."

"It sounded like you had a good time. Everyone looked happy."

"We did. I did. It's just… I don't know." He shrugged again and stuffed his hands into his front pockets. "Being around so much excess was weird. People were throwing money around like hayseed. I watched Jack lose a hundred dollars at a blackjack table in ten minutes. *Bam!* Just like that. At first I thought it was funny, but then I wanted to scream, *Dude, what are you doing?* He didn't mind, he said that was the point, to have fun and take his chances. And when we went to the strip clubs, it was insane."

"So you *did* go to some strip joints. I was wondering."

"Trey and Mark didn't, of course, but the rest of us did. Jack ran into some of his old rodeo buddies and we all went out together. I don't know, man." He shook his head. "The women down there are bold. Smoking hot, but I just couldn't get all worked up. I'm just not a one-night stand kind of guy. And looking at naked women with dollar bills hanging out of their G-strings just doesn't do it for me. I should have my man card taken away, huh?"

Ben couldn't help but laugh at Colby's hangdog expression. "You are the only guy I know who feels bad because the subjugation of women doesn't turn him on. You're fine, Colby. You're a decent, standup guy. That's nothing to be ashamed of."

"I guess so. But the whole thing got me thinking, you know? One night I'm in a strip club and the next I'm in a chapel watching Mark and Gabriella get married. Gotta admit, man. I was jealous. I want what they have. That connection with someone special. But out here, I don't know if I'm going to find it. It's not like a girl is going to fall in my lap. The right girl, anyway."

An image of Faith leaning over him as she washed his hair came to mind and he stifled a chuckle. "You never know, man. But I hear ya."

"Why haven't you ever married, Ben?" Colby asked as they climbed the front steps of their house.

Wasn't that the question of the week? "Haven't met the right girl."

"And you're forty-two. Damn. I'm going to grow to be a lonely old man."

"Now hold up. You are not going to be a lonely old man. For Pete's sake, you're only twenty-six. Look, there are a lot of reasons why I haven't married. My gene pool not taking to marriage well is one of them. But you're young. Get out there. You will find the girl who is right for you."

"May the powers that be make it so."

Ben entered the home first and drew up short. On the coffee table sat a two-foot tall container filled with purple M&Ms. "What is that?"

"Candy. Duh. Isn't it great? They have a candy store with an entire wall of M&Ms in all kinds of crazy colors you can buy by the pound."

"How much is that?"

"Five pounds."

"You bought five pounds of purple M&Ms?"

"Yeah." Colby nodded with the hugest smile on his face. "Isn't that awesome?"

"What else did you get?"

"Nothing. That was all."

And that was why he loved Colby like a brother. He was a simple man with simple needs who found enjoyment from simple pleasures.

"Actually, I did get my mom a few things. I'll take them to her next weekend."

The sentence stopped Ben with one foot on the staircase. "You're leaving town again?"

"Yeah. Don't you remember? It's my cousin's sixteenth birthday, and the family is throwing a big party. I'll only be gone for the weekend."

"Right. Right. Well, good night."

So Colby was heading across the mountains. Excellent.

As soon as he entered his room, he pulled out his phone and sent a text to Faith. It was time to introduce his girl to some more fun.

Chapter Seven

"YOU'RE HIDING SOMETHING, little girl. What is it?" Ben asked as Faith strode into the living room.

A secret smile fluttered on her lips, and mischief glittered in her eyes. Her hair was piled on top of her head in a loose ponytail, leaving tendrils of hair to skim her pink cheeks and the length of her neck. He'd never seen anyone so beautiful in his life.

She dropped her overnight bag at her feet and reached for the tie of her overcoat. "I have a present for you." Parting the sides of the coat, she pushed the garment to the floor. "Me."

"Holy fuck," he muttered and staggered backward. "That sure is something."

Faith was dressed for sex and sin with knee-high black suede boots, a little black skirt, and a matching under-bust corset. But it was the sight of her bare breasts topped by her pebbled nipples that made his blood boil.

"You drove all this way dressed like that?"

"Yes, sir."

"You're lucky you weren't pulled over. Actually, I would have liked to have seen the trooper's face if he saw you in that."

"Believe me, I have never paid more attention to obeying all of the traffic laws, avoiding every pothole, and making sure I had a full tank of gas." Her smile faded and she sucked her lower lip between her teeth. "Do you like it?"

"I love it. Sweetness, I can already think of thirty nasty things I want to do to you." But where did he begin? Images were flying at him so fast, his brain spun. "Come with me."

He guided her over to the sofa, whipping his T-shirt up and over his head and tossing it to the corner of the room, heedless of where it landed. Only Faith and her luscious tits occupied his thoughts as he eased down the zipper of his jeans to make room for his erection before he sat down and pulled her facing him between his legs.

"Put your hands behind your head. That's it. Perfect."

He took a breast in each hand and palmed the generous mass. Leaning forward, he took a pink tip between his lips and sucked, pulling the bud deep into his mouth before letting go with a *pop*. He bent toward the other nipple, but this time licked a circle around the areola, flicking the tip of his tongue against her skin.

"You're evil," she panted, arching her back in an attempt to get more of her breast into his mouth.

"Baby, I've just begun." He gripped her tight around the waist. "Don't move."

She muttered a curse and shut her eyes, but she held still as he continued his assault on her breasts, pulling and teasing as he consumed his fill of the soft flesh. The moans and whimpers falling from her lips were a sweet symphony to his ears that tempted him as well as giving him the patience to push her to the edge of sanity.

When a tear slipped down her cheek, he sat back in his seat. She was ready for the next step. "Take off your skirt."

"Finally," she sighed under her breath, and he bit back a

smile. Poor girl had no idea what he had in store for her. Relief was a long, long, long way off.

At least that was the plan until she removed her skirt, revealing a black silk thong in a pattern of fabric that matched her corset. Well, he had to give it to her, the girl knew just how to test the limits of his control. She'd have to be punished for that.

"Turn around. Let me see that ass." He landed two light taps to each cheek. To take the edge off his ferocity, he mauled her buttocks with his fingers and mouth, biting into her backside until her knees started to buckle.

He ran his hand up the inside of her thigh and cupped the pad of her pussy. The silk was damp in his palm. "You like the way I manhandle you, don't you?"

"Yes, sir. I love it."

"Such a dirty girl." He wound the string of her thong around his finger and pulled, cinching the band between her swollen folds to bite into her clit. Faith's head fell back on a sigh and her butt clenched as more cream spilled from her sheath. "I want to see you really get dirty."

A moan escaped her lips and she shook so hard, he was half afraid she'd collapse in his arms. She was so ripe, so ready to be plundered. He wanted to give her everything she desired and then some, and he knew she'd accept what he offered with unbridled enthusiasm.

He walked over to the coat rack and retrieved a length of rope. This was a special rope. Not the waxed kind he used for work, but a soft linen that wouldn't do any permanent damage to the skin.

Faith's eyes widened, her gaze glued to the line in his hands as her trembles increased tenfold.

"Easy now, darlin'. Easy." He made hushing sounds as if she were a frightened heifer. "I believe bondage was at the top of your list."

She swallowed hard and nodded, never taking her eyes off the length of line in his hands.

As he approached, her tremors strengthened, but she held still, only jerking when he trailed the end of the rope over her shoulders and down her back. She gasped each time he flicked the end over her nipples and the tops of her thighs.

He ran his tongue up her neck to breathe into her ear. "Hands behind your back."

She readily complied, clasping her hands at the small of her back.

"Hold your hands like this." He rearranged her fingers. "You'll be more comfortable." She nodded and swayed on her feet. "Bend your knees a little. I don't want you passing out before I've begun."

"I don't want to either," she said on a shaky laugh.

"I'm going to start you off easy. Just keep breathing."

Starting at her elbows, he wove the rope like a lattice down the length of her forearms and around her wrists. With each rasp of the rope, Faith's breath escalated, growing faster and faster until she started as if waking from a dream and forced deep breaths into her lungs.

"Good girl. It looks so pretty." He pressed a line of kisses across her shoulders. "How does it feel? Too tight? Too loose?"

"It feels perfect."

"Now I'm going to guide you to your knees. Let me help you down. Wait a second." He retrieved a cushion from the couch and set it in front of her. "Okay. Here we go."

Once he settled Faith in position, he stepped back and admired his work.

She stared up at him, flushed, panting, on the cusp of orgasm, and he had barely touched her. Her breasts, mottled with pink streaks from his evening whiskers, shimmied with each breath. The muscles in her thighs twitched, and the insides glistened with her arousal.

"Fuck, Faith. You're breathtaking."

Her eyes tracked the movements of his hands as he reached for the waistband of his jeans and pushed them down his legs, freeing the erection that had been aching since he woke up that morning.

He took his dick in hand, stroking up and down the length and directed the crown at her face. "Keep your lips together."

A smile broke free, then she schooled her expression, pressing her lips together in a little pout. He painted her lips with the droplets of precum that clung to the tip of his cock, stroking the head back and forth.

"That's it. Now open your mouth and stick out your tongue. Don't move."

Another huge grin broke free, but she did as instructed. He set his ball sac on her tongue, shifting his hips and working the bottom of his cock over her mouth. When the teasing became too much for him to bear, he set the crown just inside her mouth.

"Suck me."

All of the humor left her eyes as they narrowed with intent, and she closed her mouth over his cock and took him into the wet cavern. After inhaling a few of his inches, she pulled back, then sucked down again, trying to cram as much of his length into her mouth as possible.

His eyes crossed as he groaned. He placed one hand on her cheek to feel the head of his cock shuttle in and out of her mouth. With his other hand, he reached down and cupped her breast, pulling at her nipple in time with his thrusting hips.

As Faith moaned around his cock, Ben felt the pull to unload his cum down her throat. He clenched his teeth and closed his eyes tight, fighting the urge. The high of riding the edge was too great to give up so quickly. His heart might explode before he reached his release, but the pain would be so worth it.

Thunder rolled in his ears and his body temperature soared, causing sweat to trickle down his hairline. A cool draft wafted over his skin in a refreshing blast he was too grateful for to think twice about until a shout broke through his reverie.

"Holy shit!"

"Ah!" Ben jerked back as Faith choked on his cock, sputtering in surprise.

Colby stood in the doorway, eyes wide and mouth dropped open as if he were staring down the barrel of a shotgun. Well, he was staring at Ben's dick, after all. His gaze switched back and forth between Ben and Faith's heaving bosom with dizzying speed.

"Sorry," Colby stuttered. "God. Sorry. Saw car. Didn't think."

"I thought you were staying at your mom's?"

"Snow. Pass." He pointed his finger behind his shoulder, his gaze now fully focused on Faith. "Tires. Bad. I. Am. So. Sorry."

"It's okay. It's—fuck." A chuckle worked up Ben's throat that he swallowed. This was one of the most embarrassing moments in his life, but he'd bet good money that from an outsider's point of view, the scene was pretty hysterical.

Okay. Someone had to take control. Colby was still staring at Faith while doing a damn fine impression of a fish out of water, while Faith sat on her knees, still bound, aroused, her lips swollen and her eyes blazing with hunger as she looked to Ben for guidance.

The hint of an idea struck him like lightning. An idea so crazy, but so ripe with possibilities, his hard-on returned with even more strength than before. The trick was to tread with caution.

"Colby. Close the door. It's a little cold out."

The younger man's overnight bag hit the floor with a thud before he blindly reached out and caught the edge of the door and closed it behind him.

"Colby, this is Faith. Faith, my roommate Colby."

"Hello," she said, and Ben wondered if she was even aware that she had pulled her shoulders back to display her breasts in the most inviting fashion. Either way, his idea was growing in merit.

"H—hi," Colby mumbled.

"Faith is my special friend." He brushed the backs of his fingers over her cheek and down her neck. "I'm helping her explore her submissive side and all of the pleasures that come with it."

"I—I can see that."

"I think a woman who embraces her sexuality is one of the most beautiful things on the planet. Don't you think Faith is beautiful, Colby?"

"Oh yeah." His eyes scanned up and down her body, and he licked his lips. "Wow."

"And she has the softest skin. You should feel it. Come on. Run your fingers across her shoulder."

Faith's gasp puffed hotly against his arm and her eyes shot to his, but not with concern. No, it was if a bonfire erupted in her gaze and she wanted to be consumed by the flames.

"I—I don't know if I should." Colby shifted his weight from side to side. "She might—she's…"

"Mine," he stated. Loud and without question. "She agreed to do whatever I say. I take care of her and see to her needs. Come here and tell her how pretty she is, bound and on her knees. Come feel her skin and tell her that her submission is a beautiful thing."

Colby took one halting step, than another, shuffling across the floor as if caught in the tractor beam of Faith's allure. His hand trembled as he reached out and brushed his fingertips across her shoulder.

"Harder, Colby. She won't break. That's it," he encouraged as his roommate curled his fingers over her shoulder and ran his palm down her arm and back up again. "Isn't that nice?"

"Yeah," he mumbled, looking entranced as he watched his dark fingers play against Faith's milky white skin. "You're gorgeous. You're the most gorgeous thing I've ever seen."

"Yes, she is. Cup her breast. She has the perfect handful."

Colby gulped, but he reached down and cupped Faith's breast in his palm, his fingers massaging the mound.

Ben took her other breast in hand, squeezing and manipulating the nipple, and soon, Colby was copying his movements as Faith moaned between them.

Now it was time for the kill. "Do you…wanna help me out?"

"Help with what?" Colby asked.

"Take Faith to places she's never been."

Faith moaned and pressed her breasts deeper into their hands. Her eyes were half closed with desire, but there was so much trust in her eyes, his knees threatened to buckle. He'd bet his truck that if he felt between her legs, her pussy was drenched.

Colby didn't appear to be as ready to make the leap to the next step, but he certainly looked intrigued, if the bulge in his jeans was anything to go by.

"How can I help?"

Bingo.

"Lift up your T-shirt some."

A confused furrow creased his brow, but he followed, lifting his shirt enough to expose the flat expanse of his abdomen.

"Faith, undo Colby's jeans."

His furrow deepened. "How is she going to do that when her arms are tied?"

The fact that he was more concerned with the how and not the why made Ben smile. "She's a smart girl. She'll figure it out."

Faith giggled, then leaned forward and took the fabric around his button between her teeth and began to tug.

"Ah, I get it," Colby sighed, and watched with fascination as Faith struggled with the fly of his jeans.

She yanked and jerked. Shook her head back and forth and wrenched until the button popped free and she could get to the tab of his zipper to pull it down. They were all panting by the time she was finished, and she looked to Ben for further instructions.

"Keep going," he said with a nod.

It was if he had pulled the trigger on a starter's pistol. Faith dove for the waistband of Colby's jeans and worked them down his hips before tackling the band of his boxer briefs. As his cock sprung free, it bopped her on the nose, and she nuzzled the shaft.

The kid packed some impressive equipment. Not nearly as big as himself, of course, but he had a good-sized unit. Long and lean, with an arrow-shaped head and a thick shaft that widened at the base. He definitely had enough to keep any woman happy. And at that moment, Faith's happiness was the only one that mattered.

"That's my girl. Now make my friend feel as good as you were making me feel earlier."

Faith licked at her lips before settling her mouth against the underside of Colby's cock. His groan turned into a moan as she flicked her tongue up and down his length and laved at his tightening ball sac. At the second pass, she licked around the crown before gobbling him down and taking his shaft down her throat.

"Holy crap," he shouted as his hands fell to her head, holding her in place as she rocked back and forth. The bottom of his shirt fell, covering her face, and he ripped the garment up and over his head, sending it on the same journey Ben had sent his shirt on earlier.

Ben stood behind Faith and massaged her breasts while she feasted on Colby's shaft. He settled his own erection against the back of her head and rubbed the length against her silky tresses.

She was so wet, Ben could smell her pussy from where he stood, and he knew he couldn't hold out a moment longer in sinking into her humid heat.

"Have you ever been with two men before at the same time, Faith?" he asked.

Her answer was muffled, but she shook her head.

"I take it this is a new experience for you as well, Colby."

"Uh—yeah."

"How do you like it so far?"

His eyes widened, and he issued a half-laugh. "Don't know. I'm trying not to blow my load. It feels so good."

Ben agreed with the man one hundred percent.

This wasn't his first experience with a threesome, but it was his first time with people he cared about on a level that went beyond sex. Colby was his best friend. A brother. And there was no one else he trusted in helping him give Faith the ultimate experience.

"Let him go, sweetness. There's more fun to be had." He scooped her up in his arms and tossed her over his shoulder. He couldn't resist rubbing her backside as he climbed the stairs to his room. "Are you coming, Colby?"

"Sure," he replied, sounding uncertain, but he kicked out of his jeans and was hot on their heels as he followed.

Ben set Faith on her feet beside his bed and worked at the knots around her wrists. Once she was freed, he rubbed up and down her arms, to bring the circulation back to her limbs. "Doing good?"

Her gaze was hot and hungry as she looked back and forth at the two naked men before her. "You have no idea."

"Give me your hands," he ordered with a smile.

"Yes, sir."

A few moments later, she was retied with her hands bound in front of her and directed to crawl onto the bed. Ben pushed on her shoulders until she was chest to the mattress and her ass was lifted high into the air.

He turned to Colby. "Do you have condoms?"

"What?" he started with surprise. "You mean I get to— You're gonna let me? Really?"

"Really. Suit up. Our girl is waiting."

Colby dashed out of the room as Ben slid Faith's thong down her legs and over her boot heels. "Are you ready to be good and fucked, baby girl?"

"I'm so excited, I'm afraid I'm going to pass out."

"Later. You don't want to miss out on the pleasure we're about to give you."

She rested her cheek on her bound hands and smiled up at him, closing her eyes on a sigh as he smoothed his hands down her corseted-back and over the curve of her ass.

Colby returned with a foil packet in hand. He took one look at Faith and paused as a look of indecision crossed his face.

"Having second thoughts, Colby? I don't want to push you into something you don't want to do. I know kink isn't for everyone."

He looked back and forth between Ben and Faith. "I'm interested, but as long as it's okay with Faith. If she's good, I'm good."

To have his best friend show concern for his sub convinced Ben that he had chosen wisely for a partner to help introduce Faith to the darker pleasures.

He stroked the hair off Faith's cheek. "It's your choice, sweetness."

"I want this." She propped herself up on her elbows and craned her neck to look over at Colby. "I trust Ben, and if he trusts you, then I trust you. I want whatever you all want to give me."

The tense line of Colby's shoulders lessened, and his lopsided smile appeared. The rip of foil was the signal for all players to move as Faith lowered into position and Ben resumed his massage of her upper back. Colby rolled the condom down his erection then joined them on the bed.

"You heard her," Ben said. "She wants whatever you want to give her. So give it to her good."

Colby moved behind Faith, gripping his cock at the base. He dragged the tip of his cock up and down her slit that shined wetly with her cream. Faith whimpered and pushed back with her hips, encouraging him to take her. Ben felt her hunger, and he almost shouted at the man to hurry up and fuck her, the tension was so great.

Some might think it was beyond strange that he'd enjoy watching another man fuck his girl, but it was a sight that filled him with pride, especially when the couple involved were people he cared deeply about. As Colby sank into Faith's heat and the look of ecstasy came over his face, Ben knew exactly what his friend was experiencing. To know that he helped bring pleasure to Colby and Faith satisfied him to no end.

He bent to whisper in Faith's ear. "Do you like the feel of his cock inside you?"

"Yes," she panted. "Oh, yes."

"Watching his cock slide in and out of you is so hot. You are so beautiful."

Colby moaned and bucked harder. "Whatever you did just made her clench down."

"Oh, I'm planning on doing a lot more. Keep going. She likes it hard. I want to hear your thighs slap together."

With the carnal beat of sex pounding in the background, he crossed to the dresser and dug through the bottom drawer in search of a bottle of lubricant. It had been a while since he last played, and he hoped he still had supplies. Yes. Victory. And the bottle was unopened.

He crawled back onto the bed and stroked Faith's lower back. "Sorry, darlin', this is gonna be cold." Upending the bottle, he squirted a healthy dollop right over the puckered hole of her ass. "Have you ever done anal, Colby?"

Faith squealed as the cold goo hit her skin while Colby jerked as if punched.

"No," he replied. "I've wanted to try it, but never found a girl who'd let me."

"I'll walk you through it. Keep fucking her and slide your thumb into her ass. There's so much lube, it'll go right in. That's it. Fuck, that's sexy. Now curl your fingers around her ass and keep fucking. Work the lube in."

"Oh my God," Faith moaned, and pushed back into Colby. "That feels so good."

After a few more minutes, Ben added another dollop of lubricant. "Add your other thumb. Start working her open."

He looked at her face, gauging her reaction. By the looks of it, the woman was in heaven. A fine sheen of sweat covered her shaking body. With every lunge, her eyes rolled back and a moan broke past her parted lips. He reached between her legs and strummed her swollen clit. That was all it took to make her scream as she came against his hand.

Colby swore and his face twisted with a grimace as he tried to hold back his own orgasm.

"Take her now, Colby," Ben instructed. "While she's coming. Nice and slow. An inch at a time."

Colby's hands shook as if he were being electrocuted as he guided the head of his cock to her flexing hole. The tip slipped in with little resistance. "Shit, she's still coming."

"I know. It's fucking fantastic. Keep going. A little at a time. Whenever you take a woman in the ass, always, always go slow at the beginning. You need to make the experience better for her than it is for you."

"It's so tight," Colby groaned. "Faith. Are you okay?"

Faith flailed beneath him, caught in the grip of another orgasm.

"She's good," Ben answered for her. "Rub her clit."

As Colby's fingers brushed against his, Ben moved and gripped Faith by the shoulders and lifted her torso, impaling her further on Colby's thrusting shaft. He slid his legs between theirs and guided her back down to smother him with her bound hands above his head and her breast dangling before his nose.

He took a dusky nipple into his mouth and guided his cock to the sopping entrance of her pussy. With his other hand, he pulled her hips down, lunging up at the same time and spearing his cock inside.

The three of them shouted as the men fell into a rhythm, stuffing her full of their cock.

"Holy shit," Colby sputtered. "I can feel you, Ben. God

damn. I can feel you."

Ben felt the slide of Colby's dick, too. And a whole lot of other things. Like the silky insides of Faith's thighs against his hips and the rougher scrape of Colby's hairy legs against his knees. He felt the ripple of Faith's butt cheeks with each of their thrusts and the smooth texture of Colby's skin against the backs of his fingers as Colby's abdomen met Faith's ass.

He saw a lot of things, too. The unseeing stare of Faith as she looked into the distance, clearly falling into the morass of subspace. Flowing and surfing the sensual tide as her brain tried to cope with the onslaught of sensations bombarding her body. It was an expression he was familiar with but hadn't seen on his partner in a long time. He knew that at that moment, Faith would follow him to the ends of the earth and jump off if he asked her. She was a willing conduit of pleasure and his to control.

Behind her Colby was also lost to the sensation, his mouth twisting as he fought the pull of orgasm and losing the battle with every second.

He did this. He brought these two to the heights of pleasure. And it was he who would make them soar.

The rush of such power grabbed him by the balls and twisted, propelling his release up the shaft of his cock to bathe the inside of Faith's clutching sheath.

As his head twisted on the pillow, Faith screamed and shook so hard, he felt as if she'd fall apart in his arms.

"I'm coming," Colby shouted soon after. "Holy shit. Holy shit."

Through half-opened eyes, Ben saw Colby's back bow as he drilled his cock deep inside Faith who convulsed between them, her muscles milking both of their cocks for every drop of semen.

An eternity passed before Colby fell to the side, gasping for air and trapping Ben's leg beneath his hip. Faith collapsed on his chest, her gaze still unfocused as her muscles twitched beneath the skin.

Ben's eyelids felt as if they were weighed down with horseshoes, but he forced them to remain open. He had not only one, but two people to care for now, and with Faith in subspace, she faced the greatest risk of injury if he wasn't careful.

If they were to do this again, he might be better off calling his old contact at the club in the city and having a steward come over to help him with aftercare. He sure could use the help.

The thought made his breath catch. *If* they were to do this again?

He eyed Colby, who had already fallen asleep with a huge grin on his face, then glanced at Faith who shined with the glow of sexual satisfaction.

Hell, there was no *if.* The question now was *when.*

Chapter Eight

I F SHE WAS going to continue to engage in activities like the ones she had the night before, she was going to have to invest in some heating pads and Epson salts. Some extra legwork to her exercise regimen was probably a good thing to add too, although the thought of more physical exertion made her shudder with dread. But the promise of more mind-blowing sex would be totally worth the effort.

Had that really been her the night before? Her? Faith O'Leary from Small Town, Washington, sandwiched between two of the handsomest men she had ever met as they took her body ten ways from Sunday and made her orgasm so hard she blacked out?

She bent to retrieve a skillet from underneath the kitchen counter and winced. Yep, the soreness in her backside was physical proof that it had indeed been her. And she couldn't forget the lovely pink scratches and bruises on her skin from where they had held her still with their big, manly hands. She loved the marks of their possession, especially since the night still felt like a dream.

A prickle of guilt scratched at her conscience over having behaved like such a wanton hussy. For reveling in such bestial activities. Simply imagining what her father would say if he knew what she had done made her want to keel over. But if she were given the choice between walking away or doing it again? She'd eagerly drop to her knees in a nanosecond.

Huh. Now wasn't that something? Her time with Ben meant so much that she'd risk her father's displeasure. Of course, that didn't mean she didn't respect her father, but she doubted he'd understand why she wished to be sexually dominated. Heck, she barely understood the need herself. And it wasn't as if her sexual fantasies were a frequent topic of discussion around the dinner table. Yeah, her father would choke on his potatoes if she asked him what he thought about bondage. The man hadn't been on a date since her mother. And every time she brought up the subject of him dating again, he'd blush and shake his head, saying he had the best, why bother with the rest.

If he knew she had not only been with Ben but Colby too…

Colby.

Now he was an unexpected surprise. When he had walked through that door, she had about jumped out of her skin. If not for Ben's cock filling her mouth and her hands being bound, she probably would have screamed and tried to cover up her nakedness. But the funny thing was, she hadn't had that compulsion at all. If anything, her bindings had given her power. She had felt emboldened, sexy, a conduit of pleasure for a man to feast upon, and seeing the instant hunger in Colby's eyes had made her ravenous for whatever Ben had been willing to suggest. Boy, had he ever come up with a doozy. It might be a week before the smile faded from her lips.

"Oh, hey," a deep voice, husky with sleep, said from behind her. "I thought I smelled bacon."

"Hi," she said. "Um. Good morning, Colby."

Suddenly the embarrassment she might have, or should have,

felt the night before caught fire in her chest and radiated out in a wave of heat that made her achingly aware that she stood in his kitchen, wearing nothing but one of Ben's button-down shirts.

Colby didn't appear to be feeling any more comfortable. He shifted his weight from foot to foot as slashes of pink appeared on his cheeks. His gaze bounced around the room as if he wasn't sure where to look.

The feeling was mutual as she wasn't sure where to look either. His feet were bare, and between the open sides of his blue and white plaid shirt his bare chest was an enticing landscape of dips and valleys. A stolen glance at his groin made a grin tickle her lips. Was wearing your jeans with the top button undone while inside the house a cowboy thing? If so, she was a fan of the trend.

How did this man not have a line of willing girlfriends standing at the front door? He was so darn cute with his dark spiky hair, boy-next-door good looks, and all of those lean, ripply muscles. And how could she forget how good his skin tasted as she gobbled him up, and how wonderful and gentle he was as he made love to her all night long?

A burst of laughter broke past her lips that made them both jump with surprise. Once she started, she couldn't stop, even as she held her hand firmly over her mouth to control the hysterical laughter.

Were there two more ridiculous people on the planet? How could they be so shy around each other when the night before he had taken her anal virginity? Of all the people she should feel the most relaxed around, it was Colby.

"Maybe we should do this the old-fashioned way," she said as she caught her breath. She walked over to where he stood in the doorway with a questioning look in his brown eyes and held out her hand. "Hi. I'm Faith. It's nice to meet you."

His shoulders relaxed and the corner of his lips curled up in a smile that revealed the dimple in his cheek. Good lord, the man had dimples!

"Hi. I'm Colby." He took her hand and gave it a light squeeze that sent a tingle of excitement up her arm.

The sudden flash of electricity took her off guard and she felt like the new girl in school who just had the cutest boy in class smile at her.

"Um, I...oh." Flustered, she turned around in a circle then gestured to a kitchen chair. "Uh, have a seat. I'm making breakfast. Obviously. I thought you guys might be hungry, you know, after last night. I know I'm starving."

"Sure. That sounds great." He stopped by the coffeepot and poured himself a mug, flicking nervous glances her way as she returned to the carton of eggs waiting on the counter.

"How many eggs do you like with your bacon?" she asked.

"About four."

"Do you know how many Ben likes?"

He laughed. "About six."

"Right," she laughed with him. Now the three cartons of eggs in the refrigerator made sense. She had wondered if there were more roommates in the house she hadn't met yet. "Is scrambled all right?"

"Scrambled is more than fine."

"Good." She started on the eggs as Colby took a seat at the table.

"So..." he said after he prepared his coffee—cream, no sugar, she noticed. "Where did you meet Ben?"

"I've known him for years. Well, known *of* him. He's been going to my dad's barber shop forever."

"You're George's daughter?" he asked, then a glimmer of recognition flashed in his eyes. "I heard you were helping him out after he got hurt. I didn't know you were that Faith."

"Yep. That's me."

"Have you and Ben been dating long then?"

"Ah…"

Well, crap. A simple question that usually resulted with a simple answer. But what she and Ben had wasn't so simple, was it?

The frown on Colby's face deepened the longer she stood there doing her best impression of a grouper. Poor boy. It wasn't his fault his question led to an explanation of her quest for sexual liberation.

"Sorry," she said. "Your question kind of threw me. You see, Ben and I aren't really dating. We have…an arrangement."

"An arrangement? Like friends with benefits?"

"Yes. No." She shook her head with a chuckle. Although her quest was supposed to be an act of female empowerment, she couldn't stop an itch of embarrassment from heating her cheeks. By keeping her gaze on her task of making the best scrambled eggs ever, she found it easier to tell the truth. "This may sound…odd, but Ben is helping me learn about my submissive side. He's my Dom."

"Your Dom? Ben? As in whips, and masks, and leather pants kind of Dom? I thought he was being funny with that talk of submission."

His look of surprise made her laugh. "You were there last night. Do you not remember the rope around my wrists?"

"Well, yeah, but I thought that was just a guy and his girl being a little kinky, not that you were in the middle of a hard-core event or anything like that."

"We haven't done anything really hard-core. Yet." She lifted the skillet and scooped a large portion of the eggs onto a plate. "He never tells me what he has planned. That adds to the excitement."

Colby shook his head as confusion swirled in his eyes. "I still don't understand. Is it like therapy?"

The skillet in her hand slipped as she burst out laughing. "I guess so. I hadn't thought of it that way. You see, when it comes to sex, I've always wanted more. Different. All consuming. And finding someone to match that need is much more difficult than I thought it would be. Oh, darn. I forgot about the bacon," she gasped as the scent of charred pig reached her nose.

She flung open the oven door with her right hand while reaching for a pot holder with her left. Smoke rolled out in a fluffy cloud as she pulled the sheet of grease-spitting meat from the scalding interior. The larger pieces were slightly overdone, but the smaller strips looked better to use as pencil lead than fit for human consumption.

"Sorry." She turned to Colby with a sheepish twist to her lips. "I hope you like your bacon extra crispy."

"I love it that way."

She tilted her head. "Are you just saying that because it's the truth or because you're trying to make me feel better?"

"A little of both," he replied, and his dimple appeared from behind his mug. "Really, Faith. I appreciate the effort."

"Thank you." She plucked out a few of the better pieces and set them alongside the eggs and two slices of toast. Setting the plate before him, she returned to the counter. "I hope you enjoy it anyway."

"I know I will."

After fixing her own plate, she joined him at the table. Once seated, he made a big show of looking her right in the eye as he grabbed the crispiest slice of bacon from his plate and ate it with gusto. "Delicious," he said with a wink.

Man, he's adorable, she thought with a giggle and began to eat.

For several moments, they sat in comfortable silence as they replenished the many calories they had burned the night before.

Colby patted his lips with his napkin then leaned in her direction. "Faith. Can I ask you something?" he whispered.

She glanced around the room, wondering why he was whispering, but leaned toward him as she whispered back, "Okay."

"How did you know Ben was a Dom? I mean, did you just out and ask him, or did he tell you? How did you know?"

Now it was her turn to stare at him in surprise. "How long have you lived together?"

He shrugged. "A couple of years."

"And you didn't know he was kinky? Never suspected it, like, at all? What about when he brought a woman home?"

"He hasn't brought a girl home in forever. At least that I know of. I do go across the mountains often to visit my family." He blinked and looked into the distance. "But you know, I can't even remember the last time he's mentioned seeing anyone. At least romantically. Or arrangement-like, as he does with you."

"Really?" The possibility that she was special enough for Ben to grant his time and attention pleased her to no end. "But you still didn't have a clue? You never heard the rumors?"

His eyes grew wide. "What rumors?"

"Are you serious? Well." She leaned closer. "When I was in high school, my best friend Jolene had an aunt Stacy who went out with Ben for a little while. One night, during a sleepover at Jolene's house, she was there and we overheard her talking to Jolene's mom about how Ben had asked her if he could tie her up during sex. She said she agreed, until the rope hit her skin, and then she freaked out and broke up with him. I thought she was insane. Ben's hot now, but oh my God, you should have seen him fourteen years ago. Anyway, Jolene's mom said she had heard that when he had gone out with Angela Gilchrist that

Angela had said that she did allow him to tie her to the bed, and it was fun. Until she went to church that next Sunday. Then she felt dirty. It wasn't that much longer after that I stopped hearing about Ben dating anyone local. If that was the reception he was getting, I don't blame him for looking elsewhere." She popped a piece of bacon in her mouth and chewed. "You seriously didn't know any of that? Nothing at all?"

Colby blinked slowly as if in a daze. "Not. A. Clue."

"Huh. Funny." She bit into another piece of bacon and eyed the man who had lived so closely to someone for so long but didn't know a thing about his personal life. The thought made her wonder just who exactly Colby was. "Was last night really your first experience with kink?"

He froze with a mouthful of egg. His eyes widened and after a moment he swallowed hard. "Yeah. Couldn't you tell?"

"A little." She bit her lip and shrugged one shoulder. "Did you like it?"

The brown in his eyes warmed to hot chocolate, and a grin tugged at his lips. "Yeah," he replied softly. "A lot."

Heat blossomed in her chest and spread over her like a fleece blanket. "Oh. Good."

She glanced back at her plate but couldn't resist sneaking a peek at him out of the corner of her eye. Her gaze collided with his and she quickly glanced away, stifling a giggle.

She wasn't thirteen, for Pete's sake. And Colby wasn't a potential love interest. She was with Ben. Or at least, her arrangement was with Ben. There was no reason for these giddy, flirtatious bubbles to be tickling her insides with seductive caresses. No reason at all. Ben was her...man? Boyfriend? Lover?

Hmm... this was getting complicated.

"Good morning."

Ben's growly greeting made Faith jump in her seat. As she glanced his way, a shiver of pure naughtiness skipped over her body, making her aware of her nakedness underneath the shirt she wore. Colby jumped as well, and his knee bumped into hers under the table. The contact sent a row of sparks up her leg, launching her from her seat.

"Good morning," she answered, turning toward the stove. "Are you hungry? I made breakfast."

Without waiting for a response, she began to fix Ben a plate with trembling hands. Why the hell was she so jittery? All she had done was talk with his friend. It wasn't as if she had been sitting in Colby's lap with her tongue down his throat. Still, a swirl of guilt that she found Ben's roommate appealing with his sexy, shy demeanor rolled in her belly.

Attraction. That was all it was. She found Colby attractive. There was nothing wrong with that. Nothing at all. Especially since she was never, ever going to act on it again. Ben was the man she wanted.

Fortunately, or maybe unfortunately, depending on how you looked at it, that want extended to a hunger for more than just a weekend appointment. For some reason Ben seemed convinced she would grow bored of him and move on. She hoped that train of thought was not because he was expecting to have their relationship lose its luster. After their first encounter, it was clear Ben was the man for her. While playing with Colby was fun, more than fun, her prize was Ben. Only Ben.

"I thought I smelled...I think that's bacon. Right?" he chuckled as he stepped behind her and slid his arm around her waist, resting his big, warm hand on her belly.

"Would you like some breakfast or not? I do not have to feed you," she warned even as she snuggled closer.

"I'm starving, thanks to you." He dropped a kiss on her

cheek then moved on to the coffeepot. "I would love some breakfast."

After setting his plate on the table, Faith busied herself by cleaning up the cookware. Behind her, Ben and Colby murmured a greeting and fell silent with nothing but the scrape of Ben's fork against his plate filling the kitchen.

The scene felt natural. Normal. It was funny, really. She probably should have excused herself and dressed. There wasn't any reason for her to hang around, except to steal some more time with Ben. But she liked listening to the men communicate with each other in their man-speak. Ben would mumble a question and Colby would answer with a grunt or a short, one- or two-word sentence. Occasionally, she noticed he'd sneak a shy glance her way, but then he'd turn his stare to the contents of his coffee mug or back at Ben. She had no idea about what it was they were talking about, but the fact that they clearly understood each other, she found fascinating.

Was this how they spent every morning? Sitting around the table, mostly dressed and sleep-sexy as they planned the day's events? Listening to the way their voices rumbled was nice, comforting, and made her aware of just how feminine she was surrounded by so much maleness.

"Faith, darlin', come here." Ben gestured, beckoning her to his side. As she neared, he pulled her into his lap. "We have a rule on the ranch. Whoever does the cooking gets to rest while the others do the cleaning. We'll get the dishes later."

"You say that now that I'm almost finished. Besides, I don't mind. I didn't want to interrupt your morning routine too much."

"Sweetness, this is our morning routine. Especially on the weekends. You're not interrupting anything. In fact, I think you made the morning much brighter." The corner of his eyes crinkled as he smiled. "Did you and Colby get better acquaint-ed?"

"Yes." She flicked a quick glance at Colby, who was staring into the dregs of his coffee again as he twirled the ceramic mug around the tabletop by the handle. His gaze lifted to hers for a second before shooting back down in that shy way of his. "He's very nice."

"Nice?" He raised a dark eyebrow. "Just nice? Come on. You can be honest."

Heat hit her cheeks as she lowered her eyes to gaze at Ben's collarbone. "He's adorable."

At that Ben let out a huge laugh. "Adorable. Well, that's better than nice. Colby, what do you think of my girl?"

Colby started as if he'd been goosed in the seat. "I—uh. Well…"

"Tell me the truth, Colby. What do you think of Faith?"

He sank in his chair, but when he lifted his eyes, his gaze met hers. In the depths, she saw want and a touch of fear. He cleared his throat before he answered, "She's lovely. Absolutely lovely."

Lovely. She'd been called "pretty" before. "Stunning" once, but never "lovely." It was a word she didn't hear very often, especially from a man. But to hear Colby call her lovely in his husky baritone didn't sound strange at all. His compliment was like eating a spoonful of warm caramel. Sweet and delicious as it heated you from the inside out.

"Thank you," she said, unable to keep the rasp out of her voice.

"I agree, Colby." Ben ran his big palm up and down her back as he looked at her with pride and possessiveness. "Faith and I are going to be spending a lot more time together. You're my best friend, so I'm glad that you two are getting along. I want you to feel comfortable with each other." With his fingertips, he

ANNA ALEXANDER

lifted Faith's chin to stare into her eyes. "I told you last night that I trust Colby. I do. I trust him with my life. And I trust him with yours. Do you understand?"

An invisible rope tightened around her chest as she struggled for breath. Somehow she managed to answer, "Yes, sir."

He closed his eyes and muttered, "Damn, that gets me every time." He gave a brief shake of his head then smoothed his thumb over her lips. The tips of their noses touched as he ordered, "Go sit on Colby's lap."

Across the table, Colby gasped, and her own lips parted in surprise, although she didn't know why. Perhaps it was because she had thought the night before was a one-and-done deal brought on by Colby's unexpected appearance. Or maybe it was because Ben had tapped into another of her desires she didn't know she had until she had felt the heat of two men pressing her between their bodies. It seemed almost greedy of her to be so eager to await her next instruction.

"Do I have to repeat myself?" Ben asked with a stern glare.

"No, sir." She practically shot to her feet before tripping around the table until she stood by Colby's side.

Just because Ben ordered her to sit on his friend's lap didn't mean said friend was willing to participate in whatever kinky plan Ben had in mind.

At the moment, Colby looked as if he wasn't sure what he wanted, either. He glanced back and forth between her and Ben, his breath escalating as he swallowed hard.

"May I?" she asked.

With one last glance at Ben, he nodded and scooted his chair back to allow her room to slide onto his lap.

The shirt she wore rode up, and her bare bottom rested against his hard, denim-clad thigh. Unsure of what to do with her left arm, she raised and lowered it several times before

106

settling her forearm across the back of his shoulders as his hands came to rest on her waist. It wouldn't surprise her one bit if he could feel the kaleidoscope of butterflies fluttering in her tummy.

"Relax," Ben said with a chuckle. "Neither of you are going to break. Now, kiss her."

For several heartbeats, Colby stared into her eyes, and she saw the war between uncertainty and hunger wage within his brown depths. It was a battle she too was facing. Could she really act with such decadence, engage in Ben's voyeuristic fantasy as if this was something she did all of the time?

Colby's lips brushed hers and parted. His tongue swept against her bottom lip, tempting her with his coffee and male flavor, and she melted in response, sighing into his mouth as she wilted against his strong chest.

Yes. Yes she could.

"Kiss her," Ben growled. "Don't hold back, Colby. Take her mouth and feast as if she's your only source of nourishment and you'll die without her taste."

With a growl of his own, Colby speared his tongue in her mouth as his hand moved to her thigh and his fingers bit into her flesh. She gasped against his mouth and kissed him back, squirming in her seat as the fuel of her passion ignited and made her hungry for more.

"That's more like it. Take off her shirt."

The plastic buttons were no match for Colby's strength as he ripped the edges of her shirt apart and little pieces of white plastic flew in all directions. Without a word of encouragement, he cupped her bared breast in his palm and worked the nub with his long fingers.

"Do it, man," Ben said. "I know you want to."

Colby swooped his head and sucked the puckered nipple

into his mouth and lashed at the hard tip.

Over the top of his head, Faith looked over at Ben, who sat reclining in his chair. His eyes blazed and a deviant snarl curled his lip. Both of his hands were under the table, but the muscles in his right arm bulged and flexed in a rhythmic beat and she knew he had his cock in his hand and was working his length as he watched. Even from across the table, Ben was in charge. A conductor of sin, able to weave a symphony of moans and sighs with just the power of his voice.

His grin widened. "Do you want more, sweetness?"

She curled her fingers into the thick muscles of Colby's back as she panted, "Yes, sir."

"What about you, Colby? Are you ready for some fun?"

Colby drew back. His lips, full and soft, were parted, and his cheeks were dusted a rosy pink. He slid his hand up her thigh until the tip of his thumb brushed against the slit of her pussy. In that instant, the shy, hesitant man he had been not more than five minutes before vanished, and in his place was a confident man hell bent on pleasure. The metamorphosis made her shiver, and the muscles in her thighs bunched with anticipation.

He licked at her lips and brushed their noses together as he looked her right in the eye. "I'm ready."

His thumb parted the folds of her sex as he took her mouth again with a hard kiss. The sound of Ben's chair as it scraped across the tile floor joined in harmony with her moan as she parted her legs, surrendering to anything they desired.

It was official. She was a slave to her libido. But she didn't care. Never before had feeling so wicked ever felt so right.

Chapter Nine

"COLBY. ARE YOU coming?" Ben shouted at him through the bathroom door.

"Yeah. Just give me a sec," he hollered and turned to stare at his reflection in the mirror.

The image looking back was unchanged from what he saw the day before. And all the days before that too. Same dark hair. Same smooth cheeks. The same shoulders and body he'd had since the day he finished with puberty.

But his eyes... Maybe that's where it was. The light in his eyes that confirmed he had witnessed and took part in something so unbelievable, so out of character, so amazing and frightening that his view of the world had been altered forever.

Leaving him where? What was he supposed to do with this newfound knowledge? Did he even want to take all that he had learned over the weekend and apply it to his nonexistent love life?

And what about Ben? It was difficult enough hanging out with his friend once Faith had left them alone the night before. He hadn't a clue as to how to behave. Were they to have cracked open a beer and flopped down on the couch with a high five and a shout of "Good game?"

No, what he had done instead was faked a long sigh, muttered something about an early morning and sprinted straight to his room, where he had laid on his bed with his arms behind his head and stared at the ceiling as he replayed every moment since he had walked through the front door.

Even now, he still couldn't believe that it had actually been him who'd been a slice of bread in a man sandwich. Not only that, but he had laid a practical stranger across the breakfast table and allowed his best friend to instruct him on how to bring his girlfriend to orgasm. Him. Colby Jensen. A man who, up until that moment, had only engaged in the simplest of missionary-style, vanilla sex. Who needed to use both of his hands to undo the clasp on a woman's bra.

Yep. That had been him.

"Colby. I'm heading out," Ben bellowed up the stairs.

"Right. I'm coming." Because staring at his reflection was going to do him so much good.

He hit the light switch on the way out of the bathroom and raced down the stairs, grabbing his Stetson and his down-filled vest from the coat rack as he ran out the door. Ben was waiting for him on the front porch as he shut the door behind him.

"Are you feeling okay?" Ben asked.

The question made him want to laugh. His brain was so scattered that if the sun hit his thoughts, a prism of a million colors would erupt. "I'm fine."

Ben nodded and led the way down the stairs.

With each step down the lane toward the main house, Colby's heart pounded and a film of sweat collected above his lip as the fear rose that his weekend activities would be discovered the moment his coworkers got a look at his face. Or worse, he'd get so wound up, he'd just burst out with the truth. Although seeing Jack do a spit take with a mouthful of coffee would be pretty funny. Especially if Adam was the one sitting across the table from him. But was a bit of comedy worth the potential embarrassment?

The time to get his shit together grew shorter as Ben reached the back door of the boss's house first and held it open for him. Inside, the rest of the crew had gathered for breakfast, and the sounds of animated chatter seemed exceptionally loud.

"Good morning, boys," Gabriella greeted them from her place at the sink. "I managed to save you a plate before the heathens ate it all. They're in the warmer."

"Thanks," Ben replied and retrieved the plates of sausage and eggs from the hot box beneath the oven, handing one to Colby.

At the extra-large kitchen table, Trey was in his usual seat at the head of the table with Mark on his right. Jack was missing as were Rafe and Greta, but she had been sleeping in later the further along she grew in her pregnancy.

"How was the weekend with the family, Colby?" Trey asked from over his coffee cup.

He froze mid-squat above his seat. "Oh. Uh...I never made it. Late-spring snowstorm. Chains only and I wasn't prepared."

"Ah. That's a shame," Trey replied.

"Dude!" Adam slapped him on the biceps. "You were around? Why didn't you call me? We could have played Madden the entire weekend."

"Angie doesn't like you playing video games."

"And that's why Angie and I are no longer dating. She kept ragging on me about all of the stuff I like, even though I tried to compromise and do things she likes too. I even watched *Outlander* for her."

"I thought you watched *Outlander* because you liked it," Gabriella said as she placed a cup of coffee before Colby and Ben.

"You were so sad when it went on hiatus."

"I like *Outlander* because Angie is always in a sexy mood afterward. I don't get excited watching a bunch of men running around in skirts. Anyway, I figured if I cringed every time she called, it was time to end things, so now I've got free time and it's great." He squinted in thought as he munched on a sausage link as if it were the end of a cigar. "So if you weren't with your family, what did you do all weekend, Colby?"

The bite of sausage lodged in his throat and burned as he swallowed hard. It took everything within him not to look over at Ben. "I...caught up on my reading."

"Seriously?" Adam blinked with disbelief. "You were reading?"

"I like to read. Actually, I picked up this new fantasy—"

"Spare me. Please," Adam interrupted with a raised hand. "I know alien life-forms and dragons and shit get you hot, but I'm just going to get confused and tune you out anyway."

Exactly. Just what he was counting on to take the attention off himself and on to anything else.

He kept his head down and shoveled in his breakfast as the others conversed around him. It wasn't as if he were a big conversationalist anyway. He much preferred to observe those around him than contribute.

Trey stood, wiping his mouth with a napkin. "Ben, let me know when you finish moving that fence line today. I want to release some of the herd onto the new land."

"Will do." Ben stood as well. "The new fence is constructed, and we'll be pulling the old fence up first thing."

"Excellent. See you on the flipside, fellas."

"Ready, partner?" Ben asked and settled his hat on his head.

"One second." Colby went to the sink to rinse off his plate and set his dishes in the dishwasher. "See you later, Gabriella."

Mark's wife sent them off with a wave and a sack lunch. He followed Ben to the garage where they jumped into the work truck and made off for the tool shed before heading out to the far edge of the property Trey had recently acquired from the neighboring ranch. For the last week, he and Ben had been working their asses off installing the new fence bisecting the properties. The backbreaking work out in the elements with the cows and the packed earth beneath his feet was the kind he liked. It was a time to let his mind wander and think on whatever came into his head. And that morning, he had a lot on his mind.

"You're ruminating on something really hard over there," Ben remarked after they had gone several minutes with not a word between them. "I think I can actually hear your brain working."

"I guess," he replied with a shrug.

"I'm willing to listen, if you have things you want to get off your chest."

Colby looked over. "I don't. Even know. Where to begin."

A chuckle rumbled in Ben's chest and he slapped Colby on the shoulder, knocking him against the passenger door. "You did kinda have your world rocked this weekend. Didn't ya?"

Damn, the man was strong. Colby rolled his shoulder to lessen the ache. "You have no idea. A part of me still can't believe it happened. That I dreamt it all."

"I'm sorry about the way it all went down. You took me by surprise, and I scrambled. But Faith looked so hot on her knees. I knew I had to give her the ultimate experience. You know, I meant what I said. You're the only man I trust with Faith."

"Thanks. I think." He reached up and scratched at an itch behind his ear. "I just can't believe that I never knew those things about you. Does anyone else know?"

"No one that I can think of. At least around here. It's not

exactly something you go blabbing about around town."

"Yeah. I can see that." They bumped over the uneven terrain about another quarter mile before he gathered the courage to ask, "So how did you know? That you liked to do those things?"

Ben tipped his head up to look at the sky out the window. It was a while before he answered, "I don't know where or why, exactly, but I'd say it was around the time I was working at The Crescent. My dad had left when I was younger, my mom had kicked me out, everything in my life was spiraling out of control, but sex—with sex I was the one in charge. Even though I was still a kid, everyone thought I was in my twenties, and I'd have these older women throwing themselves at me. I could say who, I could say how, I controlled what my partner felt and their reactions." He paused and looked down at his giant hand that he lifted from the steering wheel. "When you had Faith in the palm of your hands, doing whatever you wanted and watching her fucking melt for you, how did that make you feel?"

The heat of his memories thickened his blood and pooled in his groin. Her sighs, the clench of her body, the way her fingers gripped the edge of the table as he sank inside her. Although Ben had been guiding his actions, it was *him* that gave Faith so much pleasure. His voice was rough as he gritted out, "Powerful."

"Damn straight. It's such a high, man. But dangerous. You're responsible for someone else's safety. That's something you can't fuck with."

"I noticed that." He shook his head to dissipate the lingering arousal. "Faith—Faith is, uh, something else."

Ben blinked a few times, then pressed his lips into a thin line. "She sure is."

With a lick of his lips, Colby voiced the question that had been eating at him most of the night. "Are you ever gonna ask her out? Like on a real date?"

Ben flicked his gaze in Colby's direction for a second then shrugged. "I hadn't thought about it."

"Why not?" he almost shouted, but kept his voice moderately even. If Faith was his girl, he'd want to take her out, show her off, and see the world through her eyes.

But she wasn't his girl. On the other hand, he wasn't one hundred percent sure she was Ben's either. Yeah. One more thing to add to his cart of confusion.

Ben sighed. "Look. Faith is great. She's smart, sexy as hell, and just a genuinely nice person. But she's young. For now she may want what I have to offer, but someday she's gonna want to settle down. Start a family. And she'll want a man who could give that to her. She deserves that."

"Why can't you be that man?"

Gravel skittered in all directions as Ben hit the brakes. "Me? Ah, no. I'm way past the settling-down age. If I had kids now, I'd be in my sixties by the time they graduated high school. Kids deserve young parents who will be around for them for a long time. At least in theory, anyway."

"Are you sure it's because you don't think you can be faithful to one woman?"

At that, Ben nailed him with a hard glare. "Make no mistake, Colby. Just because I like my sex kinky doesn't mean I can't be faithful. Never have any of my relationships ended because I was the one stepping out."

"Sorry." Colby tossed his hands into the air. "Sorry. I wasn't questioning your honor." That much. "I'm just trying to understand how the whole multiple-partner thing worked. And what if Faith wants more from you?"

"She won't," Ben said with absolute conviction ringing in his tone.

"How do you know?"

"Experience. She's gonna have her fun and move on. They always do," he muttered and looked back out the windshield.

Damn. That sounded so… depressing. How many times had Ben seen a woman he had invested time with walk away and use that newfound knowledge on some other lucky schmuck?

Actually, there was a lot more stuff Colby began to wonder about his friend. Things about his personal life he had never thought to question. It had never occurred to him that Ben might be lonely, or have had his heart broken. Was there a girl who had been the one who got away? Did she leave on her own, like Ben claimed, or did he push her away, thinking she was like all the rest?

Somehow, he suspected Faith was different. Colby would bet good money that she was falling in love with Ben, if she wasn't head over heels already. She had that same dreamy look in her eyes that Gabriella and Greta had when they gazed at their men. That look that made another man's stomach curl with the sappiness while at the same time green with envy that it wasn't directed at him. Faith was smitten, all right. How could Ben not see it?

"Let's say Faith wants more," he said. "What if she said, 'Ben, I want to be your girlfriend. Your one and only.' What then?"

"She *is* my one and only. I don't have the time and energy for more than one woman at a time."

"You know what I mean."

A pink flush raced across his cheeks as he shrugged again. "I don't know. I guess part of me would always be waiting for that other shoe to drop."

"So don't let it drop. You should ask her out on a date. A real date."

Ben shook his head and remained silent.

"What if someone else asks her out before you do? Then what?"

His head swung around so fast, the truck veered to the right. "Who's thinking of asking her out?"

Well, he had been thinking about giving it a go until Ben hit him with that glare that warned of imminent death. No way he was going to admit that out loud while trapped inside the cab of a pickup truck with nothing but miles of open pasture land around them.

But if Ben wasn't going to make his move, why shouldn't he? His nervousness around women stemmed from his lack of confidence in the sex department. With that part between him and Faith already settled, the rest should be a breeze.

Of course, he did suspect Ben was talking out his ass when he claimed he'd let Faith go with nothing more than a hearty handshake and best wishes. Ben liked her a lot.

"Anyone might ask her out," he said, knowing full well he could be poking the beast. "We both agree she's great. And if you're not going to stake a claim on her, what's to stop someone else from trying?"

"Stake a claim," Ben scoffed. "She's not a piece of land."

"No. But you know how guys are. If they think there's a shot, someone will take it. Besides, you heard what happened when she first returned to town. Adam said his dad had to go down to the barber shop and retrieve half his workforce one day. Do you really want Faith to end up with one of those guys?"

Ben grunted but kept his gaze straight ahead. Colby let the thought sink in as they approached a section of pasture where the new and old fence converged.

With each rail and section of barbed wire they removed,

hundreds more acres of grassland would be opened up for exploration. More land for the cattle and more land for the men of the Sprawling A to maintain. Growth was difficult sometimes. Challenging as much as it was rewarding. Ben had opened Colby's eyes to passion, domination, and obedience. Maybe he could return the favor by giving his friend the confidence to hope for more. To not be planning for the end before giving the beginning a chance to develop.

He knew by the time he got to be Ben's age, he wanted a family of his own. Someone to come home to and hold in his arms at night. His other half. Ben deserved the same, and Colby had a hunch that girl was Faith.

If only he could get Ben to take the chance. "Ask her out. You know she'll say yes, and you know you both will have a good time."

"Why are you so concerned about me and Faith this morning?" Ben asked, giving him the side eye.

"Because you're my best friend, and I like Faith. I think you two are good together and I'd hate to see her slip away because you were being too much of a chicken shit."

"Chicken shit, huh?" He shook his head but smiled. "I'll think about it."

"Don't think, Obi-Wan. Do."

They climbed out of the truck and retrieved their shovels and pickaxes from the flatbed. Colby would give Ben a week to ask out Faith. That would give him plenty of time to make sure there was room for him to move into the main house, because if Ben didn't ask her out, he would take that chance.

Chapter Ten

"WHO IS SHE?"

"Ah!" Ben jumped with a shout and almost lost his grip on the broom. "Jesus, Greta. Are you trying to put me in an early grave?"

The boss's wife stood in the entrance to the barn with her hands planted on her hips. With the sunlight spilling in behind her, she looked like an avenging angel, and Ben had an idea of who she might be avenging.

Still, he could play dumb with the rest of them. "She who?"

"Don't give me that, Ben Castillo." She stomped closer. Her pregnant belly jutted out as if the baby in her womb was also wagging its finger at him in reprimand. "For the last three weeks I've seen an car I don't recognize drive down to your and Colby's place. As soon as I saw a flash of red hair in the distance I knew it was a woman and she was probably there to see you. So who is she?"

"And why does it matter?" he asked and focused on sweeping every piece of hay off the cement floor and out into the yard.

"Because you matter. If you are seeing someone, and your relationship has progressed to the point that she is spending the weekend with you, then I would hope that you'd want to introduce her to the rest of the family."

Right. The family. In other words, everyone who lived at the Sprawling A.

It had been way back when Trey's parents were still alive and running the ranch that he had stopped bringing girls to the main house. Mrs. Armstrong would fawn all over the girls and when the relationship ended, she wanted to dissect every conversation and action Ben had had with them to see where he had gone wrong. It didn't take him long to figure out it was best to keep the girls away.

"You'll land a wife one of these days, Benjamin," she'd say. "I know you'll be a good husband for some lucky girl."

While her concern over his love life was at times a little over the top, he knew Mrs. A was only acting out of love. She pretty much adopted him the moment her husband brought him home the night a couple of drunks had jumped the young man outside The Crescent. They hadn't taken too kindly when Ben had tossed them out for harassing the waitresses.

Doug Armstrong was leaving a cattleman's association meeting that was being held at the restaurant across the street when he witnessed the altercation. Mr. Armstrong had shouted, scaring the attackers away. When he had taken Ben to the emergency room and discovered that not only was Ben without medical insurance, but also underage and working at the bar, he decided that Ben would come home with him and gave him a job on the ranch. Mrs. A immediately took on the role of mother, especially when it came to smothering him with affection.

Sure, he'd brush off her attention, full of all the arrogance a boy of nineteen who thought he was wise to the ways of the world would do. But at night, he'd hug his pillow tight and refused to fall asleep for fear that he'd wake up and he'd find himself back on the flatbed of his truck with only the thigh-high grass off the side of the road for a bathroom.

Now, he wouldn't trade a second of Mrs. Armstrong's fussing, just as he wasn't about to tell Greta to go mind her own business. Deter her, sure, but he wasn't going to bite her head off because she cared about what was going on in his life. He was a private man, not an asshole.

He straightened and leaned on the tip of the broom handle. "I may be entering into a relationship with a female. It's new."

The motherly glow surrounding Greta turned up a notch as she bounced on the balls of her feet. "Who is she?"

"Her name is Faith. Faith O'Leary."

"O'Leary? As in George's daughter Faith? But isn't she—" she broke off as her eyes widened as if she just stepped into something one of the nearby cattle left behind. "I mean, she, uh—"

Ben caught what she was laying down. "Yes. She's younger than me. That's why we're keeping to ourselves and taking it slow."

"Right." Greta snorted. "That's why her car is at your place *all weekend.* I bet Colby's met her."

He choked on a laugh, remembering how during the previous weekend he had taught Colby how to hogtie Faith and they teased her so much, she broke down in tears before they fucked her silly. "Of course. He lives there too."

Greta harrumphed and folded her arms above her belly. "Is she nice?"

"She's really nice."

"Good. Then you will invite her to join us for Trey's birthday so I can welcome her to the ranch."

"Greta—"

"I hope that the only reason you haven't invited her over is because you are taking it slow and not because you are ashamed of us in any way, or because you think she isn't special enough to meet your family." Her eyes widened again. "Or is she just a booty call? Is that what's going on, Ben? Is she just an easy lay?"

For the love of Pete. "Damn it, woman. Why do you have to go and practice your mom guilting skills on me for?"

"Stuart's Steakhouse. Friday night," she said with a smile and a flutter of her lashes. "I'll expect to see you both there."

"I'll ask her. But she may already have plans."

"Then I'm sure you'll do your best to convince her to come." She turned away with a wave. "Enjoy the rest of your mucking."

Ben gazed out onto the pasture, and he swore the weight of the phone clipped to his belt grew heavier and heavier. He had been dragging his feet over asking Faith out on a real date, partly because he wasn't sure if their chemistry only lasted within the confines of their arrangement, but mostly because he was afraid she'd say no. What they had going was good, and it would be a shame if something as innocuous as a dinner invitation ruined everything.

But when Greta labeled what he had with Faith a booty call, yeah, that stuck in his craw something fierce. Faith deserved more than that from him.

On the other hand, dinner with the family was a lot different than dinner in a restaurant with just the two of them. Faith might not be prepared to face the onslaught of four inquisitive cowboys and the two women who'd do anything to protect them. Then again, she might be even less prepared to face a pregnant Greta who he wouldn't put past going around him and seeking Faith out on her own. Or have Gabriella join her in her quest.

No contest. He reached for his phone and dialed Faith's

number. If those two women reached his girl before he did, for certain he'd be the one on his knees the next time they met up.

FIVE MINUTES. THAT was all she'd give her. If her last appointment didn't walk through that door in five minutes, Faith was closing up shop and starting her weekend early. The night to come was too important to spend wasting time for a last-minute call-in that never showed.

Ben was taking her out. On a date. In public.

Not only was he taking her out, he had invited her to spend time with the friends and coworkers she knew he considered to be family. This was a big deal. Huge.

Wasn't it?

In her head, she tried to stay practical and not read too much into the invitation, but her heart had soared when he had called her the other day. Maybe they were progressing to something that included more than hot sex.

When they had first started out together, she had been so eager to learn from him, she didn't dare hope that the arrangement might become more permanent. And after the last month, becoming his one and only had blossomed to become her greatest wish. He was just so...so amazing. Sexy. Smart. She loved his laugh and the way he made their time together both intense and fun. Even when he pushed her to the point she felt as if she were dangling on the edge of the unknown, she trusted that he'd keep her safe, and he did.

Even though she'd been with him for such a short time, she knew she loved him. Now all she needed to do was convince him that she wasn't using him to explore her sexual nature and that she truly wanted all of him. After talking with Colby and gaining what little insight she could about Ben's past, she knew he'd been stung enough times by other women. She was probably going to have to hit him over the head with a frying pan to make her point. For now, she'd go the more subtle route and show him how much she loved being in his company. Hopefully the man would get the hint.

The bell over the door chimed, signaling an arrival, and Faith had to restrain the urge to shout "Hallelujah," especially when she saw Meredith Belhaven, Faith's preacher's wife, enter the barber shop.

"Good afternoon, Mrs. Belhaven. Did you get stuck behind a cattle drive?" Faith asked with a smile.

"Sort of. The Benedictos were moving their sprinklers from one end of their farm to the side across the highway. That was a lot of pipe blocking the roadway."

"That's life in the country for you."

"It's the price we pay for peace and quiet, so I don't mind." She shrugged off her overcoat and hung it on the peg by the door. "I'm so glad you could fit me in. Gloria at the Cut and Curl called out today with allergies and I just couldn't miss my hair appointment. Dave and I are taking Jennifer to tour colleges during spring break and I just have to look my best."

"Wow, Jennifer is old enough to be looking at colleges? I remember when I used to babysit her as a toddler."

"She graduates next year. It's all very exciting. Her younger sister is thrilled." She paused and glanced around the room with a wary eye. "So. This is where Dave has his hair cut. It's very...rustic."

Why did the woman look as if she smelled something funky? "I call it minimalist. As Dad says, the men come here to knock a chore off their list and talk to the other fellas. They don't come to discuss the décor. Let's get you shampooed, and you can tell me what you want done."

Mrs. Belhaven sat gingerly in the chair in front of the sink. "I'm partial to the style I have now. I just need it reshaped so it's not so shaggy."

"No problem." Faith popped the release on the back of the chair. "Lean back here and relax."

"Oh. Now this is nice," Mrs. Belhaven remarked as Faith dug her fingers into the bleach-blonde tresses and massaged her scalp. "I can see now why so many of the men folk have been coming in while you're working. You do give a good shampoo."

"Thank you," she replied, although the praise sounded more like an accusation than a compliment.

Once Mrs. Belhaven was seated in the barber's chair and pumped to the correct height, she asked Faith, "Speaking of fellas, are you seeing anyone special?"

"Well, there is one guy. But it's new and I don't want to jinx it."

"Is he of good stock? Decent family? Career oriented?"

"He's a ranch hand—"

"Oh no, dear."

Faith paused mid-snip. "Excuse me?"

"Stay away from the cowboys. Don't you know, dear? They may be fun for a little slap and tickle in your youth, but they are not husband material."

"About half of the town is made up of cowboys, Mrs. Belhaven. They can't all be bad."

Her snort suggested otherwise. "The Maguire family is the closest to being civilized, but they are so concentrated on making money they at times forget they're family and not business partners. Especially after Scott was killed in action. Such a brave soul. But that Adam is a loose cannon."

"Adam works for the Armstrongs."

"Humph. Now don't get me started on the Sprawling A."

"What's wrong with the Sprawling A?"

Mrs. Belhaven rolled her eyes. "To start, not one of them attends church, and after the way the entire community rallied around them after their son passed away, you'd think they'd feel some attachment to the church. And the way Mark shacked up with that woman before she was divorced? Shameless. And then there's Benjamin."

"Ben?" The scissors in her hand felt as if they weighed ten pounds as she stood there and listened to this supposedly Christian woman speak so unkindly about her neighbors.

"Yes, Ben. He was a wild one when he was younger. Drinking, fighting, hooking up with all sorts of women. If not for the Armstrongs' generosity, he would have ended up in jail, of that I have no doubt. And..."

And... what other hateful rhetoric was this woman, who until a few minutes ago Faith had held great respect for, going to spout now?

Mrs. Belhaven's eyes lowered to half-mast and her lips pursed, clearly enjoying having an ear to listen to her malicious gossip. "I have been told that he is perverted and indulges in sins of the flesh."

"Uh—I. What?"

Mrs. Belhaven nodded and shifted in her seat. "That's right. Benjamin Castillo is a sinner."

Well, who the hell wasn't? "I don't understand."

"I had heard rumors for a long time, but a few years ago Helen Renner came crying to my husband about her son Ryan. He moved to the city right out of high school and seemed to do nothing but drink beer, hang out with his friends, and date questionable women. He rarely came home or returned her phone calls. So she and her husband went to surprise him with a visit. He was just leaving when they arrived and they followed him to a nightclub, only it wasn't a nightclub. It was a sex club! Helen about dropped dead of shock when she saw what he was up to."

"They went inside?"

"Why, of course. All who enter are welcomed and told they'll get exactly what they need. Well, Helen needed to be taken out on a stretcher, that's what she did. When they got Ryan home, they asked how he had heard of such a place. That is not the kind of behavior a boy from Mission indulges in. And he told them Ben Castillo told him about the club. Apparently he's a regular there."

Although she knew Ben had connections to the lifestyle in the city, to hear it confirmed made her a little bit queasy. But what overrode the lick of jealousy was the hurt that her pastor and his wife thought ill about the man she was falling in love with. "Was it illegal, what he was doing?"

Mrs. Belhaven blinked as if struck dumb. "Well, not in the sense of the law, but what he was engaged in was morally illegal. And his downfall was all on the account of that no-good cowboy."

Really. From what she remembered, Ryan Renner was a charmer who used his blond good looks to his advantage many times. In Faith's opinion, Ryan would have found that club with or without Ben's help.

She set the shears in their holder on the counter before she gave in to the urge to cut a section of Mrs. Belhaven's hair down to the scalp.

Restraining the tremor in her voice she said, "Ben Castillo has been a customer of my father for over twenty years. He is one of the most polite, loyal, upstanding men I know."

"Don't let your lady parts steer you down the path of sin, Faith. I know that man is a handsome devil, but he's just that. A devil. What you need is a nice Christian boy. You know, Deacon Brady's son has just returned from the Peace Corps. He was mentioning just the other day how he was looking for a wife to settle down with."

"It's time to style your hair," Faith said with a shout and picked up the hairdryer, turning the appliance to full blast to drown out any more blathering by the hateful woman.

Why didn't she remember Meredith Belhaven being such an awful person? So judgmental and holier than thou?

As a child, she remembered church being a welcoming community. Sure, at times it was as boring as watching ice cream melt in the sun, but everyone was friendly and kind. Perhaps she had been naïve in thinking Mission was without prejudice. That because of the size of the population, any hint of bigotry would come to light immediately, and she hoped squashed just as quickly. From the sound of it, Mrs. Belhaven and her group of cronies had been brewing ill will for a long time.

Faith couldn't get that woman out of her chair fast enough, whipping the cape away and brushing the woman down without a single concern if she had removed all of the little hairs.

"Yes. I think that will do," Mrs. Belhaven said as she smoothed her hand over her hair then picked up her purse. "What do I owe you?"

"Thirty-five will do."

"Thirty-five?" she exclaimed with a gasp. "Gloria only charges me twenty-five."

"At the salon in Yakima we charge forty-five. I gave you a discount."

"And that there's another reason why I prefer to live in a small town." She thumbed through the small stack of crisp bills. She withdrew the asked-for amount and some additional ones. "Here you go."

A three-dollar tip? The woman needed to pay her more for having tortured her with her rhetoric. "Thank you, Mrs. Belhaven."

"Will you be attending service this weekend with your father again?"

"Perhaps. I had errands planned and was thinking of sticking close to home."

"Well, don't be a stranger. We'd love to see you."

Faith forced a smile and clasped her hands behind her back to keep from pushing the woman out the door.

The second the door closed, she threw the deadbolt and leaned against the wood with a weary sigh. "Good. God."

She needed a drink.

No. She needed to be held, and kissed, and hug and kiss in return. Thankfully there was a cowboy waiting for her just a few blocks away who only cared if she was happy. She'd gladly take one Ben Castillo over a million Meredith Belhavens any day.

Chapter Eleven

STUART'S STEAKHOUSE WAS crowded with its typical Friday dinner crowd. As Faith walked through the main dining room toward the banquet area, she waved or nodded a greeting at those she recognized. Seeing so many friendly faces as the scent of steak sauce and grilled meat filled her nose, the memories of her time with Mrs. Belhaven blew away like a cloud of steam in a windstorm.

Boisterous laughter spilled through the open archway, causing her to hesitate just inside the entrance. As welcoming as the sound was, she wasn't yet ready to make a grand entrance into a room full of mostly strangers.

Over the heads of everyone else in the room, she spotted Ben standing in the corner. The seams of his dark blue cotton shirt looked ready to pop as the fabric hugged the slope of his broad shoulders. His cheeks appeared freshly shaved, and she swore she could smell the scent of his aftershave over the aroma of garlic and pepper. In her opinion, there was nothing better than snuggling against his strong chest and inhaling his citrus-cedar fragrance. No doubt about it, he was one scrumptious specimen of mankind.

As if he sensed her gaze, he turned in her direction and a

smile curled the corner of his mouth, and she melted against the doorway. With his easy, long-legged stride, he crossed the room, his gaze eating her up from her head to her toes as he came to a stop before her.

"You're wearing my favorite boots of yours," he said.

"I'm wearing other of your favorite things too, but you'll have to wait until we're alone to see them."

His smile widened and he held out his hand. "Come on in and join the circus."

Conversation died as he drew her deeper into the circle of people, and she felt her face flame as all eyes turned in her direction. Was it really such an anomaly for Ben to bring a date to meet his friends? And why did the possibility of that being true make her so deliriously happy?

Ben brought them before the birthday boy and his beaming wife. Greta Armstrong was the epitome of glowing mom-to-be with her sparkling eyes and a smile so wide, Faith wondered if her cheeks were sore.

"Faith," Trey exclaimed and stepped forward for a brief hug. "Long time no see. It's been a while."

"It has. Happy birthday." She handed him a gift bag. "Ben mentioned how much you all enjoy watching football and baseball, so I put together a bag of goodies for the next game."

"Thanks, Faith. That was awfully sweet of you." He stuck his nose in the bag and inhaled. "Is that Cracker Jacks? Yum. Oh, hey, have you met my wife, Greta?"

"Yes, once years ago," Faith replied. "It's good to see you again."

To her surprise, Greta enveloped her in a big hug. She wasn't used to near strangers initiating physical contact. "It's good to see you too. When did you move back to this side of the mountains?"

"A few months ago."

"Did you grow tired of life on the road, traveling with the theater?" she asked as she stepped back, keeping a grip on Faith's hand.

"Exactly."

"Well, come sit with me and tell me about some of your adventures." She leaned close to whisper with a wink. "Of both your travels and of the local kind."

Faith looked over at Ben, who smiled and shook his head as if to say, *Do what the lady wants.* "Can I get you anything to drink, Faith?" he asked.

"A white wine would be nice."

"I'll be right back." He pressed a kiss to her cheek then whispered in her ear, "Don't be scared. She's curious."

"I kind of figured that," she said with a smile.

While Ben left to fetch her a beverage, Greta pulled her to where the restaurant staff was setting up the buffet.

"I'm starving," she announced and handed Faith a plate before getting one for herself. "I don't know what everyone else is waiting for, but I'm digging in."

A server approached them from the other side of the table. "Excuse me, Mrs. Armstrong, but we're not ready to serve yet."

"But everything is set out."

He shook his head. "Not yet. We're waiting on the dressings and butter. You'll have to wait."

Greta's eyes narrowed and shifted the fork in her hand into a stabbing position. "Did you just tell the hungry, pregnant woman who is paying you good money to wait?"

Faith choked on a giggle as the server paled. "No. No," he sputtered. "Please go right ahead."

"Damn straight," she muttered and jabbed her fork into a thick cut of steak. She turned to Faith with a smile. "I do love being pregnant."

"It suits you. You look absolutely radiant."

"Why, thank you." She stabbed another piece of meat. "Steak?"

"Yes, please."

As Faith filled her plate, she jumped as two hands came out of nowhere from behind her and cupped her shoulders. She detected the familiar scent of Colby's aftershave a second before he dropped a kiss on her cheek. "Hi, Faith. Talk to you later. Hold up, Adam. That pie is mine."

"Hi bye?" she replied as Colby let go of her so quickly, she swayed on her feet.

"I swear," Greta said with a laugh. "Those boys think of nothing but their stomachs. Well, sometimes girls, but the conversation always seems to return to food."

"I wish I had their metabolism," Faith said as she followed Greta to a table and sat down.

"You and me both, sister."

Ben set a glass of wine by her place setting before heading off to join the buffet line while Greta helped Faith reacquaint names with faces of all of those who were in attendance to wish her husband a happy birthday.

"So all of those men right there work for your ranch?" Faith asked, gesturing to the group of spruced-up cowboys.

Greta nodded with a smile and her mouth full of food.

The group of seven men squabbling over who got what cut of beef were just as delicious looking as the hunks of meat they fought over. There must be some kind of magic spell over at the Armstrong ranch in order to attract such fine-looking gentlemen.

"That is ridiculous," she said with a shake of her head.

"Uh-oh. I recognize that look," said a beautiful brunette who joined them at their table. "Yes, they are that obscenely good looking, and even worse, they're really nice too."

Greta laughed. "Faith, have you met Gabriella?"

"No, I haven't." She wiped her hand on her napkin before extending it. "But I've heard lots about you. I'm Faith O'Leary. It's nice to finally meet you."

"Oh, yeah. I've heard of you, too. Welcome home."

Faith raised her wineglass for a toast. "And congratulations on your nuptials. I wish you lots of happiness."

Gabriella laughed and raised her glass in return. "I will gladly accept it."

"Holy hell." Melody Webber plopped down in the last seat at the table and blew her bangs out of her eyes. "You'd think they hadn't just eaten a few hours ago. Those animals."

"Hey, Mel. You stole my seat," her brother Mark grumbled right behind her.

"You snooze you lose, brother mine."

He snorted. "Move. I want to sit next to my wife."

"Nope," Greta said and shooed him away. "This is a girls-only table. You and the boys go sit somewhere else so we can gossip about you."

His lips barely moved as he murmured, "Is that right?" And his dark eyes sparkled with laughter. "Then why isn't Stacy sitting with you?"

He nodded over to a table in the corner where Jack Cannon sat snuggled next to a blonde. Faith would have considered her pretty, if she didn't have such a sour expression pinching her features. She picked at her plate of food as if it wasn't fit for consumption and sighed with undisguised boredom as Jack talked with the other people at the table.

"I think Stacy will be more comfortable where she's at," Greta said with a tight smile.

Faith leaned closer to whisper, "Is there something about

this Stacy I should be aware of?"

"She's really pretty," Gabriella answered. "And that's about the extent of her appeal, aside from her parents' bank account. But Jack's happy, so we keep our opinions to ourselves. For now."

"You can do without your bride for twenty minutes," Greta said to Mark. "Take the men folk to that table over there and talk about how great we are."

Gabriella blew a kiss at her husband. "I'll miss you."

"Don't worry, Gabriella. My brother can survive without being joined with you at the hip."

"I think it's sweet," Faith said.

"You don't have to see them kissing on each other all of the time." Melody dusted the breadcrumbs off her fingers then did a double take as her gaze finally met Faith's for the first time that evening. "Faith, that *is* you. Sorry I'm being such a space cadet and haven't even said hello. Hi. Hello. So what have you been up to lately?"

"Ben," Greta said with a snicker. "They're dating."

"Get out," Gabriella exclaimed as Melody added, "No shit. Since when?"

Technically? All of ten minutes. "Oh, about a month now."

Greta turned her chair to better face Faith. "Tell me everything. He's such a private guy, he won't say a word. The jerk. How did you meet?"

"Well, I've known Ben for, like, forever. But we crossed paths again when he came into the barber shop while I was covering for my dad."

"And he asked you out right away?"

"Actually, I kind of had to ask him out."

"You go, girl." Gabriella raised her wineglass in a salute. "I swear these boys are dense sometimes. I practically had to tie

Mark to the bed before I could get him to agree to go out with me."

"You *did* tie him to the bed," Melody reminded her with a shiver of disgust. "A fact I could have gladly gone my entire life without knowing."

"You're into bondage?" Faith asked excitedly, almost adding the word "too" before she caught herself.

"Cover your ears, Melody," Gabriella warned. "Not hard core, but Mark and I like to spice things up now and again."

"Eww." Melody made a gagging noise. "Do you want me to tell you about my time with *your* brother?"

Gabriella's smile dropped. "No."

"Wait." Faith raised her hand. "You're dating Gabriella's brother?"

"Dated," Melody clarified with a hard pronunciation on the past tense. "Very briefly dated. He's a nice guy and all, but for me, the biggest appeal was how it irked Mark to see us together. What we lacked was spark. I want spark."

"I hear you." Faith nodded. "Spark is everything."

"And you spark with Ben?" Greta asked with stars in her eyes.

Faith glanced over to where Ben sat with his friends, but his gaze was fixed on her, stripping her down to her soul and letting her know without a movement or quirk of the brow that when he got her alone, there was not one part of her he wasn't going to possess.

"Yeah," she sighed. "We spark."

"No kidding." Gabriella laughed. "You're smoking. I've never seen that look on his face before."

"Me either," Greta added. "Makes me hungry for some man loving of my own. Okay, now I'm regretting the 'no boys at the table' rule. Finish up, girls. Let's go get our men."

"That's it. Remind the single girl that she's all alone," Melody grumbled.

Gabriella patted her hand. "For now. Just keep that in mind. For now."

How long had it been since Faith sat with a group of women and giggled as if they had been friends for decades? Melody she knew from school and had always been on friendly terms with, but Greta and Gabriella were new to her circle but she already loved them to pieces. Especially when they made an effort to welcome her to their world.

Throughout the evening, they laughed, traded stories, and made sure she was either introduced or reacquainted with everyone in the room. When Ben joined them, he kept his arm was around her, and she sensed his sigh of relief as she integrated with his ranch family. Apparently she hadn't been the only one worried about fitting in.

Just when she thought she couldn't eat another bite, a massive two-tiered cake was rolled in on a cart complete with candles, sparklers, and decorated with cowboy boots and spurs cut out of fondant. The crowd erupted into a rousing chorus of "Happy Birthday" as Trey's cheeks turned pink and he laughed so hard at the off-tune caterwauling, he doubled over.

"Speech. Speech," Adam shouted when the song was over and clapped his hands. Soon the entire room was clamoring for some words from the birthday boy.

"Wow." He wiped a hand down his face. "You guys…you guys have no idea what it feels like, being here with all of you. Celebrating with my friends and family, especially knowing that this day almost never was." As his eyes filled with tears, the reflection of the sparklers made him look as if he beheld magic. His voice was raspy as he choked out a heartfelt, "Thank you for being with me today."

And with that, he turned toward his wife and pulled her in for a hug so tight, Faith was almost afraid their unborn baby was being squished, but she knew there was no better place for that baby to be. She remembered hearing about the death of their first child, and she could only imagine how they must be feeling as they waited for their second go-round.

She always liked Trey. And his parents. His mother had made the best chocolate chip cookies ever. Whenever her husband came to the barber shop for a haircut, she always made sure to send a batch for the O'Learys. Her father, knowing how much Faith loved those cookies, would guard them from his hungry customers and make certain not a one was stolen. For Faith's sweet sixteen, Mrs. Armstrong sent her a box of cookies and the recipe on a laminated card—a gift that soon turned bittersweet when Mr. and Mrs. Armstrong were killed in a car accident just a few months later. Those cookies were the only thing Faith could bake with absolute certainty that would not burn or turn into rocks, and to this day she still had that card tucked into her family recipe book.

It warmed her heart to be surrounded by so much love and joy. To be included in something so special as the connection these people had with each other was such a wonderful change from being around the negativity she had been subjected to with Meredith Belhaven, she was ready to shed a tear herself.

A squeeze around her waist brought her attention up to Ben's warm gaze. Good thing he had a hold on her, or her weak knees would have sent her sprawling to the floor.

"I'm glad you're here," he said softly.

"I'm glad you invited me."

He smiled and leaned in for a brief kiss on the lips that heated her blood quicker than any of the more ardent kisses they had shared before. It was a simple kiss that gave her hope that maybe her wish of them being more than sub and Dom was actually on the path of coming true.

The cozy moment was lost when Jack's girlfriend Stacy bumped into her from the side as she turned toward him with a flounce. "Jack, honey, let's go someplace to have some real fun."

"We will, Stace. I want some cake first."

"How can you want cake when you just had half a pie?"

He looked at her in shock. "It's from Dolce Vita. They make the best cakes."

"Fine," she said with a roll of her eyes. "Have your cake, then let's go meet up with my friends over at The Crescent."

A hush fell over those in the immediate area, and Faith felt the hairs on the back of her neck stand at attention. She wasn't sure what had been said to cause such a reaction, but she sensed it was something big.

After several tense seconds, Jack scratched at the pink scar bisecting his right eyebrow. "The Crescent, huh?" he asked with a slight tremor in his voice.

"Of course," Stacy said. "That's where everyone hangs out."

"Right. Right," he nodded somewhat absentmindedly. The faraway look in his eyes made Faith's arms itch to give him a hug, but since that wasn't really her place, she tightened her hold on Ben's waist and waited.

"Jack." Gabriella stepped forward and placed her hand on his arm. "Mark and I will come with you."

He looked surprised at the offer. "Really? You don't have to."

"I want to." She looked over at Mark, who nodded and came up behind her to enfold her in a hug. "It'll be good for us."

"Okay." His smile was bit forced, but his shoulders slumped as if a weight had been lifted.

"We'll go too," Ben said. "If that's all right with you, sweetness."

"Absolutely." Even though she didn't know why, instinctively she understood that it was important for them to show their support.

"That's my girl."

Oh, she did love it when he smiled at her in that soft and dreamy way of his. He could have asked her to go watch cattle sleeping and she would have happily agreed if it meant spending more time with him.

After cake had been consumed, they had a small crowd ready to go across town to the honky-tonk. Trey and Greta headed home, claiming the baby was sapping her strength, but Faith suspected they wanted to have a little personal celebration of their own.

Colby drove Ben's truck so Ben could ride with Faith to the bar. Watching him try to adjust the seat to make room for his long legs was quite comical.

"Is there something I should know about Jack and The Crescent Moon?" she asked as they got under way.

"Gabriella's ex-husband and his friends jumped Jack and Gabriella when they were leaving the bar one night. They kidnapped Gabriella and beat the shit out of Jack."

"Oh no." The car swerved as she jerked in shock. "That's terrible. I thought it looked like Jack's nose was broken recently."

"And his cheekbone and a few ribs too. They really did a number on him. That was back last fall, and neither of them have been back to the bar since."

"I don't blame them. I hope Gabriella's ex was put in jail for a very long time."

"All parties involved are in jail and will be for a while, just not long enough, in our opinion."

"Does Jack's girlfriend know this?"

"The whole town knows. It was all anyone talked about for months."

"And she still suggested they go to a place where he was attacked. What is wrong with her?"

Ben turned to her and flashed a plastic smile. "She's really pretty."

"You think she's pretty?" she asked, allowing her shocked tone to convey her doubt of his intelligence.

He raised a dark brow. "You don't think she's pretty?"

"She's thin and blonde. That's about it. I guess she's pretty in that bitchy, popular-girl way."

"Please, don't hold back." He began to laugh so hard, the windows practically rattled with his booming bass. "Seriously, I agree with you. But Jack likes her, so we deal. But I'll let you in on a secret. Trey's mom refused to say anything unkind about anyone, but you knew there were times when she really wanted to let loose, so whenever anyone asked her opinion about someone she didn't care for, she'd just smile and say, 'They're really pretty.' That was code for 'I'd rather lick a dollar bill than spend any time with them.' We've carried on the tradition since her passing."

"Do you think Mrs. Armstrong would have liked me? The me I am now and not the kid she knew?"

"Oh yeah," he rumbled in that way that felt as if he had dipped her in warm syrup. "She would have adored you."

Do you adore me?

She bit her tongue on the question and instead said, "I like your family. I've known most of them from high school, but it's been so long, and we're such different people now, it's nice to get to know them again."

He reached out and wound a lock of her hair around his

finger. "I like that you called them my family and not my friends."

"They are, aren't they?"

"Yeah, but not everyone sees it that way. You're a special person, Faith."

Ack! Why did she have to be the one driving? She wanted to launch into his arms and kiss those firm lips and feel the purr in his chest as he sighed.

She pressed the accelerator and sped the last remaining blocks to The Crescent's parking lot, spraying gravel all over as she hit the brakes and turned off the car with Ben chuckling by her side. She swallowed his laughter as she threw off her seatbelt before the car stopped rocking and climbed over the emergency brake, sealing his mouth over hers in a hot kiss. It was a tight squeeze in the front seat of her little SUV, but she didn't care as long as his taste filled her mouth and the heat of his body surrounded her.

Ben was feeling the heated urgency with her, trying to wedge his hands between the dashboard and her backside as he groped her butt and hips. He sank his teeth into her fleshy lower lip and she howled in pleasure.

"Hey, you two." A pounding fist at the window broke them apart as she yelped in surprise. Adam's blond hair was all she could make out through the fogged-over glass. "If you're going to copulate, do it at home where us single guys don't have to watch."

Ben popped open the door. "Who said you have to watch? No one asked you to look in the window."

"Please, like I'm going to ignore a car rocking in what is obviously a good makeout session."

"Come on, sweetness." Ben shifted her on his lap until she spilled out of the car. "The anticipation will only make it sweeter."

"I don't know if I can hold out that long," she grumbled even as she smiled.

God, how she loved this. Spending time with him like a normal couple. Laughing, teasing, talking about future plans, even though the future he spoke of was only a few hours away. As he took her hand in his, she wished with all of her might that every night could be spent in the same fashion. Judging by the way Ben held onto her tight, she hoped he felt the same way.

The next few hours inside the beer-soaked wood-paneled walls, with the cover band playing country songs and having to shout at the top of her voice to be heard, were some of the best in Faith's life.

Ben's family accepted her as one of their own, chatting and treating her as if she'd been one of them all along. Never before had she laughed so hard, especially when she witnessed Adam on the dance floor.

"What is he doing?" she asked as she caught sight of his failing limbs.

"We ask ourselves that all of the time," Ben replied and cupped the side of her face, turning her away and tucking her against his chest as if he was shielding her from a violent crime scene.

Ben liked the slow songs, holding her in his arms and making her feel like a princess, even with the hay on the floor and cages in the corner for the wilder girls to climb in and shake their asses. When a fast song came on, he'd sit those out, setting her on his lap as they talked and sipped on their beers. Occasionally, Colby would ask her to dance, and to her surprise, they'd tear it up as he dipped and twirled her across the dance floor. The man had some serious energy that kept her laughing until she grew too hot to keep going.

"I need some air," she shouted to him over the music. "I'm going to step outside."

"I'll join you," he shouted back.

Clouds of cigarette smoke greeted them as they walked out the front door.

"Twenty feet, guys," she muttered at the smokers loitering on both sides of the doorway and headed deeper into the parking lot. "Twenty feet from the door, not millimeters."

"Wow, it's loud in there," Colby said with a shake of his head. "My ears are ringing."

"Mine too. I can't believe Ben worked in there every night."

"I know. And back then it was even rowdier. Of course, Ben is pretty bad ass. All of that sound probably bounced off all of his muscles."

"That would have been awesome to see. Woo." She swayed on her feet. "I haven't had tequila in a long time. Gabriella and Rafe can sure put it away."

"They claim it's their Mexican blood. Are you going to be okay? You look a little tipsy."

"I'm a lot tipsy."

"Here. Have a seat." He lifted her up and set her down on the hood of a beat-up Chevy pickup.

"What if I dent the hood?"

"This piece of shit belongs to Jack. He won't notice another dent."

"Be nice to Jack. He's a hero. With really bad taste in women."

Colby snorted with laughter. "I know. If we hadn't come along tonight, he'd be on his own while she ignored him for her friends."

"I know," she agreed, perhaps a little too loudly. "I'd never ignore my date."

"You kind of are now," he pointed out.

"Then let's go back inside." She tensed to jump off the truck when Colby stopped her with a hand on her thigh.

"Don't. Not yet." By the light of the streetlamp, his Adam's apple cast a shadow on his neck as it bobbed. "I like being out here with you. Like this."

The combination of the dreamy look in his eyes and the husky timbre of his voice drew her in like a socialite to a shoe sale, hypnotizing her with his seductive charm until she found herself pressed against him breast to chest. "I like being with you too. Is that bad? That I like it?"

"Truthfully, I don't know," he admitted with a wary chuckle, then leaned closer, so close his breath brushed her lips as his fingertips dug into the flesh of her thighs.

"Hey!"

They broke apart with a shout and Colby stumbled on his heels as Ben approached them from the shadows.

"Were you two getting frisky without me?" Ben asked.

"No, no," Colby stuttered. "I was just, we, uh, talking."

"Colby, I was joking." Ben scratched at his jaw as he frowned. "Sort of. I guess I should have laid it all out when I first asked you to join us. If you two want to be affectionate with each other, that's fine by me. Just let me know if you want more time with each other."

Maybe it was the tequila talking, but did she just hear Ben give the green light for her to kiss on his roommate whenever she wanted?

Apparently Colby had the same thought, but he phrased his confusion with much more clarity than she had the ability to at the moment when he asked, "Wha—?"

Ben chuckled. "You know how much I like seeing you two together. And it's only natural that you would grow close. Faith, do you want to kiss Colby?"

Way to put me on the spot there, buddy. But how could she answer with anything less than honesty as Colby stood there with his heart in his puppy-dog brown eyes as they waited for her to respond?

"Yes."

Colby let out a sigh of relief but snapped back to attention when Ben asked, "Do you want to kiss Faith?"

He blew out another breath. "Yeah. I do."

"Then kiss her," Ben said with a shove at Colby's back.

Was it really so simple? Could she hold affection for both men and be only in love with Ben?

She'd like to think her heart was big enough to care for more than one man, but this was taking "care for" to a new extreme.

Perhaps she needed to put a stop to whatever was happening between them at the moment. Perhaps she needed to jump off the truck, go back inside, and lose herself to the beat of the music until she passed out and woke up to a new day and a fresh perspective.

But then Colby lifted her chin with his finger and fit their mouths together so perfectly, it was as if they were two parts of the same whole. Her bones and muscles felt as if they liquefied under the sensual heat. If not for the arms of the two strong men on either side of her, she'd have slid right off the hood of the truck.

As Colby sampled her mouth with long, drugging kisses and languid strokes of his tongue, Ben ran his lips down the column of her neck. The collar of her blouse delayed him but only for a moment until he tugged the fabric down, exposing her lace-covered breast. With a jerk of his fingers, the cool night air hit the newly exposed nipple a second before being engulfed in his mouth.

It was almost as if the two men shared one mind as they each ran a hand up the inside of her thighs. One pushed the damp fabric of her panties aside while the other ran his fingertips over the puffy lips of her sex.

"You are always so wet," Colby marveled between kisses. "That is so hot."

"Yep." Ben popped off her breast for the brief moment to add, "She's always ready for us." He pushed a finger into her sheath as he drew her nipple deeper into his mouth. His thick digit sawed in and out for several strokes before he withdrew and began the invasion of her tight asshole. "Fill her pussy with your fingers."

"Oh God," she moaned and bit her lip as Colby took possession of her hungry channel as Ben continued taking her ass.

It was impossible to hold still as the two brought her to the brink of orgasm and left her dangling there while they took turns kissing her mouth and sucking at her nipples. Soon, the entire front of her shirt was pulled down and both of her breasts were out for them to feast on as she laid back on the hood of Jack's Silverado with the moon and the stars and the parking light of The Crescent Moon bar shining above them.

Her hands clutched at whatever she could grab onto—a fistful of hair, a contracting bicep, a bit of cotton straining over a slab of flexing muscles.

The stars seemed to swirl, and she swore she saw lights flashing as the men filled her body again and again.

"Are you going to come for us, sweetness?" Ben growled in her ear. "Right here? Right now?"

"Yes," she panted. "Yes."

The tension inside her grew to the point she was near tears. Just as she was about to crest the peak, a truck sped by on the nearby road. The old beater rattled past them on worn-out shocks and the breaks squealed as it slowed to round the corner.

The clatter broke the sexual haze they had all succumbed to as the men jumped and formed a barrier around her and any passersby.

"Let's take this inside," Ben said as he helped her sit up and right her clothing. "I know just the place."

"Your home?" she asked hopefully.

"I'm not that patient," he replied with a wink. "This late at night, the kitchen is closed, which means the pantry is empty. And plenty big enough for the three of us."

"The three of us to, what? Have sex? In public?" Faith gasped even as she skipped at his side to keep up with his long-legged stride.

"Naw, out in the parking lot was public." The curve of his smile sent a lick of heat over her body. "This will be a private party, just for us to get a little naughty."

Fooling around in a restaurant kitchen while a packed house was partying on the other side sounded like more than getting a little naughty. Ben had led her down some pretty bold paths lately, but did she have the courage to be so brazen?

She glanced behind her to see Colby right on their heels. His gaze caught hers, and in his eyes she saw everything she too was feeling, including the nerves, but most of all the glitter of excitement. With a big grin, he wiggled his eyebrows as if to say, "I'm game if you are."

She winked at him and let loose with a peal of laughter. She couldn't wait to see what else Ben considered to be "a little" naughty.

Chapter Twelve

GETTING OLD FUCKING sucked.

Okay, maybe he did overdo it a bit by trying to muscle an entire flatbed's worth of feed on his own. Now the only part of Ben's body that didn't hurt was his scalp. He wasn't quite sure why he was so sore. It was the same work he'd been doing for the last twenty years. Huh. Maybe that was the problem.

His body wasn't bouncing back like it used to. In the lifespan of a ranch hand, he was most certainly nearing the age of retirement. But as long as he kept up with the younger guys and performed the work, the reality of his age was easy to ignore. However, with each passing day, a constant ache had taken up residence in his lower back, and the last time he was at the doc's, the word "arthritis" had been mentioned when he had difficulty clenching his fist.

He opened the back door of his home to the scent of burnt toast and a chorus of hoots and hollers coming from the living room. The reason he had rushed through his tasks that day was because Faith had stayed over since she had Sunday off, and he wanted to continue where they had left off after crashing the moment they returned from Trey's party.

All of that dancing, drinking, and having a banging good

time in the pantry of the bar had wiped them all out. As it was, it had taken a monumental effort to climb out of bed to start his chores. It was his turn to manage the feed truck, a task he wasn't going to pawn off on one of the others, and the cows didn't care if he had a warm, willing woman in his bed.

Apparently Colby had the same idea, as he had already returned and was sitting next to Faith on the couch.

Ben paused in the kitchen door and took in the sight of the two adults bouncing on the sofa with game controllers in hand as they cursed at the images kart wheeling across the television screen.

"How did you do that?" Colby shouted.

"I got skills," Faith replied.

"No. Seriously, how did you do that? I've never seen that player do that move before."

"I don't know. I moved my thumb like this." She twirled her thumb over the controller.

Colby gaped with a mixture of shock and disgust. "You're just randomly pushing buttons? How are you beating me?"

"I told you, I've got skills." She tossed him a grin before moving her thumbs wildly over the controller. Her shoulders rolled as if she were on a crazy, twisty roller coaster.

The ninja character on the right side of the screen landed a series of punches and kicks to its opponent, knocking the head clean off. As the body fell to the ground, Faith jumped to her feet, her arms raised in triumph. "Woo-hoo! Oh! Hi, Ben."

She dropped the controller and sprinted to him, launching herself straight into his arms with enthusiastic laughter.

Oh shit.

He almost didn't catch her in time, barely getting his arms around her backside as her legs wrapped around his waist. A groan of pain burst past his lips as he stumbled into the wall.

"Oh my God, Ben." She jumped down. "Are you all right? Did I hurt you?"

"Nope," he wheezed. "Just caught me by surprise was all. I'm learning I can't party as hard as I work anymore."

"Are you sure? You don't look so good."

"I'm fine. Just fine." He forced a smile to his lips. "So, you two having fun?"

"Yeah. Colby introduced me to the joys of Ninja Warriors in Space." She leaned in close to whisper. "I think he regrets asking me to play. Can I get you anything? I can heat you up some soup. Or make you a grilled cheese."

Behind her, Colby shook his head and made the kill signal with his hand across his throat.

"Naw, sweetness. I ate a little bit ago. What I need is a long, hot shower. Get the stink of cattle off me."

She snuggled up against his chest. "When you're done, I'll give you a nice, deep massage and work all of those kinks out."

"Now you're talking." He took her lips in a brief kiss. "I'll call you when I'm ready."

Her smile never faltered, but he saw the concern in her eyes as she rejoined Colby on the couch. Although his thighs burned and knees ached, he kept his stride steady as he crossed to the stairs.

A few steps up, he heard the pings and whistles from the video game resume. Sheer curiosity brought him back down to peer around the corner.

From his spot on the stairs, he was able to see their faces as they moved their torsos in time with the actions on the screen. Colby wore the most serious expression Ben had ever seen from him, with a snarl on his lip and brows drawn low. Every so often he'd flick his gaze toward Faith, his lips pressing tighter together the longer the round lasted.

By his side, Faith was just as focused, but she had a smile that twisted and turned as she manipulated her character. When she performed a maneuver that gave her unexpected results, her eyes would widen and she'd hoot with surprise.

Colby began to growl, his thumbs flying faster and faster until he jumped out of his seat with a shout. "Yeah! Take *that*, bitch."

"Excuse me?" Faith screeched.

He dropped the controller and fell to his knees at her feet. "Sorry. I am so sorry. I got carried away."

"No shit." She crossed her arms, and her lips puckered into the cutest little pout. "You didn't hear me call you names when I won."

"I do take my games a little too seriously. I'm sorry." He leaned forward and pressed a series of kisses to the firm line of her lips. "I'm sorry, sweetheart."

Sweetheart? When did Colby start calling her nicknames?

She turned away from his kisses. "You don't get to be sweet to me after you call me a bitch."

"I've never called anyone a bitch. Well, except Adam, but he calls me a motherfucker when we play. But never before have I called a woman a bad name."

"So I'm supposed to be glad to be your first?"

"No." He laughed. "You're supposed to forgive me, because I'm really, really, really sorry."

Each sorry was punctuated with soft kisses until Faith melted and kissed him back. Colby moved next to her on the couch and reclined into the corner, coaxing her to drape over his chest. Cupping the back of her neck with one hand, his other hand skimmed over the curve of her ass and back up again. Soon the sounds of their soft moans drowned out the tinny bass of the video game.

Not for a second did Ben feel a speck of jealousy watching his girl make out with his best friend. They looked so natural together, so...so in love. At least on Colby's part. Faith, well, with Faith it was a little harder to decipher how exactly she felt about the man. There was definitely affection on her part, as well as desire. It didn't take a great leap of imagination to think that with a little more time, she'd be in love with the young man who watched her as if the day wasn't complete without being witness to one of her smiles.

Whenever it was just the two of them out in the field, or at night after a day of hard work, Colby would ask Ben if he heard from Faith that day, or if they had made any plans for the weekend. He was so eager for information, he reminded Ben of Trey's dog Daisy when she sat at their feet under the breakfast table, hoping for a piece of bacon to drop to the floor. The boy was most certainly smitten.

Leaving them to their passion, Ben hobbled up the steps, keeping his footfalls light so as not to be heard, although the two were locked so tightly together, he doubted they'd hear anything at the moment.

In his room, he flopped onto his bed with a groan, then looked down at his shoes. "Aw, shit."

Probably would have been a good idea to ask for some help in removing his boots before heading to his room.

God, what a sorry example of manhood he was.

Suck it up. Just suck it up.

He took a few puffs of air as if he were a weightlifter about to perform a clean and jerk. With a grunt, he bent and as quick as his aching muscles allowed, worked his boots off, tossing them into the corner before dragging his ass off the bed and stumbling into the bathroom.

After cranking the water up to high, he pulled off his clothes as the room began to fill with steam. Jumping into the stream, he bit back a curse as the scalding water hit his battered body. Damn, it hurt, but he knew if he were patient, the heat would start to work its magic and help dull some of his aches.

As he stood under the spray with his head hung low, he began to question everything.

What could he offer a woman as vibrant and full of energy as Faith? He could barely stand, let alone be someone she could rely on for strength and protection.

Someone like Colby.

It was only a matter of time until Faith decided she was ready to find a steady boyfriend, a potential husband. If Ben had to hand her off to another man, he'd prefer that man to be Colby. Colby would treat her right, treat her like a princess, and only call her a bitch during a scene when she asked for it. Yeah, the look on her face when he had lost his head had been pretty damn funny.

With a little more training, Colby could become the Dom Faith needed. Allowing her the freedom she craved, but guiding her submissive desires with a nurturing hand. He'd be loving and kind, and a great father when they decided to start a family. They'd most certainly make beautiful babies.

Now that thought did bring a pain to his chest. The idea of the two of them, going off, building a life together that didn't include their old friend Ben Castillo. It just about tore his heart out thinking they might leave him behind.

Didn't matter, he decided with a shake of his head. Those two were deserving of a happy ending, and he'd do anything in his power to ensure their happiness.

Anything.

"I DON'T KNOW about you," Colby mumbled as they neared the main house for breakfast. "But I could use another ten hours of sleep."

"I thought you liked the early morning," Ben said.

"That was before we had a woman in the house who made staying up late way too enjoyable."

"But the lack of sleep was worth it, right?"

The satisfied smile that stretched his lips was answer enough.

"That's what I thought." Ben slapped him on the back then held the door open for Colby to enter first.

As he walked through the mudroom, he pounded his feet as he stepped to shake loose any excess dirt before tracking it inside the kitchen.

"Good morning, fellas," Greta greeted them from her place by the waffle iron. "I saw Faith's car going down the lane about thirty minutes ago. You could have at least asked her to join us for breakfast. I swear, Ben, I thought you had better manners than to let your girlfriend starve."

"I didn't let her starve. Thank you, Gabriella," he said as Mark's wife handed him a cup of coffee. The two women often worked in tandem making the morning meal for the ranch at the beginning of the week. They said it made Mondays more enjoyable. "Faith cooked breakfast for the three of us."

"Then why is Colby loading up a plate as if he hasn't eaten in a week?"

He almost choked on his sip of coffee. "Faith has a great many skills. Working our stove so it doesn't burn everything to a crisp is still a work in progress. Right, Colby? Colby?"

He glanced to the side and frowned at the sight of Colby standing stock still, plate in hand with a look of confusion stamped on his face. The source of the expression appeared to be from Jack and Adam, who were sitting at the table and staring back with equally inquisitive faces.

Jack had frozen in place with a strawberry clinging precariously to the tines of the fork hovering before his mouth while Adam had paused mid-chew. His eyes were wide and a sausage link protruded from his lips as if it were a cigar.

"What's up with you two?" Ben asked.

"Is that Ben?" Trey's voice came from down the hall a moment before he and Mark spilled into the kitchen. They had identical creases to their brows and worry in their eyes, as if they had just been witness to a bad car accident. "Are you guys all right? How's Faith taking it?"

Alarm burned down his spine as he snapped to attention. "How's Faith taking what? Did something happen to her dad?"

"You don't know?" Mark asked.

"Know what?" Ben noticed the rest of the men appeared to be equally as shocked as Mark that he was in the dark. Well, all except Colby, which kicked the unease in his gut from rolling to tsunami-sized waves.

"Uh, magpie," Trey said to Greta. "Can you and Gabriella give us a moment alone?"

"Trey, what's going on? You're freaking me out."

"It's guy stuff. We'll take care of it."

"Excuse me?" She propped her hand on her hip while Gabriella stood next to her with her arms folded and her stiletto-clad feet set apart as if she were preparing for a brawl. "You did not just say the equivalent of *Not now, little woman*, did you?"

"I—uh, no," he sputtered. "It's just sensitive information."

Mark matched his wife's stance. "And it's not really your business. Gabriella, don't you need to head off to work now anyway?"

She narrowed her eyes and nailed him with a glare. "Oh no. We're staying. If Faith is involved, we need to make sure she's all right. Just spit it out."

With each second that passed with furtive glances between Mark and Trey, and Jack and Adam, Ben's heart pounded so hard, he thought his ribs would crack.

"Tell me," he said, his bass so deep, it rumbled through the room like a crack of thunder.

Trey swallowed hard. "There're some racy pictures going around the Internet of you and Faith. And Colby."

"What?"

"Here." Adam handed his phone over the table. "If you break it, you owe me a new one."

Ben's hand trembled as he reached for the phone and turned the screen to face him as Colby came over to look over his shoulder. The both were tense as if whatever they saw would jump out and bite them like a poisonous snake.

It was worse.

"Fuck," Ben bit out.

There it was. Lit up with the brightest flash he'd ever seen in all its depraved full-color glory. A picture of Faith sprawled across the hood of Jack's truck with Colby nuzzling at her exposed breast while Ben was leaning over her and giving her a look that left no doubt he had every intention of fucking her silly. Her legs were spread and it was obvious both men had a hand up her skirt.

"Oh my God," Colby gasped, dropping the plate in his hand. Waffles and strawberries exploded as it hit the floor like a grenade, shooting sticky shrapnel all over their legs. "Where did that come from?"

"No one knows for certain," Trey replied. "Mike at The Crescent called me the moment he found out about them."

"Stacy told me," Jack added. "Some friends of hers messaged them to her."

"They were in my media feed," Adam said.

"Why do you all keep saying *them*?" Ben asked.

"Swipe your finger across the screen. There's more than one."

"Oh God," Colby moaned again as Ben flipped through one picture more lewd than the one previous. If he swiped fast enough, it looked just like a motion picture. Dear lord, how many photos were there?

Who would do such a thing and why? Ha. Silly question. The *why* he already knew. This town was starved for good gossip, and with his carelessness, he had fed the beast and tossed his best friend and Faith into its gluttonous clutches.

Faith.

"Shit, Faith." His grip on the phone tightened until the screen cracked. "She went to fill in for her dad at the barber shop. It's why she stayed the night. She can't be ambushed like that."

Colby was already heading for the door. "We have to get her."

Ben took a step to follow, then turned around only to spin again in a circle. Damn, he didn't know which way was up or down. "Trey, I don't know when I'll be back."

"Take your time and go be with your girl."

"Or is it their girl?" he heard Mark mumble under his breath.

"I'm not sure," Trey mumbled back.

Let them debate semantics. The only thing that mattered was Faith was about to walk into a shit storm and it was all his fault.

Chapter Thirteen

L ORD HAVE MERCY, it was a beautiful day. The sun was out, the morning no longer carried the chill of winter, and she had had the best night of sleep snuggled in Ben's arms.

Their evening together hadn't included any acrobatics. There had been no toys or restraints brought out for the evening's enjoyment. The only thing Ben did was hold her close, his big hands moving over her body as if he were trying to imprint all of her curves to memory as he pressed kisses to her cheeks until she had fallen asleep. Never before had she felt so safe, so secure and cared for. She had fought with everything she had not to close her eyes, but exhaustion had won out in the end.

At this rate, she wasn't going to want to leave his bed at all. As it was, the forty-minute commute from her apartment in Yakima to the ranch was far too long. Fortunately, she was working extra days at the barber shop while her father was in the city for some intensive physical therapy, which meant more opportunities to stay the night with Ben. Would he notice if she left her toothbrush next to his in the bathroom?

Okay, maybe she was being a little presumptuous, but she just loved being with him so much. Hell, she just loved him. She was in love with Ben Castillo.

She was in love. And it felt glorious.

Now if only she could get him to quit acting like she was going to grow tired of his company. Behind his smiles and soft caresses, she sensed a wall building between them. Kind of like the plastic film on a new television. The picture was still visible, but distorted. It was as if he expected her at any minute to tap him on the head and say, "That was great. See ya." And walk away. What did she have to do to convince him she wanted forever?

Hmm. Looked like time was not on her side to conjure up a plan. Cal Brotherton stood outside the shop with his hands in his front pockets, leaning against the side of the building. Funny, she didn't remember him having an appointment on the books that day.

"Faith, Faith, Faith, Faith, Faith," he sang as she approached.

"Good morning, Cal." She unlocked the door. "What brings you by?"

"I'm here to collect on that date you owe me," he replied as he followed her inside, walking a little too close behind her for comfort.

"What are you talking about? I don't owe you anything, let alone a date."

His low laughter was like a bucket of ice water sluicing down her back. "So you say. But I know what kind of a girl you are. I've seen it with my own eyes."

She glanced at the door and really wished it hadn't shut behind them when they walked in. The creepy vibe rolling in her direction made her clutch her purse in front of her like a shield. Fat lot of good that would do her if she actually needed protection.

"Stop being cryptic and just tell me what you're doing here, Cal."

He slithered a step closer, then another. "I heard you've been a bad girl, Faith. A dirty, naughty girl. A girl who thinks she needs more than one man to satisfy her. Well, I'm here to tell you, baby, all you need is me."

As he moved closer, she backed away until the wall stopped her progress. "Well, *I'm* telling *you* I'm not interested. And my boyfriend won't appreciate you talking to me in such a fashion."

"Your boyfriend," he snorted. "You mean those two losers from the Sprawling A? Oh yeah, I know all about them. The entire town has seen the pictures of you three. I have to tell you, Faith, seeing you laid out on the hood of that truck gives new meaning to the word *sprawling*."

"Pictures? What pictures?"

"The ones of you looking like the slut you pretend not to be. Now if you're looking for a good ride, I'm more than ready to give it to you, darlin'."

"Back away now, you asshole," she shouted and pushed against his chest as he tried to crush her against the wall.

Determination glittered in his eyes and in the curl of his lips as he shoved aside her arms as she tried to get in a punch or a slap. "Does fighting get you hot? I'll fight ya. I know *no* doesn't mean *no* to a woman like you. It just means you want me to try harder."

Oh my God. He's not going to stop.

Terror and disbelief funneled adrenaline into her limbs, making her punch and kick blindly as she fought to evade Cal's grabbing hands. But the battle was one sided as he laughed and grabbed at the collar of her blouse with both hands, ripping it open to her navel. No matter how hard she fought, it was not lost on her that he was taller and bigger and stronger. As her energy sagged, for a moment, just a moment, she thought about giving up.

Then a wisp of memory stuck her like a bolt of lightning.

Gabriella hadn't given up. She had fought. Jack had fought. Neither of them had given up until there was nothing left for them to give. By God, she wasn't going to give up either.

A scream tore through her throat as she curled her fingers into claws and scored a hit with a scratch down the side of his face.

"Ow!" He pulled back and touched his wet cheek. As he looked at the blood on his fingers, his lashes fluttered as he looked surprised that she had drawn blood. Surprise quickly turned to pissed off as his gaze narrowed and he raised his hand. "You bitch."

The door burst open. "Get your hands off her, you son of a bitch."

The shout was still echoing in the room as Colby flew into her field of vision and grabbed Cal by the back of the shirt, using his momentum to throw her attacker against the wall, barely avoiding ripping the sink off the wall with his body weight. Bunching the front of Cal's shirt in his fists, Colby pulled him forward and slammed him into the wall again as her knees buckled and she slid to the floor.

"Who the fuck do you think you are, touching her that way?" *Slam.* The walls rattled with the force. "Huh? Huh?"

With murderous intent etched into his granite-like features, Colby pulled back his fist, ready to let it fly with when Ben caught his hand before he could follow through.

"Hold up. Don't give this son of a bitch any reason to put you away."

"He hurt Faith," Colby shouted and fought Ben's hold. "The fucker has to pay."

Ben wrapped both of his arms around Colby's struggling body. "Cal won't hesitate to have you arrested for assault. You won't do Faith any good in jail."

"It'll so be worth it."

"Go to Faith. Colby." Ben shook him as Colby snarled. His bass dropped so low as he rasped near Colby's ear, she barely made out the words. "I'll take care of this piece of shit. Faith needs you. Take care of her."

That seemed to burst through the chains of anger surrounding Colby, and he stepped away, falling to his knees by her side. "Faith, baby, where are you hurt?"

She couldn't answer. Couldn't make a sound. Not then. Not with Cal still in the room, watching them with a smirk.

He might have thought he was getting off scot-free with the removal of Colby's in-your-face ferocity, but now Ben stood before him. All six-foot-four, two hundred fifty pounds of solid muscle and quiet, barely leashed anger.

"Get out," Ben snarled. "You don't touch her. You don't talk to her. Ever."

But Cal was still full of piss and vinegar and stupid enough to behave as if he was in the right as he snorted, "I don't get what the big deal is here. I was just giving her what she wanted until you two bozos showed up."

Ben's nostrils flared. "Get. Out."

Cal still didn't get the hint. "You know, I should call the cops. The bitch drew blood." He turned his gaze on her. "All you sluts are the same. You want to play hard to get, and when we give it to you, you freak out."

Bam! Ben jabbed Cal with a finger to the chest that sent him flying back against the wall.

"I will tell you one more time. You come near Faith again, you even *think* about her, and I will hunt you down, tear you apart with my bare hands, and eat you alive. And that goes for any other woman you try to bully. I'll gladly go to prison if it means assholes like you are off the street. Now get out."

The vibration in Ben's warning made the hairs on her arm stand up. And she wasn't the only one who watched in fascinated fear as the muscles beneath Ben's shirt flexed and pulsed like Bruce Banner just before he hulked out.

Now Faith saw the man who as a youth had to fight for his livelihood. Who, out of necessity, had become a man at far too young an age. It was a side of Ben she wished he didn't have to tap into, yet she was so, so grateful he did.

Cal took a look at all that flexing muscle and swallowed hard. "She's nothing special, anyway," he muttered and stormed out of the shop.

The lingering silence wasn't really silent and left her feeling as if she was standing in the aftermath of a tornado. Blood rushed in her ears, and her heart pounded so hard it hurt.

Ben and Colby were raging bulls, their breaths billowing, and they held so still, so tense, she was afraid that with the slightest provocation they'd snap and take off like an arrow launched by an Olympic archer.

Colby was the first to move. His hand hovered near her cheek. "Faith? Talk to me, please."

"I—I." Her teeth began to chatter so hard, she was afraid she'd bite her tongue off. "I don't. Understand."

"He's an asshole. Period," Colby spat, but his hands were gentle as he ran his palms up and down her arms. "Did he hurt you?"

"He—he tried," she replied with a hiccup and glanced down, moaning in dismay at the state of her blouse.

The sight of the shredded silk and the pink scratches marring the curve of her breasts was the final straw. Tears spilled down her cheeks and pooled into her cleavage as she tried to pull the ripped fabric together. Only once before had she been so frightened, and that was when her mother took a turn for the worse and she knew the end was near. But this was different. Cal's attack came from so far out from left field, it might as well been from another state.

"Ah, baby girl." Colby scooped her up into his arms and sat in the chair by the sink, settling her on his lap. "I've got you. I've got you."

Try as she might, she couldn't stop the tears and huddled against his chest, seeking shelter and the warmth of his arms. In the background, she could hear Ben's deep murmur as he spoke into his phone and the clomp of his boots as he paced inside the little shop.

"Look at me, sweetness," Ben said softly after he hung up the phone and urged her chin up with his finger. He used a wet towel to blot away her tears. "I called Gabriella. She has a client coming in, but she will be down here right after."

"That's a good idea," Colby said. "After what her ex did to her, she'll know what to do."

"Why?" she stuttered, still in disbelief over the last few minutes. "Why would he do such a thing?"

Self-recrimination filled Ben's eyes as his lips tightened into a thin white line. "It's all my fault."

"No. It's not," Colby emphatically replied.

"I still should have known better."

Their arguing confused her further. "He said there were pictures. What did he mean?"

"Fuck." Ben stood and wiped his hand down his face. "Someone took pictures of us outside of The Crescent. On Jack's truck."

"Oh." Well. Didn't this day go from great to holy effin' hell. "Do I even want to know how bad they are?"

"They're bad," Ben confirmed in a grim tone.

"Actually," Colby cut in. "They're not that bad. I mean, if they weren't taken by a stranger and spread all over the Internet. They're kinda hot."

"They're on the Internet?" she barely refrained from shouting. "Oh my God. What's my father going to say?"

Ben dropped to his knees before her. "I'll make this right, Faith. I'll talk to George and let him know this was all my fault."

"No." She refused with a voice that sounded much stronger than she felt. "Unless you told someone to take those pictures and post them online, this was not your fault."

"But I was supposed to protect you—"

"And you have." She climbed off Colby's lap and clutched the front of Ben's shirt until his gaze rose to meet hers. "I chose *you*, Ben. And I chose the relationship we have. I'm not ashamed of being with you or of what we've done. I just wish... I just wish it wasn't coming to light in such a freaking, spectacular, Jerry Springer fashion."

The look in his eyes suggested he didn't believe her. His mouth was still set in a firm line, and there was such sadness on his face she wanted to start crying again.

"Let's get you home," he said in that same low tone that frightened her in an entirely new way. His shoulders slumped and he appeared to be much older than his forty-two years of age.

This defeated, dejected man wasn't the Ben she knew. Where was her thoughtful, seductive champion? Where was the man who always had a mischievous glint in his dark eyes? Where was the man who told her that her desires were not weird or strange and that she could be a strong woman in charge of her sexuality?

Where was the man who believed in her?

"I'm not going home," she said as she gathered all of the remaining pride and dignity she could muster while standing there in torn clothing. "I won't be bullied into tucking my tail and hiding. No." She stopped him with a finger raised in warning as he opened his mouth. "You told me not to be ashamed of who I am, of what I want. I have customers coming in any minute and I will not let Cal Brotherton, or you, make me feel less than worthy to be out in public."

"Dammit, Faith," he groaned and pulled her into a hug so tight, she couldn't breathe. She didn't mind. In fact, she clung to him so hard, her arms ached. "I can't leave you alone with these animals. That bastard almost—he almost..." He choked on his words and squeezed her even tighter. "Maybe we should have called the sheriff."

"I can still go get him," Colby offered.

"Not yet." She pulled away before she passed out from lack of oxygen. "I want to talk to Gabriella first."

"It's your call, Faith," Colby said and crossed his arms over his chest. "But if you insist on staying, then so do I."

"Me too." Ben matched Colby's stance.

"But your jobs. You should be at the ranch."

"Trey will understand."

How did the morning spin so out of control? They shouldn't be there having to watch out for her like a security detail. Then again, she shouldn't have to worry about being attacked in her place of work. And what if Cal did came back?

"One of you can stay," she agreed, not feeling half as courageous as she had just claimed to be. "But only for today."

"We'll see," Ben muttered.

She glanced around the shop in search of anything to help remind her of her normal routine. In the mirror's reflection, the sight of her torn shirt made her rethink her demand for only one of them to stay.

"I'm going to need a new shirt. And fast. Mr. Gomez is due

any minute."

"Take mine." Colby unbuttoned his plaid shirt and handed it to her, leaving him dressed in a plain white T-shirt.

"Thanks. I'm just going to go freshen up."

"I'll help," Colby said as he followed her.

"I can wash my face on my own."

"I want to make sure you really are okay. Physically. I do have medical experience. Remember?"

"With animals. I'm not one of your cows."

He squeezed into the small restroom with her. "I want to be certain you're okay."

The moment he shut the door behind him, he pulled her into his arms, holding her just as tight as if not tighter than Ben had done just a few minutes prior. He trembled in her embrace, and his breath stuttered as if he couldn't catch a breath.

"Thank you," she said against his chest. "Thank you."

When he pulled away, his brown eyes shimmered with unshed tears. "I think I know how Mark feels now. I'm going to have nightmares forever."

"Me too," she admitted in a small voice as her own eyes burned.

He cupped her face in his hands and smoothed his thumbs over her cheeks. "Ben isn't going to stop beating himself up for this."

"I'm afraid you're right. How can we help him?"

"Let us take care of you. I know you want to prove that you're brave, but that was one of the most frightening things I've ever seen, and I've seen far too much violence lately. Let us take care of you, not because we don't believe in you, but because we...we care about you, Faith."

When he looked at her that way, held her as if she were the most precious thing in the world, she couldn't deny him anything. "Okay. But I meant what I said. The ranch needs you too."

"I know." He gathered her close, cradling her head to his chest. "We'll work something out. But for now, let's see how the dust settles."

Out in the shop, she heard the murmur of voices. "That'll be Mr. Gomez."

She almost whimpered as she broke away from Colby's embrace and changed her shredded blouse for his work shirt, which was actually quite a pleasant replacement. The cotton was still warm from his touch and smelled like his aftershave. As she tied the tails into a knot around her midriff, it was as if he still held her in his arms.

There wasn't enough time to wash her face, so she dabbed the wet towel she held under her eyes and headed back out, stopping short as she saw Mr. Gomez staring up at Ben with wide eyes. Ben was looking quite formidable with his arms folded and a stern frown carved onto his face.

"Where's Faith again?" the older man asked and twirled his cowboy hat in his hands.

"She's in the back with Colby."

A humorous light blossomed in the man's eyes. "Colby's here too?" He chuckled and waggled his brows. "Do you—"

"Don't. Even. Go there, Daniel," Ben warned with a slow shake of his head. "Don't."

Mr. Gomez paled and dropped his hat as he hastily stuttered a retraction.

Great, Ben. Let's just add more fuel to the fire. She pasted on an overly bright smile and swept into the room like a 1950s housewife in one of those old television sitcoms. "Good morning, Mr. Gomez. How are you this morning?"

"Fine. Fine." His gaze bounced back and forth between

them. "If you're busy, Faith, I can come back another day."

"Of course not. This is your appointment and I'm here for you." She gestured to the shampoo chair while she retrieved his hat from the floor and set it on the hook by the door. "Have a seat and we'll get you shampooed."

He looked again at Ben and Colby, who stood like two sentinels on either side of the barber's chair. "I don't think I'm supposed to."

"Oh for heaven's sake." She urged the man toward the chair with a hand on his back. "I'm sorry, Mr. Gomez, it's been kind of a distressing morning and the boys here are worried about me. I'm very lucky to have such wonderful friends, but as you can see, they are very protective." She went over to her purse and pulled some cash from the side pocket then pressed the bills into Ben's hands. "Can you go to the diner and bring us back some coffee, please? I think we could all use some."

Oh, he wanted to argue with her, she could tell. The fight was in his eyes, but he shifted his gaze and shot a glare at Mr. Gomez, as if to say, "I'm watching you," and stomped to the door.

With a sigh, she returned to the sink and turned up the wattage on her smile. "Shall we?"

Happy frickin' Monday.

Chapter Fourteen

C OLBY RAMMED THE tines of the pitchfork into the bale of hay and tore into it while imagining it was the gullet of one Cal Brotherton.

After talking to Gabriella, Faith decided not to call the sheriff on that sleazy son of a bitch. It was an unfortunate reality, but the odds of Cal being charged with anything concrete were slim to none. It was her word against his. Well, their word. But with the rep the three of them were building, Faith was afraid the sheriff would be more likely to believe Cal than them. Especially after she heard the conviction rate on sex crimes was a paltry four percent of those cases that even made it to trial.

While he didn't agree with Faith's decision, he understood why she chose not to move forward. At this point, they were all trying to maintain a low profile, which was difficult enough to do as word got around that Colby and Ben were guarding Faith like two rottweilers protecting a herd of cattle from hungry wolves.

The barber shop had been full to bursting the day before with people eager to stop by to say hello. There had been so many visitors, Ben refused to head back to the ranch and insisted they take turns looking out for Faith for the rest of the week. Hell, by the way people stared at them, it was as if they expected the three of them to fall to the floor and perform a sex act at any moment. It was creepy.

And it didn't make it any less creepy when it was your own friend staring at you in the same way.

"What?" he shouted and looked over at Adam who was standing a few feet away. Although the other man held a pitchfork, he wasn't doing a thing to break up the truckload of hay bales they had unloaded.

Adam jumped then shook his head. "Nothing."

"Well, you're not staring at me like it's nothing."

"It's just...well...I was—I was just wondering." He licked his lips. "Um, are you and Ben gay?"

"What?" When did his world turn ass over head? Was this how Alice felt like when she fell down that rabbit hole?

"Are you guys gay?" Adam asked again with a shrug, getting a little bolder. "You've been naked together. And you've probably touched each other's junk, so I was just wondering."

"Jesus, Adam," Colby muttered with a shake of his head. Now he knew why Ben didn't tell anyone anything about his private life. "We're not gay. And does it matter if we were?"

"It doesn't. I guess. I'm just trying to picture how you all fit together and I don't know if I have it right in my head."

"Why are you picturing it at all?"

He gave him the boggle-eyed, are-you-stupid face. "Are you serious? I'm a red-blooded male, in the prime of my youth. All I think about is sex. And Faith is hot. Of course I'm going to wonder what it's like. Repeatedly. Like I can't think about anything else."

"Well, stop it. You're weirding me out."

Adam jammed his pitchfork into a hay bale and sat on the tailgate of the truck. "Come on, man. You gotta fill me in.

What's it like? How long have you guys been holding orgies at your place?"

"When did you become such a dumbass?"

"I'm just asking what everyone's thinking."

The truth of that statement made the bile churn in his belly. "We don't have orgies. It's not like that."

"Then what *is* it like?"

Colby tossed his pitchfork to the ground and went to the truck to take a swig of water from his canteen. Obviously, they weren't going to get any work done until some of Adam's curiosity was appeased.

"Look. I hadn't done anything like that before," he began, trying to find the words to describe something that he himself was struggling to understand. "It just kind of happened. And it's not about the sex. It doesn't matter who's naked or who's touching who. It's all about Faith. How she moves, the look on her face, the sounds. When all of us are together, it's incredible. It's like a melding of the souls."

"That's really beautiful, man. You should put that on a greeting card."

He picked up a handful of hay and tossed it at Adam's smirking face. "Fuck off."

"I'm just teasing. Lighten up." He flashed a grin and looked down at the toes of his boots. "And maybe I'm a little jealous. I've never experienced anything like you've just described. Sounds like you've got quite a girlfriend there."

"She's not my girlfriend. She's Ben's."

His blond brows shot up so high, they disappeared under the brim of his hat. "Could have fooled me. Sounds like you're in love with her."

That's because he was.

Somewhere along the way, he had fallen in love with Faith

O'Leary. It didn't matter that she was Ben's girl. As unconventional as it seemed, the three of them worked well together. He was just going to have to get them all to see it like he did, which was near to impossible with the rest of the town watching them as if they were an episode of some trashy reality show. No matter how badly he wanted to throw up two big middle fingers to those who thought their relationship was an abomination, he knew it was best to keep to the status quo, or whatever it was that was equally acceptable until the storm blew over.

"I care about her very much." He picked up the pitchfork and returned to his work. "She's great. And she's great for Ben too."

"I'm sorry about what happened with Cal yesterday. That son of a bitch should be beaten to a pulp."

"I'm with you, but it was Faith's call. But if he touches her again, he's a dead man."

Adam jumped down from the flat bed. "I'll help you hide the body."

"Thanks, man."

Apparently Adam had gotten all of the answers he needed, because he picked up his pitchfork and started in on the next bale of hay.

"How about we go to your place after this?" he asked. "Grab a few beers, play a round of Ninja Warrior, and you can tell me about some of the kinky stuff you, Ben, and Faith have done."

"Not going to happen," Colby replied with a shake of his head. Yeah, his buddy was not going to let it go.

"You have to share something. I'm dying for details."

"I don't have to share anything. And I'll tell Ben you keep asking."

That brought Adam up short, and his spine straightened with a snap. "Don't tell Ben. He'll pulverize me."

"Then quit being a jackass and get to work."

"You'd think having all of that sex would put you in a more agreeable mood," he muttered under his breath.

Yeah, he would have thought so too. But that was before he understood the difference between sex and making love. Between having sex to experience physical pleasure, and making love and feeling your entire being come alive.

Who knew what the future held for him, but he was certain that if he wanted it to include Faith, he would do anything to ensure she was a part of it.

"WITH A SPRING like this, who needs summer?" Mark grumbled and ran the handkerchief he had soaked in water over his face before tying it around his neck.

Ben agreed. The valley had fallen into a heat wave with temperatures soaring in the low nineties by mid-morning. Usually this type of weather was reserved for the middle of summer, and after the winter they had just experienced with record-breaking days in a deep freeze, the heat was a jarring change. Thankfully, the blast was only supposed to last until the end of the week, but knowledge of the upcoming reprieve did little to help Ben's current mood.

Faith decided to work at the salon in Yakima for the rest of the week, which meant both he and Colby could return to their jobs on the ranch. On the one hand, it was a relief to have her away from the prying eyes of the town busybodies, but the physical distance apart was harder to cope with. He couldn't check in with her as often as he wanted, unless he had a live feed from the salon to his phone. Every time he paused for more than two seconds, he remembered the way Faith looked as she slid to the floor, shirt torn, scratches marring her perfect skin.

Shock wasn't even the word for it. It was a gut-twisting conglomeration of horror, confusion, and humiliation.

Cal Brotherton didn't know just how close he had come to death. One more word, one more little twitch of the eye, and Ben would have landed a jab straight to the middle of the fucker's face that would've taken his head clean off.

Logically, he understood that the entire situation was not his fault. He didn't tell the coward who took their pictures to post them online. Just like he didn't tell Cal that he was free to be an asshole and treat Faith with such disrespect. But he still felt as if it was his fault, and the shame of allowing Faith to experience such nastiness bore a hole into his soul.

It was his job to protect her, and although she could argue that his protection extended only to the bedroom, he'd give his life to ensure nothing and no one harmed her again.

His hope was the scuttlebutt surrounding the pictures would die down soon and be attributed to a few drinks and a beautiful night. After all, the photos depicted nothing more than some kissing and groping. It was the viewer's imagination that filled in the rest of the lurid details. As long as they laid low, hopefully the clamor would end, and they could all go back to normal. Whatever normal was for them. A decision he was afraid was going to have to be made sooner rather than later.

But not right then. Now he had his hands full rounding up the male calves for castration. Usually, he'd rather do any other job on the ranch than wrap rubber bands around a set of bovine testicles, but if he imagined each one as belonging to Cal Brotherton, he found himself actually looking forward to the task.

"Where's the boss man?" Adam asked. "I thought he was helping us with this round."

"He'll be by later," Mark answered. "He had to run into

town and pick up our order from Bingham's."

"Lucky guy." Adam repositioned his hat on his head and took up his position near the end of the shoot. "This part always makes me squeamish. Watching a cow being slaughtered, no problem. But slapping a pair of bands on a ball sac just to watch his nuts shrivel up and fall off, I don't even want to think about lunch."

"I don't want to either when you put it that way," Jack said from his perch on the rail. "Can we get on with it already?"

Mark placed his fingers in his mouth and whistled. "Send 'em on down, Rafe," he shouted at the rider at the other end of the paddock "Go get 'em, Daisy."

The Australian shepherd took off with a yip, charging through the collected herd and helping Rafe separate calves from adults.

For the rest of the morning, it was business as usual. Colby and Rafe guided the herd on horseback while Jack and Adam traded insults and dirty jokes, leaving Mark and Ben to do the real work. The sun beat down, making it feel as if they were slices of bacon on a skillet, and the work was dusty and strenuous. Overall, an unexciting, normal morning, which was just how Ben liked it.

And then Trey arrived.

They were all gathered by the horse barn, using the outdoor washroom to hose off their hands and arms of dirt and animal when Trey pulled up in his beloved Ford F-350. The silver beauty was polished to a high shine, and carried enough horsepower to pull whatever load the ranch required, including the four hundred pounds of seed Trey was to have picked up from the supplier.

"Where's the seed?" Mark called out as Trey climbed out of the truck.

"They didn't have it," Trey replied, turning his back on them to head to the main house.

"What do you mean, they didn't have it?" Mark slapped his wet hands on his jeans as he took off after him. "I confirmed with Marshall two days ago that they had the stock and we could pick it up today."

"Well, he didn't have it," Trey said with a slight turn of his head and kept walking.

"Hold up," Mark shouted. "Did he say when he'd get some in?"

"He's not getting more in."

On any other day, Mark and Trey talking administrative stuff about the ranch washed right over him. But the crease in Trey's brow and the troubled set of his lips made Ben's gut clench, especially when Trey's blue gaze shifted to him for just a little too long.

"What are you talking about?" Mark asked. "We've been ordering that seed for years. How does he just stop ordering it, and how did the stock he did have disappear?"

"Let it go, Mark," Trey muttered.

"Trey." Ben cut in before Mark's ire gathered more steam. Like a dog before an earthquake, he sensed trouble was on the horizon, and there was more going on than Marshall Hodgins losing the ranch's order. "What's really going on?"

Trey blew out a breath as his gaze scanned the horizon before landing back on him. "Marshall wanted to know if I reprimanded you and Colby about Faith. I told him it was none of my business. After a bit of an argument, he refused to sell me the seed. Said he doesn't do business with people who allow perverts and deviants to work for them. I told him to fuck off."

"Jesus," Mark groaned with a wince.

Behind him, Ben heard an accompanying chorus of curses

and muttered oaths. If he turned around, he wouldn't be surprised if they all looked as if they'd been kicked in the nuts.

"So what now?" Mark asked. "We needed that seed to plant for the fall harvest."

"I'll order it from somewhere else," Trey replied with a shrug. "It will only set us back a few days. I hope."

A few days of lost money and productivity, and all because some small-minded merchant wanted to impose his beliefs on his customers. It was a shitty situation that was one hundred percent avoidable, and all his fault.

Ben couldn't let Trey take the fall for his actions. "Trey, I'm sorry. I'll cover the cost of finding new seed."

"No. You won't," Trey shot back immediately.

"I can't let my actions hurt your business."

"It's *our* business, and you're family," Trey shouted in a voice that vibrated with restrained anger. "It's no one's business who you choose to be with. I don't care if you're fucking everyone on the ranch, as long as they're consenting. Except Greta, of course. You stood by me when I was at my lowest, and I'm gonna stand by you, because you're my brother. I don't care if I have to spend twice as much for grass seed and order it in from Europe. Marshall Hodgins and anyone else who talks smack about you, any of you, can kiss my ass. All right?"

"Amen, brother," Mark added.

Well, shit.

Never before had Ben felt pulled in so many different directions. Part of him wanted to hug the stuffing out of Trey. Another part wanted to head down to Marshall's and punch the fucker in the face, while inside he fought the need to fall to his knees and cry like a baby. And he didn't dare look at Colby for fear that he actually would give in to the tears that stung his eyes.

Trey never should have been brought into this mess. None

of them should've. And as much as he wanted to apologize and make grandiose gestures for forgiveness, he knew Trey wouldn't accept them, and he'd just end up embarrassing all of them. So he did nothing but nod and wait for someone to say something, anything to break the tension and help them all move on.

It was Jack who broke the silence and slapped Ben on the back. "Let's head inside and cool off. Greta said she left a few pitchers of lemonade in the refrigerator. I say, let's add some whiskey and take the afternoon off. What do you say, boss?"

"Yes to the lemonade. No to the whiskey," Trey replied. "We still have work to do. But later, we're cracking open a case of beer."

Mark nodded. "Amen to that too."

Getting buzzed might take the edge off his troubles, but no longer could Ben deny the truth. He had to make a decision about his relationship with Faith. And he had to make it now.

Chapter Fifteen

F AITH PULLED INTO the driveway of her childhood home and almost threw the car in to reverse to back right out.

All of her nervousness was entirely due to her imagination. The phone conversation with her father the night before was brief, as was his norm. He had returned from his week with the physical therapist. All was well, and he wanted to make sure they were still on for attending the Rotary Club fundraiser together. There was no mention of Ben, or Colby, or those damn pictures, which made her think he might not have heard about them. Impossible as that might seem.

She loved her father, and they had a great relationship, but who wanted to face their parent when there were compromising photos running around?

And her father wasn't the type to ask about the intimate details of his baby girl's relationships. On the night she went to prom, he had stayed up late, like most fathers do, and waited for her to come home. He had asked if she had a good time and where they went to dinner. Then he had stared at her real hard for several minutes, as if he could tell by sight alone if she had engaged in any post-prom activities of the sexy variety. She had, but she wasn't going to say it out loud. Instead, her cheeks had burned hot and she couldn't look him in the eye.

After several awkward minutes he had swallowed hard, nodded and mumbled, "Glad you made it home safe." And left it at that.

To not say anything to him now about her relationship with Ben would be a chicken thing to do. On the other hand, what her father didn't know gave her more time for those photos to blow over and for her to solidify her status with Ben as his one and only.

Ugh. It was times like this when being an adult sucked.

She blew her hair out of her eyes and climbed out of her car. "Time to be a big girl."

From facing the sunlight all morning long, the doorknob was hot to the touch as she opened the door, knowing he wouldn't have it locked. "Dad? It's me."

"Hey, darling." Her father limped out from the kitchen dressed in a pair of black jeans and a red button-down shirt, the fanciest outfit he owned. But he spruced up his appearance with freshly shaved cheeks and a good amount of gel slicking his thick hair off his face. The plaster cast around his foot was gone, replaced with a walking cast.

"Where's your cane?"

"I'm not using no cane." He held open his arms. "Now where's my hug?"

"You'll heal faster if you keep your weight off it." She squeezed him tight around the middle, inhaling the familiar scent of his Old Spice aftershave. "Did the doctor say you can go without the cane?"

"He said I'm stronger than men half my age. A few of the nurses even thought I was only forty."

"Uh-huh." She could imagine her father getting a kick about that, especially given all of the times he used to tease her about giving him gray hair before his time.

George O'Leary was built like a cowboy with strong thighs, a barrel chest, and toned arms formed from working with livestock and the land. His once-copper locks were almost all white, and he had wrinkles carved around his blue eyes from spending most of his time squinting in the sun. To her he was Superman. Able to lift any weight, open any jar, and fix anything she needed repaired.

Although she still carried that invincible image of him in her heart, there was no denying that the years of working whatever odd job he could find was taking its toll on his body.

From the moment he could walk, he was riding horses, and the only reason he took up barbering was because of the easier hours and the chance to make a quick buck to support his young family. After her mother passed away, he took classes on tax preparation to earn extra income. And soon that might be the only work he'd be physically able to do. Arthritis was settling into his hands and wrists, and all of the time in the saddle was causing him issues with his back. If he weren't careful, he'd end up in a wheelchair. Or worse.

Realizing your parents were mortal was a tough truth to swallow and burned the entire way down. As an ache bloomed in her chest, she hugged him again, just to imprint more of his touch to memory.

"I'm glad you're back, Dad."

He patted her on the shoulder. "It's good to be back. As much as I love your aunt's pot roast, I was missing my bed. She says to tell you hello, by the way. So…" He paused to scratch at his cheek. "When I went out to pick up my mail from the Ortegas, Martina asked if I had heard about your boyfriend. Or was it boyfriends? Her accent is so thick, and you know my Spanish is bad, I was only catching half of what she was saying."

"Oh." Dear lord, the time was now. "Well, I've been seeing Ben Castillo lately."

His brow crinkled. "Seeing?"

"Yes. Seeing. As in dating."

The furrow in his brow deepened. "Ben Castillo? From the Sprawling A?"

"Yes."

"But he's twice your age."

"He's not *that* much older than me."

"Then how much older is he?"

"About twelve years."

"That's plenty old enough," he said as he staggered back. "You were playing with your Barbie dolls while he was out drinking."

"I'm not ten anymore, Dad. I'm thirty. We have more in common now. Besides, you like Ben. You've always said he was an upstanding guy, well mannered, and reliable."

"Well, that was before I knew he wanted to get his hands on my daughter. Say." He sucked in a breath and grew real quiet as he squinted at her hard.

Ah, there it was. The probe. But this time she met his gaze full on with all the confidence of a woman who knew her heart, but for the life of her she couldn't stop the heat from climbing up her neck and burning her cheeks.

His mouth twisted as he looked away. "We should probably get going to the picnic," he mumbled.

Sorry, Daddy. Your daughter has needs.

Fortunately, the ride to the VFW hall was uneventful, and she was able to concentrate on the fifteen-minute drive as her father filled her in on his visit with the family. While the change of subject was welcomed, part of her wondered if she should be hurt he didn't seem more interested in her relationship with Ben.

Or maybe she shouldn't go begging for trouble. It wasn't as if the discussion was over forever. Just on hold.

Yeah. There would be plenty of time to dig deeper later.

The parking lot of the VFW hall was crowded, but with her father's handicapped parking placard, they were able to get a spot up front.

It had been ten years since she last attended the annual Rotary Club fundraiser for the school district. Farm owners, ranchers, and merchants turned out for the spring picnic and silent auction that was the main moneymaker to supplement the district's tiny budget.

Stuart's Steakhouse sponsored the grills and provided the cooks who were already creating clouds of mouth-watering goodness over the area. The rolling garage doors along the side of the hall were open for the attendees to walk from the silent auction to where the picnic tables of food lined the flower beds. Underneath a big, white tent were tables covered in blue or red checkered tablecloths and pots of colorful Gerber daisies.

The sun was shining. The air was warm, but the reception was chilly as she stepped out of the car. Those in the immediate vicinity paused in their conversations to openly gawk at her as she walked up the sidewalk with her father.

Most of the men she recognized from her father's shop, and they greeted him with a hearty handshake and a slap on the back. Their wives, on the other hand, smiled with their lips as their eyes scrutinized her as if she were a deep wrinkle in their silk blouse.

"So, Faith. Did you bring your men with you this afternoon?" Mrs. Ortega asked with a snarky curl to her lips.

"If by 'men' you mean my father, then yes. I'm spending quality time with my dad today," she replied with a smile that felt as sincere as a pair of waxed lips. "Excuse me. I spotted a Coach handbag and want to see where the bid is at. Coming, Dad? Looks like the butcher has a basket of jerky up for auction. All kinds."

His eyes lit up as he licked his lips. "The Folletts do make some damn fine jerky. Let's go take a peek."

The day was going to end in a disaster if snarky questions like that were going to keep popping up. Her father's love of jerky would save her bacon only a couple more times at best.

She guided him through the auction as quickly as manners allowed, giving him just enough time to say a quick hello or chat for a bit then moving him on before any serious questioning could begin. "Dad, let's go find you a seat so you can take the weight off your leg."

"I'm doing fine, Faith. Don't you worry about me. Why don't you go find some of your friends?"

Friends? So far all she'd seen were sharks circling, waiting for someone to draw first blood before pouncing.

"Faith. Faith. Over here."

"Look." Her father pointed to a spot over her shoulder. "Isn't that Trey's wife waving you down?"

Greta stood under the tent with Gabriella by her side. Both of them wore identical frowns on their faces and held worry in their eyes.

"Go on, honey. I see Hamish Maguire over there and I want to catch up with what's been going down at the ranch. Save me a seat."

"Sure, Dad." As much as she wanted to stick by his side, she knew she couldn't monitor all of his conversations. Hopefully Mr. Maguire wasn't one to pass along gossip.

"Faith. How are you holding up?" Gabriella asked as she neared.

"As well as expected." She gave a weak chuckle. "You two

have the exact same look on your face. Did you know you could pass as sisters?"

"Yes," Greta practically shouted as Gabriella groaned. "We've heard that before. But let's talk about you. Sit. I haven't seen you on the ranch much this week. We've been worried about you. I really do need to get your phone number."

"Between the salon in Yakima and the barber shop in Mission, I've been busy." She took a seat at the table then scanned the dining area before asking, "Did you all come on your own?"

Gabriella sat between them and waved her hand toward the refreshment stand. "Nah, the boys are off getting us something to drink. Have you had any more trouble at the shop? Getting information out of Ben is like trying to juice a rock. I think I could break Colby, but we keep missing each other."

"How can I have trouble at the shop when I have a big, strapping man staring down every person who comes in as if they're already guilty? On the plus side, the tips have been huge, but seriously, I just want all of the hoopla to die down and life to get back to normal."

"Don't we all, sister. Don't we all." Gabriella nodded then waved at Trey and her husband who were circling the edge of the dining area, wine glasses in hand.

Greta sighed with longing. "Oh, I miss my wine. Thank you, sweetie." She accepted the glass of grape juice and turned her face up for Trey's kiss.

"Where's my seat, darlin'?" Mark asked his wife.

"You and Trey sit across the way. We're having girl talk."

"I see." He turned Faith's way and smiled. "How are you doing, Faith?"

"I'm fine. Thank you."

He flashed her a wink. "I know the real reason my wife wants me across the table is so she can admire my good looks better."

"You know it, baby." She slapped him on his denim-clad ass.

"Down, woman." He chuckled.

"So, um, Faith." Greta bit her lip and looked to Gabrielle once their husbands were settled. For several seconds the two women did some nonverbal sparring with pointed glances and raised eyebrows before she continued. "We were wondering which of the guys it is, exactly, that you're dating?"

"Ben," she said, maybe a little louder than necessary. "I'm dating Ben."

"Right." Greta giggled. "Right. We—uh. That's what we thought."

"No, it isn't." Gabriella interrupted. "Look, it's no one's business who you date. We just wanted to make sure we're, I don't know what's the word, treating you all appropriately. So if you are dating both, then more power to you, girl."

"Gabriella," Greta gasped.

"What? You know those are two fine, fine gentlemen. Hmm. Can you imagine being the filling in that sandwich?" She raised her glass in salute. "As I said, you go, girl."

"No." Faith dropped her head in her hand with a groan. "It's not like that."

Gabriella leaned forward to whisper. "So you aren't sleeping with both of them?"

"Well...I." She glanced around and saw Trey and Mark acting as if their attention were diverted elsewhere, but they were most definitely trying to listen in on the conversation. She lowered her voice. "Kind of. It's complicated."

Gabriella toasted her again. "Uh-huh."

"No. Really." She sighed. "Look, I'm with Ben. I want to be with Ben. Colby, well, Colby is a friend."

"I'm friends with Colby too," Greta said. "But we've never

been cozy like that."

"No, really. We're friends. When I'm with Ben, it's stars and fireworks. What we have is so intense, I shake inside. Colby is more like my best friend. I can share almost anything with him. I don't feel the need to impress him, like I do with Ben. It's different. Does that even make sense?"

"It does." Gabriella reached out and grabbed her hand. "You found a lover and a friend. They just happen to be two different men. But, honey, at some point in the near future, you may have to make a choice with how *friendly* you are with Colby. People are talking. A lot."

Greta nodded at a spot behind Faith's shoulder. "And that time may come sooner than you think. Your dad is headed this way and he looks, well, *confused* may be the best way to say it."

Faith turned to see her father limp toward them with a frown etched on his brow. His jaw was set as if he were angry and his blue eyes appeared troubled. Her stomach sank as she noticed Mrs. Belhaven just behind him, watching them with unbridled interest.

"Hey, Dad," Faith said with an overly bright smile. "Have a seat. I wondered where you went off to."

He glanced at Greta and Gabriella, who flashed him big smiles, then back to her. "Faith, can I talk to you for a minute in private?"

She pointed to the small stage that had been set up, and the group of students from the high school orchestra class who were setting up their music stands. "In a minute, Dad. It looks like they're about to start the program. Have a seat." She patted the chair beside to her. This conversation was best held anywhere but in the immediate vicinity.

"Faith," he started again in a hushed tone once he sat down. "You told me you were dating Ben Castillo."

"I am."

He leaned closer and his lips barely moved as he asked, "Then how does Colby Jensen fit in?"

She batted her lashes. Surely he wasn't making a dirty joke. "He's Ben's roommate and best friend."

A flush rose on his cheeks. "And what's he to you?"

"He's become a good friend to me too," she said through a tight throat. "He's a really sweet guy."

"Is that all? Because I've been hearing things, Faith. Disturbing things."

Fortunately for her, the school district's superintendent tapped on the microphone, calling the group to order.

"Welcome," he said with his hands raised. The breeze picked up and flapped the ends of his tie and the length of his extra-long bangs that he used to hide his balding pate. "Welcome, everyone. First, let me thank the ladies and gentlemen with the Mission PTA for putting this event together, and the Mission High School home economics department for their decorations. Thank you also to Stuart's Steakhouse for donating their time and making us all these delicious vittles."

Gabriella snorted softly. "Did he actually say 'vittles'?"

Faith too choked on a chuckle, then bit her lip when her father looked sharply in her direction.

The superintendent continued, "Before we begin our programming, we have asked Pastor Dave Belhaven to come on up and say a few words in dedication."

There was a polite smattering of applause as Pastor Dave stepped onto the stage. His neatly pressed suit hung a little large on his medium-built frame, and the only object of bling he wore was his wedding ring that caught the sunlight when he waved his hands around.

Faith wondered if there was something in Mission's water

supply, for she noticed a large percent of the men in the forty to fifty-year-old range had lost a good portion of their hair, including the pastor, whose bald head gleamed from a fringe of dark hair trimmed above his ears. Thank the lord Ben hadn't fallen prey to that trend.

"Thank you, Superintendent Goldberg." Pastor Dave turned to the crowd with a dazzling white smile. "And thank you all for being with us here today as we celebrate our youth on this beautiful Saturday afternoon. As you well know, the proceeds that are received today from your generous donations go directly to our schools and to the education of these bright children sitting here before us."

As he looked amongst the crowd, his gaze landed on Faith, and his eyes widened for a split second. She didn't know why, but that brief sign of recognition caused her stomach to tighten.

Pastor Dave spread out his hands. "Let me tell you, folks, we need these programs to keep our children active and set on a positive course in life. Right now our children are in more danger then they ever were. Technology has softened their minds and bodies. Electronics and the media have given our children access to material that encourages them to engage in illicit activities and sins of the flesh."

Oh. God. No.

"And I'm not just talking about these youngsters here." He gestured to the students behind him. His bald head grew shinier the more animated he became. "Our adult children are in more trouble than our youth. Yes sir. Right here in our community our neighbors are fornicating. Our employees are fornicating." He looked directly at Faith and his eyes narrowed as he loudly proclaimed, "Our daughters are fornicating."

Well. Why didn't he just shine a spotlight directly on her, paint a giant "F" on her chest, and call her a raging slut?

On her left, her father shifted in his seat. While on her right, Gabriella and Greta sucked in a collective gasp. As the pastor continued to pontificate on the evils of social media and reality television, Gabriella placed her hand over Faith's and gave it a squeeze. Faith latched on to that gesture of support, squeezing the other woman's fingers in turn as she concentrated on forcing the air through her tight lungs. On keeping her tears in check, and willing the heat in her cheeks to subside.

How dare this man make her feel as if she had done wrong? All but call her out by name in the middle of a school function? Who did he think he was? Never before had she been so embarrassed in her life, but she'd be damned if she let him think he got to her in any way. Hell, by the way he was going on, she was already damned.

The rest of the afternoon was a lesson in patience as Faith smiled politely at those who whispered about her behind her back, or made snide comments right to her face. She couldn't bring herself to eat a single bite, and when her father excused himself, hobbling away without waiting for her to respond, she slumped in her chair and wondered if she should just arrange for the Armstrongs to take him home while she went to her favorite bar to try to gather the last of her dignity.

Thank God she had Greta and Gabriella by her side, especially when Gloria from the Cut and Curl said loudly enough for her to hear from the next table over, "I heard the reason the barber shop has been so busy lately is because Faith is giving men more than just a haircut."

To which Gabriella shot back in voice loud enough for all to hear, "Bitchiness and jealousy doesn't suit you, Gloria. Maybe if you woke up to the fact it's no longer 1955, you may be able to get more clients before the ones you have up and die from old age."

"Well I never," Gloria huffed. "You've just cost yourself my business at the golf course, Gabriella. See if I ever work an event for you again."

"That's *Mrs.* Webber to you," Gabriella said with a toss of her thick wavy mane of hair. "And don't forget, it's *my* brides who call *you*, not the other way around. A fact you may best remember."

"Gabriella," Faith said, reaching out to touch her arm. "Thank you, but I don't want to cause trouble for you."

"You're not doing anything. It's these small-minded hypocrites who need to check themselves." She took both of Faith's hands into hers. "You're my friend. I don't have very many, and those I do have, I'm sticking by. No matter what."

When Greta laid her hands over their clasped ones and nodded with solidarity, tears hit Faith's eyes. "Thank you," she managed to whisper. "Ben was right. He said he you all were the best family in the world."

"He said that?" Greta asked and instantly became teary-eyed. "That sweet, sweet man."

"Magpie?" Trey was at his wife's side the moment her tears began to fall. "What's wrong?"

"Just hormones," she wheezed between sniffling sobs. "We're friends with some really good people."

"That we are, magpie." He turned to Faith and smiled. "The best. We're lucky people."

Faith swiped at her cheek and stood. "Thank you all again, but I think I've had about as much civic responsibility as I can take for one day. I'll see you all later."

"Call me if you need anything," Gabriella said. "Call any of us. I mean it. And let's do a girls' night out soon."

"I'd love that." She waved one last time and went in search of her father, who was already heading her direction. "Dad, I'm going to take off. Are you ready to go, or can I find you another way home?"

"I'm ready," he rasped, and made it a point not to look her in the eye.

Oh, great. This was going to be an awesome ride home.

Uncomfortable was the best description of the silence that rode shotgun with them in the car on their way to her father's house, making the drive feel as if she were driving across the country than town. As she pulled into his driveway, he muttered, "Come inside for minute."

"Sure," she mumbled back, noting how his jaw was set with resolve, the way he usually looked when he had come to a decision and was about to act on it.

She took a breath and straightened. It was time to be a grownup. No stammering, no blushing. She was going to own up to her actions, no matter how embarrassing the conversation was going to be.

She followed him into the house but remained standing as her father took root in the center of the living room. If he weren't nursing a game leg, she knew he'd be pacing a track in the well-worn area rug.

"I gotta tell you, Faith. That was one of the most awkward afternoons I've spent in a long time. And I was in the delivery room with your aunt when she gave birth to your cousin Charlie."

Uncertain as to how to respond, she kept it simple. "Oh?"

His lips tightened before he said, "I got an earful today, about you and Ben Castillo and Colby Jensen, and it wasn't lady-like in the slightest. What do you have to say to that?"

Okay. There it was. She sucked in another breath and laid it on the line. "Well, Ben and I have a great relationship where he recognizes I am a sexual woman with needs, and sometimes those needs include inviting Colby to join us during our more intimate moments."

"What?" His white brows shot up before he grimaced with distaste. "Jesus, Mary, and Joseph, Faith. I don't need to hear about my daughter and her sexual needs."

She wanted to laugh, but she stayed the course. "But you do. You see, I enjoy being with Ben, and with Colby. The other night when we were out, someone took advantage and took pictures of us in a private moment without permission then posted them all over the Internet. I'm sorry if it caused you embarrassment, but I'm not sorry I was with them."

"A private moment?" he asked incredulously. "You were outside. In public. With two men falling on you like hungry wolves with a side of beef."

"They were racy, but not that bad."

"That's because it wasn't your child in the pictures."

Damn. He had her there. "I'm sorry. We'll be more careful in the future."

"There isn't going to be a future. You won't be seeing those two men again."

"Of course I will."

"No, Faith, you're not. I shudder to think about what all you got into being around those theater people, but this here is God-fearing country. This type of behavior will not be tolerated. I forbid you from not only seeing those two men, but from going to the Sprawling A at all."

The statement struck her as being so ridiculous that for a moment, she couldn't even form a thought. When her lungs began to burn from holding her breath for so long, she barked out a laugh. "You can't forbid me from seeing anyone. I'm thirty years old. I can see who I want."

A streak of red spread across his cheeks. "Not if you're going to run around, acting like a whore."

She drew back in shock. "That's not fair."

He drew up to his full height and pointed a blunt finger at her. "I will not have my daughter consorting with a bunch of perverts."

"The world is full of perverts," she shouted. "You show me a man who claims not to be a pervert, and I'll show you a liar. Even you're a pervert, Dad."

His eyes boggled as he drew in an indignant breath. "Why, I—"

"Don't you even lie to me. I've seen the dirty magazines you hide in the bathroom."

His mouth snapped shut, and his earlier flush of anger morphed into a pink shade of embarrassment. "That's different."

"It's only different because I'm talking about you and you're talking about me. There is a double standard in this world when it comes to sex and women, and I will not kowtow to it." She pinched the bridge of her nose and tried to quell her frustration. Engaging in a shouting match wasn't going to accomplish anything. "Dad, do you know how many women I've had sit in my chair and talk about their husbands or boyfriends? About the men in their lives who either ignore them, or make them feel worthless, or lacking? How many women who think if they change the color of their hair or curl their lashes, the men in their life lives would stop treating them like garbage? And here I am with two wonderful, generous men, who treat me like a princess. Can't you see how lucky I am?"

"All I see are two men taking advantage of you, but no more. I'm drawing the line in the sand, Faith. You are not to see those two again."

Draw the line, her ass. She wasn't thirteen. "Or what? You'll ground me?"

His nostrils flared and the hair on her arms stood on end, as if sensing the impending strike of lightning of her father's anger. "This is my last word, Faith. Either you stop seeing those men." He drew in a breath. "Or you're no longer welcome in my home."

He might as well have dumped a bucket of ice water on her head. Shock wasn't a strong-enough word to describe the riot of emotions swirling inside her. She must have misunderstood.

"What are you saying?" she asked in a low voice.

"I'm saying I will not have my daughter whoring around and being an embarrassment to this family."

The vehemence in his words was like a knife to the stomach. Who *was* this man before her?

"Let me make sure I understand. You want me to choose between two men who support me, cherish me, encourage me to be anything I want, and you. My father. The man who is supposed to do those exact same things, but who is instead telling me that I am an embarrassment because of whom I choose to love. Is that what you are saying?"

A tick started near his left eye, but he crossed his arms over his chest and set his jaw. "Until you decide to act like the lady your mother and I raised and not some tramp, I don't want to see you in my home or my shop."

It was a toss-up as to what flayed her insides the most, the words he spoke or the disappointment in his eyes. Especially when she had never done anything to cause such a rift between them. Until now.

She shook her head and scrubbed the back of her hand over her eyes. This was not happening. This man was not her father, and if there was any chance of salvaging their relationship, she needed to keep her cool.

"I know it must be tough seeing your little girl as an adult," she said in a voice thick with tears. "And I like to think that I have been a kind, loving daughter who makes you proud. This right here is not the man I know to be my father. I hope that your anger is only because you are confused, or scared, and not because you value a bunch of rules set forth by a society of hypocrites over my happiness. I love Ben. And Colby has become one of my best friends. If you can't accept that, then I don't want you in my life either."

The three seconds it took her to turn around were some of the longest in her life. In her mind she knew her father wasn't going to call her back or suddenly recant his ridiculous ultimatum, but her heart broke when he allowed her to walk out the door without another word.

Despite the brilliance of the midday sun, she shivered from a cold that came from deep inside, where grief and loss flowed in a current that threatened to breach the dam of self-control and pull her under.

She didn't remember climbing into her car, or pulling out on the road. It was pure instinct that guided her to the highway and in the direction of the only place on Earth where she had ever felt truly accepted.

Chapter Sixteen

B EN'S GRIP TIGHTENED on his phone, nearly shattering the plastic into pieces. "Thanks for letting me know, Mark."

"Sorry I had to be the messenger, but we thought you should be on notice," he replied.

"No, I understand. I'll take care of it."

"Let us know if you need anything."

"Will do."

As he ended the call, Ben gave in to the rage and disbelief boiling inside him and threw his phone at the fireplace with a furious howl. The poor phone didn't stand a chance and shattered to smithereens upon impact. Unlike Adam's phone, which had been an easy repair, there was nothing that would bring this particular piece of technology back from the dead.

Who the hell did Dave Belhaven think he was, calling out Faith in front of most of the community? How dare he ambush a defenseless woman whose only crime was falling for someone the likes of him? He'd like to have seen the little prick try a stunt like that with him. He'd have had that self-righteous bastard on his knees asking him for forgiveness.

But poor Faith had to endure the embarrassment on her own, with her father sitting next to her. God, what must George be thinking now? Ben had always liked and respected the man. He'd hate it if George thought his daughter was caught up with some degenerate lowlife, even if it was mostly true. Okay, so he wasn't a lowlife, but he was a degenerate. And Faith was better off with someone far more worthy than he.

The crunch of tires on gravel brought his attention to the front window where he spotted Faith's car coming down the lane.

Shit. He knew this day was coming, but he had hoped he'd have a little bit longer in paradise before the powers that be kicked him out into purgatory. Foolish thinking on his part. More than once he'd seen life kick a man in the groin just when he thought the getting was good. Why did he think he'd be spared such pain?

Using one of Colby's video game cases like a scoop, he picked up the remnants of his phone off the floor then dashed into the kitchen to throw away the evidence of his anger.

The tremors of his fury morphed into nerves as his fingers curled into his fists and he contemplated his next move. At the forefront of his thoughts was his love for Faith. Nothing else mattered but her happiness, even if it meant he had to push her in the right direction by any means necessary.

The clip of her heels coming up the steps preceded her knock on the door and the creak of the knob turning. "Ben? Ben, are you home?"

With a mental picture of her future happiness in his mind's eye, he concentrated on slowing his breathing and loosening the tension in his body.

The man who walked into the living room to join her was nothing more than a façade of who he was on the inside. To stay the course, he locked away his heart and filled the void with righteous determination.

"Hey," he said as if he hadn't a care in the world. "I thought you were spending the day with your dad."

She looked up at him with her big, watery eyes and his knees almost buckled at the sight of her distress. His thighs tensed in preparation of running to her side, but he locked his knees in place and curled his fingers around his belt.

"Oh, Ben," she cried and flew to him, throwing her arms around his waist and burying her head against his chest.

The walls he had thrown up cracked under the onslaught of her tears, but he remained steady, keeping contact to a minimum by patting her on the back with light taps of his fingers as she shuddered against him. "What's this all about?"

"It was awful. First, Pastor Dave practically pointed his stubby finger at me and called me a fornicator in front of the entire town, and then my father..." she hiccupped. "My father forbade me from seeing you. He said it was either you or him. Can you believe that?" She pulled away, lifting her tear-stained face with indignation. "He actually said it was him or you, like I was a teenager and we were in some sappy movie."

Her words were as effective as a blast chiller, freezing his blood and encasing him in ice. "What did you tell him?" he asked quietly, fearing he already knew the answer.

"I told him he was being unreasonable, and if that was how it was going to be, I chose you."

Fuck.

What didn't she just kick him in the nuts too? The pain would have been more bearable. As it was, he barely restrained the groan that welled from his gut.

Was the idea of Faith being in a relationship with him really so horrible, her own father was ready to disown her? He figured George might be a little out of sorts when he found out, but the extremity of his objection shocked the hell out of him. No wonder Faith was near hysterics.

"Faith, sweetness." He set her away from him and took a step back. This would be easier without her soft heat to tempt him away from his objective, but there was no way he'd allow the rift between Faith and her father continue any longer than necessary. "You need to go back to your dad. Tell him you're sorry, and that you choose him."

Her lashes fluttered for several moments. "What?"

"Choose him. Faith, he's your dad. I'm just your current lover."

"You are more than just my current lover," she shouted.

"No. I'm not." He made a big show of heaving a bored sigh as he crossed his arms. "I think we got sidetracked from what this arrangement was intended to be. I was going to help you explore your submissive side, which I've done. And then some. But you and me were never supposed to be a permanent couple."

"I'm hearing words, but it's like you're speaking in a foreign language." She shook her head. "What are you saying?"

Stay strong, dude. Stay strong. Don't let those big blue eyes suck you in.

"I'm saying that you've grown too attached. I'm sorry if I led you on in any way, but I'm just a passerby in your life. And it's time for us to part ways. We're done, Faith."

Again with the flutter of the lashes. Beneath her pretty green dress, her shoulders slumped and she looked as if she were a young girl and he had just ripped the head off her favorite doll.

"We're done?" she asked quietly. "What does that mean?"

He shifted his weight on his feet, tightening his arms across his chest to keep from reaching out for her. "It means that we're done. It's been fun, and you're an excellent lover, but seriously, all the fuss that has been kicked up all over the place—well, I don't think it's worth it."

She began to resemble a bobble head doll, and he could actually see it in her eyes as she withdrew into her mind, seeking protection as he broke her heart.

"Worth it?" she repeated on a whisper so soft, he barely heard the words.

"Yeah." He cleared his throat. Time to be the supreme asshole. "It's one thing to have the town all in an uproar because I was the bastard who smudged your squeaky-clean image. But if your dad's now going to be up my ass too..." He shook his head. "I think I'd rather take the time to drive across the mountain for an easy hookup than have to deal with irate fathers. No amount of pussy is worth that much trouble."

Never before had he spewed such disrespectful words, and he hoped to God he never had to do so again as Faith stared at him as if he had taken a knife and gutted her. Her mouth dropped open and the pink faded from her cheeks, leaving her looking like a ghost version of her usual glorious self.

Bile burned his throat, and for a moment, he almost said fuck it all and beg for her to forget everything he just said, but she deserved better than what he could offer. Better than a few nights a week of hot sex in return for the loss of respect from her community. For fuck's sake, even her father turned on her because she dared to embrace her darker side.

Faith wasn't cut out to be shunned from society. She hadn't been hardened by the injustices of life like he'd been. People had been giving him the side-eye since he was sixteen years old. It came with the territory when you were a big silent guy. But Faith was like a beautiful rose that needed to bloom in the sun, and he refused to be the one to block her light.

"It's been a great run, kid." His voice rumbled as if he had rocks in his throat. "But we're done."

"Just like that?" Her voice sounded just as scratchy. "You

feel like I'm crimping your style, so now we're done?"

"I'm a simple man, Faith. There's no need to drag this out and make things more awkward than necessary."

"No. Of course not." She reminded him of a sleepwalker as she stared blankly at him as she spoke. "Best to keep things civil."

The low cadence of her speech tore him apart. He knew her well, recognized she was devastated, but he loved her. So much so, he knew he had to let her go.

He cleared his throat again. "Thanks for being an adult about this. I know whomever you end up with next will be the guy you've been looking for. Now, if you'll excuse me, I, uh, I have to get back to work."

She started as if waking from a dream. "What?"

"You can go now." He placed his hand on her shoulder and guided her toward the door. "I wish you well."

"Right. I'll just…let you get on with your life." With a gait as jerky as her speech, Faith shuffled out the front door.

The soft catch of the lock closing behind her was like a bullet to the chest, but the pain exploding within him hurt a thousand times worse.

WHAT WAS GOING on? What the *fuck* was going on?

Just the other week, her stars had been falling in line and the world was a bright and shiny place. Then in what felt like five minutes it was as if the frickin' Death Star had orbited into her universe and blown everything to smithereens. Which way was up? Which way was down? She hadn't a clue.

It felt as if the strength had been sucked from her limbs, but somehow she managed to walk down the front steps of Ben's house without adding the further disgrace of falling on her face.

A strange, yellowish haze stole across her vision, and in her head, she heard nothing but a dull roar that struck her stupid. She was done. Absolutely done.

"Faith? Faith!"

It wasn't until she felt the touch of a hand on her arm did she find the energy to blink away some of the fog. Her eyesight blurred and shifted, bringing into focus Colby's handsome face that was marred with ripples of fear.

"Faith, sweetheart, what's wrong?" He took her into his arms. "I heard about what happened at the fundraiser. That cowardly son of a bitch pastor. I'd like to throw some rocks at his glass house."

"Ben. Ben. He—he." She couldn't even utter the words. All of the humiliation of the last week sucked her under and she lacked the power to paddle to the surface.

"Ben what? Faith, you're scaring me. What happened?"

"He—he broke up with me," she stuttered.

"He what?" He looked over her shoulder to the house in surprise. "What happened?"

Tremors took root in her bones and her teeth began to chatter. "He said our relationship was causing him too much trouble, and that my, that my pussy wasn't worth it," she finished on a sob and collapsed in his arms.

"What? Ben said that? I don't believe it."

"I—I never—" She buried her face against his chest and let the tears that had been building all day pour out.

"Son of a bitch," Colby muttered and bent to scoop her up. "I don't know what's going on, but let's get you someplace more comfortable where we can talk."

She didn't want to talk anymore. All she wanted was to curl into a ball and travel back in time when no one called her bad names and she was cuddled in the warmth of Ben's arms.

Although Colby's arms were just as nice as he carried her to his truck and set her in the passenger's seat as if she were fragile. He didn't need to be so careful, she was already broken.

After he settled into the driver's seat, he pulled her against his side before taking off down the lane. As she wept a wet patch into the fabric of his T-shirt, he rubbed his hand up and down her thigh while cooing nonsensical sounds of comfort between the shifting of the truck's gears. He drove so fast down the lane, every bump and rut in the road had her bouncing in the seat, nauseating her.

"You don't have to go so fast," she said, and swiped at her tear-drenched cheeks. "It's not worth driving into a ditch because Ben made me feel bad."

"Sorry, darlin'. We're almost there."

Colby brought them to a stop beside a giant willow tree.

She had never seen a tree so massive. The trunk alone would take four people with their arms stretched out fingertip to fingertip just to circle the circumference. A few feet away, the creek moseyed past them. The ripples where water met rock glittered so brightly in the afternoon sun, she could barely look at them without squinting.

Underneath the stretching branches, the grass was shorter than the surrounding area, as if that area was clipped regularly and not available to the path of the grazing herd.

"Where are we?" she asked.

"This is *the* tree. That's what we call it, anyway." He stepped out of the cab and pulled a thick wool blanket from the flatbed of his truck. "If you want a quiet place where no one will bother you, this is where you come. Of course, Trey and Greta come here to have some sexy, outdoor time, but I know they're still at the fundraiser."

She followed him to where he spread out the blanket beneath the abundant foliage and sat where he gestured. "It is pretty here. Peaceful."

"I figured you could use all the peace you can get." He sat beside her and handed her a bandana he had pulled from his pocket. "I'm sorry Ben said those horrible things to you, but something doesn't add up. He loves you. I know it. I've seen it. I don't know why he pushed you away, but I'll get to the bottom of it, I promise you."

"I feel like I'm in a snow globe and a giant bully is not only shaking it to death, but kicking it all over to hell and back. First those pictures, then Cal, and the fundraiser, then my father disowns me."

"What?" he exclaimed. "He disowned you?"

She nodded with a sniff. "He said I had to choose between being with Ben and being friends with you or being a daughter who wasn't an embarrassment. I stupidly thought Ben cared about me, so I chose him."

"That's the thing, Faith. He does care about you." He pushed the hair off her damp cheeks. "I've never seen him with a woman the way I've seen him with you."

She snorted. "Yeah, but you also didn't know he was into bondage either."

"It's more than that. He loves you. How could he not? You're wonderful. Smart, sexy, funny. I know he loves you." He paused to take a breath. "Because *I* love you."

"I love you too."

"No." He tilted her chin up with his finger and gazed into her eyes. "I love you, Faith. Like a man loves a woman. Like you are my heart and my soul and will be until the day I die. I. Love. You."

There was so much love and emotion in his eyes, it was as if he had reached into her chest and squeezed. She could barely breathe, barely think. Was he really saying what she thought he was saying?

"Colby, I—I. What?"

"I know." He released her and looked off into the horizon and ran his hand through his hair. "I didn't plan on falling for you, especially as hard as I have. And I know your heart belongs to Ben. It should. You two are perfect for each other. But I love you, Faith. Whether you're with Ben or not, I'll still love you, crazy as that sounds. And I hope that someday you may grow to care for me, too. As something more than a friend."

Crazy? Yeah, the entire situation was crazy. What woman hadn't fantasized about a man professing his love while gazing at her as if she were the moon and stars with chocolate sprinkles and angels singing hallelujahs? She certainly had. In fact, very recently she imagined hearing the very words Colby said, except being spoken by an entirely different man.

Or were they?

From the first moment she met Colby, she liked him, and over the weeks they had grown close enough that she considered him a friend. He always found a way to make her smile, and they never lacked for conversation. And when she needed a champion, he was right there, ready to defend her to the death, without question. She cared for him, but did she love him? Like, *love him* love him?

Sweet baby Jesus. She did.

"This is horrible," she broke out on a sob. "I am a horrible person."

"Faith, please don't cry." He raised and lowered his hands several times before gingerly placing them on her arms. "I didn't mean to upset you further. I understand if you don't feel the same way."

"That's just the thing," she stuttered. "I do love you. I love you the same way I love Ben. And that's why I'm a horrible person."

"Why does loving us make you horrible?"

"Because I can't love both of you that way. It's a terrible thing."

"Says who?"

"Says everyone. Says all off those people who—" she broke off as if a million-watt lightbulb had been clicked on and she realized the insanity she was about to spew.

Suddenly, it was as if the support beam inside her keeping her upright had been demolished, and she deflated, curling her knees against her chest as she admitted in a quiet voice, "Says all of the people who will think that me loving two men is wrong. All of the people who have called me names or thought I have no right to any respect. All of those people will think I am a horrible person because I love you and Ben."

His lips tightened as he nodded. "Does their opinion matter?"

"Not all of them. My father's does. So would your family's."

"Darlin', my family thinks of Ben as one of their own. And if you haven't noticed, Greta and Gabriella have already kind of adopted you."

"It's still crazy. And a moot point. Ben doesn't want to have anything to do with me."

"You let me take care of Ben," he said with a tight smile.

"What does that mean?"

He cupped her face in his work-roughened palms. "It means I want you to trust me to make everything all right."

"Yeah, it's been a really rough week. I'm going to need more than that."

He smiled his little lopsided smile and she melted. "All I ask is for you to grant me two things. One, your trust. And two, thirty minutes. For the next thirty minutes, I don't want you to think about anything or anyone outside of what we can see around us. I want you to let me hold you in my arms and love you. Later, well, we'll deal with the rest later."

Man. He was really good at making a girl feel special. For the first time in a long while she felt like smiling. "Only thirty minutes?"

"I'll take longer, but I'm trying not to be too greedy."

She climbed into his lap and hugged him tight. "Be as greedy as you want."

"Are you sure?"

"Absolutely," she whispered against his lips. "I love you, Colby Jensen."

His eyes sparkled as if she had just handed him a fortune.

"Damn, that sounds good." He reached up to cup the back of her neck in his palm and settled his lips over hers.

Kissing Colby always felt as if she were being wrapped up in a big warm fur blanket. She was safe in his arms. Cherished. With Ben there was an air of danger. At any moment, he could turn vicious and pull her hair or sink his teeth into her flesh, exciting for certain, but at times exhausting.

Of course, that wasn't to say kissing Colby was boring. Oh no. The languid heat flowing through her body like hot caramel made her skin tingle and set her erogenous zones pulsing in a primal rhythm. She couldn't sit still, wiggling her hips against the hard ridge behind his fly. His kisses teased with the promise of more, hinted at the hunger lying in wait to pounce. The anticipation drove her mad with the need to tear off their clothes until they were skin to skin. To feel something other than shame or embarrassment.

"Impatient, are we?" He laughed against her skin before trailing a string of kisses down her neck.

After the week she had endured, she needed the closeness of his touch, of his love. Craved it like a flower needing sunlight to banish the darkness of her sadness. "I need you. I need you to love me."

"Done, sweetheart."

He bunched the skirt of her dress in his hands and pulled the garment up and over her head. With his teeth, he yanked the strap of her bra off her shoulder as he popped the clasp, spilling her breast into his waiting palm before rolling her onto her back.

Above them the tiny leaves of the willow rustled in the slight breeze, playing a melodic accompaniment to her gasps and sighs as he nibbled on the curves of her breasts. His hands followed his lips as he stripped her naked and worshipped her with his tongue.

It was so decadent, so hedonistic, lying in the open with the sun shining through the branches like little spotlights, and with him still dressed. The wash-worn fabric of his jeans and shirt rubbed against her belly and inner thighs as he crawled down to settle between her sprawled legs.

He separated the lips of her sex with his thumbs then ran his tongue between the damp folds. "Is all this for me? You're so wet and delicious." He speared two fingers into her sheath and stroked the sensitive nerves. "Play with your breasts for me. Tug on your nipples."

"If I do that, I won't last long."

"I'm not planning for you to have only one orgasm. Come for me, Faith. Make me drown."

Her breasts felt so heavy in her hands. So swollen and needy for attention. The sight of Colby between her legs, with his tongue working her clit as he watched her pluck and pull at her nipples, sent her to the edge at breakneck speed.

"That's it. Come for me." He wrapped his lips around her

clit and sucked hard as his fingertips tapped the spot near the neck of her womb.

Her back arched as she screamed and turned liquid in his grasp. The breeze picked up the sound of her shouts and scattered it across the meadow while cooling her hot flesh.

But Colby wasn't done with her yet. With a twinkle in his eye and his lopsided smile, he kept up the come-hither motion of his fingers against her g-spot and a gentle suction on her pulsating clit. He reached up with his free hand and took over the playing of her nipple, and together they built up the rising tide of passion until the dam broke and she came on a groan, hitching her hips up against his hungry mouth, desperate to draw out the exquisite pleasure until tears fell from her eyes.

"No more," she panted. "I can't take any more."

"You've got one more in you." He sat up and pulled his shirt over his head. As he released his fly, the hard length of his erection bounced free and slapped him in the belly. "I think you have three or four more in you."

"I'll die."

"Maybe." He gripped the base of his cock and paused. His gaze flicked back and forth between the tip of his swollen cock and her open sex. A frown formed on his brow as he stroked his hand up and down.

"Colby? What's wrong?"

He nudged her clit with the damp crown of his cock. Slowly, so slowly he rubbed a path around the lips of her sex over and over again.

When he spoke, his voice was deep and husky in a way she never heard from him before. "I want to take you bare, Faith. Nothing between us."

Bare. Flesh on flesh. Filling her with his seed. Changing the chemistry of her body for a brief moment of time.

That intimacy was a privilege she had shared only with Ben. A man she had suspected she'd fall in love with, and she had. Now here was Colby. A man she *did* love.

She took his hand gripping his cock and guided him down to lodge the blunt head against her opening. "Take me, Colby. Make me yours in every way."

He chuckled and drew little circles, teasing her opening. "I can't decide if I should bury myself inside you quick-like, or draw it out nice and slow."

"Whatever you do, do it now. I'm empty without you."

"Aw, now, we can't have that." He braced both of his hands on either side of her head, and thrust his hips forward, filling her to capacity with one mighty lunge. As their pelvises kissed, he shuddered with a curse. "Shit. This was a bad idea."

"Why?" He felt divine, all hot and hard inside her.

"It's too good. You're so hot and wet. And tight. I'm going to spill before we get started."

"You've got one more in you." She scored her nails down his back and dug them into the curves of his ass. "Maybe even three or four."

"Smart ass." He lowered to his elbows and thrust again, establishing a steady pace where he pulled almost all of the way out before plunging to the hilt inside her. With each thrust, he'd arch up his pelvis, stroking the head of his cock against her g-spot and making her eyes cross with the pleasure.

Not to be outdone, she fondled the crease of his ass then dipped her fingers inside to rim the edge of his hidden hole.

"Jesus," he bit out. "You don't play fair."

"I like to see you sweat. I love it when you're mindless with lust and the feel of your cock jerking inside me when I do this." She probed the hole with her fingertip.

"You little witch. I want to make this good for you."

"It's good. Believe me, it's good." On an extra-deep lunge, her eyes rolled and her pussy fluttered in preparation of another orgasm.

"That's more like it." He rolled her over so she sat astride him.

"I was so close," she wailed.

"I know." He smiled wickedly. "Grab onto that branch above you."

The nearest branch was so far above her head, she had to rise up on her knees in order to reach it. Colby took advantage of the space between them and dug his heels into the ground, lifting his hips to impale her on his length as he drove inside her again and again.

He cupped her bouncing breasts in his hands. "With the sun behind you, you look like a pagan goddess. My goddess. And I want to worship you."

She gave herself over to his keeping. Her head fell back as she moaned and luxuriated in the feel of his caresses as he plucked and strummed her body like a harp. Beneath her, his body grew slick with sweat as his muscles flexed. Fire burned in his gaze as he watched her undulate on his cock. His lips drew back in a grimace and the skin over his cheeks tightened the more he swelled inside her.

Like a pendulum, she swung from one extreme to the other. The tension within her was delicious, addictive, heightening her senses even as it blocked out the world around her. She was loath to leave the cocoon, but she knew that once she jumped, the fall would be just as sweet, if not sweeter.

"Are you ready for me?" he asked as he settled his thumb over her clit, rolling the nub with a firm touch. "Ready for me. To make you. Mine?"

"Yes. Oh God, yes."

Colby held onto her hips, his fingers digging into her flanks as he bucked like a madman. His back arched, and he cried out in a string of curses as he erupted inside her.

Leaves rained down upon them as she followed him into the flames. The branch in her hands bowed as she bucked and jerked. It wouldn't surprise her one bit if they generated so much energy, the entire tree burst into a giant fireball.

How long they stayed locked in the throes of ecstasy, she hadn't a clue. The only things she was aware of were the fire in her lungs and the throbbing strength of the man embedded in her body. Only when the once-refreshing breeze turned icy and her teeth began to chatter with the cold did she recognize the fall back to earth.

"Come here, baby," Colby murmured and pulled on her shoulders.

Her fingers wouldn't budge from their hold around the branch. Even the tiny muscles of her fingers refused to cooperate, and she needed Colby's assistance to help pry them loose. Once free, he curled her into his body and pulled the edges of the blanket around them.

His thumb stroked her cheek as he cradled her head against his chest. "You know I'm never letting you go, don't you?"

For fear of saying something stupid or potentially hurtful if she opened her mouth, she nodded with a slight smile and cuddled closer.

Forever with Colby sounded lovely, but she couldn't ignore her feelings for Ben. Her very confused and twisted feelings for Ben. She promised Colby thirty minutes where nothing existed but the two of them. Hell, she'd give him an hour, even an entire day, but soon, all too soon they were going to have to address the presence of the big cowboy who broke her heart.

Would Colby still love her then? Or would he have to

choose between a woman he claimed to love and the man he regarded as a brother?

Did she want him to?

Chapter Seventeen

"ARE YOU SURE you don't want me to come home with you?" Colby asked Faith through the opening of her driver-side window.

"I'll be fine," she said, but the tightening of her hands on the wheel gave him cause to worry about her well-being. "I just want some time alone with a hot bath and my friend Jose Cuervo. Besides, you have to work in the morning."

The forlorn look in her eyes as she glanced over to the house tore his heart out. If this had been yesterday or the day before, the comfort she sought would have been with him and Ben. Not in the depths of a bottle of tequila.

"Don't drink and bathe at the same time. Please. For my sake."

Her smile was more like a grimace as she nodded.

"Hey." He reached in and tilted up her chin for his kiss. The fingers of his free hand curled over the frame of the door, transferring to the metal the energy he wanted to use to climb through the window and drag her back into his arms. She was so determined to be strong, and at the moment he was willing to give her whatever she wanted. Even time away from him, although it killed him to do so. "Call me when you get home.

And when you wake up. And if you need anything."

"Colby." She latched onto his wrist and dropped a kiss in the center of his palm. "I'll be all right. I am an adult who is facing an adult situation. In the grand scheme of life, things could be much worse."

True. But she was his girl, and she was hurting. Until she found her smile, his world wasn't right. He pressed another kiss to her lips. "I love you."

A burst of blue flame lit up in her eyes, and a little bit of the Faith he knew returned as the corner of her lips lifted and her lashes fluttered. "I love you too."

With a heavy heart and a stomach full of dread, he backed away from her car and watched her disappear behind a cloud of dust as she drove down the lane. He blew out a breath and grabbed a handful of his hair, pulling at the strands until his eyes watered. What a total, utter, clusterfuck the last few days had been.

He liked to consider himself a patient man. A calm, steady presence his friends and family were able to draw strength from in times of trouble. He had always followed the rules, done well in school, and respected others, even when they might not have been deserving of that respect. But the events of the last week had given him a hair-trigger temper, and at that moment, the eye in the cyclone of the fury whirling around him was his best friend.

What had Ben been thinking, hurting Faith that way? Abandoning her in her time of need. Not only that, Ben managed to ruin the moment he was going to tell Faith he loved her.

Of all the ways he imagined telling Faith what lay in his heart, having her tear-stained and crying because Ben insulted her was not one of them. To have her know of his love was probably more important than how she came to learn of his affections, but he had wanted the moment to be romantic, magical. Not with the specter of Ben's assholiness playing a supporting character.

Hell, to be truthful, he was completely clueless as to how any of this relationship was supposed to work. He wasn't supposed to fall in love with his best friend's girl. He wasn't supposed to be mad on her behalf because his friend broke her heart. And he most certainly wasn't supposed to march into the house and demand that said friend beg her forgiveness and get back together with her. Without a second thought, he was marching across the gravel and climbing up the front steps to do just that.

The house was stone silent as he entered, and he wondered if Ben had bugged out to avoid a confrontation. Fat lot of good that would do him. As soon as word got out that he broke up with Faith, there wasn't a place on the ranch he'd be able to hide. Everyone loved her, and Greta and Gabriella would be on his case for sure.

From room to room he crept, covering the first floor before climbing up the stairs.

There he was. Sitting on his bed. Elbows on his knees, his hands hanging limply and with his eyes closed.

Damn. It was hard to stay pissed at a man who appeared to be so broken. Ben was larger than life, so massive, so strong, that sometimes Colby forgot his friend was fallible. Human. But he still deserved a kick in the ass.

"Would you like to explain what went down between you and Faith?" Colby asked as he leaned against the doorframe.

Ben drew in a long breath then straightened. "It was time to move on. We'd run our course."

"Right. And I call bullshit. What's really going on?"

"It's not that difficult to understand." He rose to a stand then shrugged. "She's not the girl for me. It's best we parted ways now."

"Is she not the girl for you, or are you not man enough for her?"

The muscles in his jaw flinched. Ah. A direct hit. "Doesn't matter. We're done."

"Are you?" He shifted to fill the doorway as Ben tried to walk past him. "Tell me something, Ben. Did you tell Faith that she wasn't, well, I won't disrespect her by repeating such foulness. I just need to know if you did."

Ben's lips tightened and he glanced away. Answer enough.

Fire sizzled down Colby's right arm as his fist tightened. The punch he launched flew so fast, he almost missed the motion himself as his fist connected solidly with Ben's strong jaw with a loud *crack*.

Ben stumbled back, bouncing off the wall as he regained his footing. Shock flared on his face before his brows lowered and his nostrils flared.

Colby widened his stance, his hand throbbing as his muscles tensed in preparation of the answering swing, but it never came. After a few deep breaths, Ben nodded then continued down the hall.

"Is that it?" Colby shouted and followed him down the stairs. "You're just going to let her walk away? You're not going to fight for her? She loves you."

"No. She loves *you*."

"I know she does. She just told me so herself, right after I told her I loved her. Then we had the best sex of my life right by the river. Happiest moment of my life."

Ben drew up short then rounded on him. A parade of hurt followed by jealousy and confusion marched across his face. "What? Then why the hell are you yelling at me to go back to her? She's your girl."

"No. She's *our* girl. She loves you just as fiercely as she loves me. She's meant to be with both of us."

"Are you insane?" Ben asked with wide eyes. "Are you even listening to yourself? She can't be with two men at once."

"Why not? She's been with the two of us all this time. People engage in ménage relationships all of the time."

"What the fuck do you know about triad relationships? Until recently you knew jack shit about the lifestyle. And what you're suggesting isn't about being in a scene. You're talking about every single day, chores around the house, PTA meetings, and the like. It isn't normal."

"Oh ho!" Colby crowed. "Since when does the great Ben Castillo worry about being normal or about what other people think?"

In an instant, Ben was standing toe to toe with him, towering over him with his eyes narrowed in warning. "When it's about keeping Faith safe. When it's about keeping assholes like Cal Brotherton from targeting her, or having her father speak to her again. When it affects Trey or the ranch. That's when I care."

Okay. So he had a point. But still. "We will protect her. No one understands Faith like we do. No one will love her like we do. She needs us. And we need her. Am I saying it'll be easy? No. Hell no. But nothing worth having ever is. I'm not going to give up on a chance at happiness because of what some dumbasses in town think. And you deserve your happiness too. Someone to lie beside you at night, or kiss you hello, or burn your bacon every morning. I won't live my life for those fuckers, or give up something special because it doesn't fit into convention. And you shouldn't either."

"That's very Pollyanna of you," Ben said in a rough voice. "But the world doesn't work that way. Over time, the sneers and the whispers will wear on her. They'll wear on you too." Tears glittered in his eyes. "Then that light within her that I've—you've—come to love will be extinguished. I'm not going to let that happen."

"Then you're a coward."

He shook his head and backed away. "Then I'm a coward. And Faith will have some chance at happiness. With you. You're what's best for Faith, Colby. You're right. No one will love her like you will. That's why I have to walk away. I wish the best for both of you. I really do."

He spun on his heel and stormed out the door. The heavy tread of his boots on the stairs sounded like an echo in an abandoned mausoleum and felt just as welcoming.

Ben was crazy if he thought this conversation was over. It wasn't. Not by a long shot. Oh no. All of his arguments about what was best for Faith convinced Colby that Ben loved her. Loved her enough to set her free. Fortunately for Ben, she was going to fly back home. With a little outside help, of course.

Chapter Eighteen

IT WAS A sad state of affairs when the highlight of a man's day was mucking out the barn.

Ben allowed himself a moment to wipe the sweat off his brow before shoveling out the last bit of dirty straw from Temptation's stall. His mare was not pleased she was the last to have her bed cleaned, but she was the most patient, and therefore the most pleasant to be with at the end of a long morning.

It wasn't yet ten a.m. and he'd already put in a full day's work. After all, it wasn't as if he had anything else to do or anyone to talk to at the house. The women of the ranch were indeed giving him the cold shoulder after they heard he ended things with Faith. Hard work was going to be his saving grace over the next few days.

He hoped.

"Hey."

Now there was a voice he hadn't heard in a while.

For the last week, Colby had been spending almost every night at Faith's place and commuting in to work. Although Colby wasn't one for lengthy conversations, Ben missed the sound of his friend walking down the hall and cursing at his video games. Those noises that reminded a person that they weren't alone. Who knew that there'd ever be a time when he missed the sound of someone brushing their teeth.

He glanced over his shoulder at the man standing in the doorway. Maybe it was the way he was silhouetted by the morning sun, but Colby appeared older somehow. More mature, with a confident posture and a thoughtful look on his face. Maybe that was what the love of a good woman did to you. Made you man up to be the person she needed. It looked good on him. The fucker.

He nodded and replied, "Hey."

It was on the tip of his tongue to ask how Faith was. To say he missed him. Missed them. Instead, he pinched his lips together and continued with his work.

Colby ambled closer. "I don't suppose you've had a change of heart and decide to come back to Faith, drop to your knees, and ask her to take you back?"

Too many times to count.

"Nope," he said, turning his back on him to hang up the shovel on the wall of tools before heading to the sink to wash his hands.

Colby followed as he continued on to the hay storage. "Positive? She misses you."

"She'll stop soon."

"I was afraid you'd say that. Good thing I'm prepared to talk some sense into you."

A familiar whirring sound reached his ears the second before a rope fell across his vision and dropped to encircle his arms before it was cinched tight.

"Colby? What the hell?" he shouted as his hands were tugged behind his back and bound.

"As they say," Colby panted as Ben struggled like a rabbit

caught in a snare, "sometimes you've gotta take the bull by the horns. Especially when that bull is being bullheaded."

"I am going to kick your ass," Ben snarled and dug his heels in as Colby dragged him by the length of the rope to a support beam.

He looped the rope around a hook screwed in the overhead beam and used his full body weight to pull it down and around the joist, tethering Ben into place.

Colby dropped a hay bale behind his feet. "Sit down, cowboy."

"Whatever fool plan you've got cooked up isn't going to work. Let me go before I tear the whole damn barn down."

"We'll see." Colby smiled and backed away. "Sit tight. I'll be back in a minute."

"Colby," he shouted. "Colby!"

Well, fuck. His wrists were already starting to chaff but his fingers weren't tingling. Thank the lord he taught the kid how to tie a decent knot that wouldn't kill his blood circulation. The length of rope trailing behind his bound hands offered just enough resistance for him to stand, but that was about all of the movement he could manage.

As it was, he figured he had two options. Scream his head off until one of the other hands came to untie him, or wait it out until Colby returned. Either option was its own version of hell.

"Right this way, sweetheart," he heard Colby say from the direction of the stalls.

"Why did you ask me to meet you in the barn?" Faith asked.

Oh shit. This was another level of hell altogether.

"I thought it would be nice to take out the horses and have a picnic by the stream. Doesn't that sound romantic?"

"It would," she said with a giggle. "If I knew how to ride a horse."

"I've got something better in mind for you to ride."

Good God. He was going to be sick.

Faith's laughter was cut off then quickly replaced with a soft moan that soon turned into a series of whimpers that went on and on. And on and on. Each little gasp was like a series of one-two punches to his gut.

He knew that if he stayed on the ranch he'd be subjected to watching Colby and Faith as they reveled in their love, just as he knew it might be painful to bear witness. He just never anticipated the acid-like burn of jealousy eating him up from the inside by only imagining what they were doing on the other side of that wall.

"Have I told you how much I love you?" Colby asked.

"Yes. But it's still nice to hear. I love you too."

Gah. Another punch, this time to the kidneys.

"I've got a surprise for you. I hope you like it."

"Ah, Colby. You didn't have to get me anything. The jewelry was more than enough."

Jewelry? What jewelry? Was she talking a necklace or a ring? Had he asked her to marry him? What the fuck?

As the shock of that possibility reverberated in his mind, the partition wall slid open.

Faith stopped in her tracks with a gasp as she spotted him trussed up like a calf in a roping competition. She looked back at Colby. "I don't understand."

Colby stepped between them. "This is what my mother would call a 'Come to Jesus' moment. Faith, you've walked around brokenhearted long enough. And Ben, it's time to get your head out of your ass."

"Colby," he gritted out. "Untie me now."

"Only the truth will set you free, my brother." He took Faith's hands in his. "Faith, sweetheart. I know you love me, but

I know you love Ben, too. You love him the same way you love me. Don't you?"

"You know I do," she whispered, stealing a guilty glance in Ben's direction.

Colby turned her to face him. "Tell him. Tell Ben how you feel."

"What?" she gasped and looked at him as if he were crazy. "Just like that?"

He cupped her face in his hands. "Behind your smiles you're miserable. So much was left unsaid and now you have a hole in your heart. Tell Ben how you feel. How angry and disappointed you are that he turned you away. That you hate him. Once the truth is out, we can move on and I can fill that hole."

"But I *don't* hate him." She backed away from his touch. "I just—I—yes, I was angry and disappointed. But I don't hate him."

She closed her eyes and drew in several breaths as her lashes grew wet and spiky. Just when Ben thought his lungs were about to burst, she shook her head and turned to stand before him.

"I don't hate you." A pink flush raced across her cheeks but she met his gaze with so much love swimming in her blue eyes, he got choked up just looking at her. "I love you. And I miss you. You were my everything." She looked back at Colby. "Well, almost my everything. But you saw right to the heart of me, Ben. The parts I knew were inside, but didn't know how to embrace. I don't love you because I'm grateful, but because you're a good man. You're a good friend. What woman wouldn't fall in love with you and want you for their own?"

He'd have liked to think it was the dust making his eyes water, but the love and the passion with which she spoke tore his heart out. With only a moment's hesitation, she laid her soul bare. Faced the possibility of his rejection again with her heart on her sleeve. If only he could be as brave.

"Don't," he rasped. "Don't waste your love on me. I don't deserve it."

"How can you say that?" she asked with anguish in her voice. She crossed to him, placing her hands on either side of his face. Her fingers were cool against his hot cheeks. "How can you say you're not deserving of love?"

"When it causes you harm. When people think they can treat you poorly, or hurt you. You deserve better."

"Those people don't deserve my affections. I love you, Ben Castillo, and I will until the day I die. Even if you never return my love, I will love you."

"You can't, Faith." He shook his head, the only means he had to communicate besides his words, and at the moment he wasn't able to string a simple sentence together.

"Can you handle the alternative?" Colby asked him, stepping behind Faith.

He wrapped the length of her hair in his hand and pulled, exposing the long line of her neck. Her lips parted on a gasp, and her eyelashes fluttered as he dropped a line of kisses across her skin.

"Can you handle watching another man kiss what was yours?" He ran his hands over her belly and up to cup her breasts. "Touch what was yours? Love what was yours? And knowing that you threw it all away because you were a coward?"

The rush to refute the label stung his lips, but it was the truth. It was all true. He was afraid to allow Faith to love him. If he disappointed her, caused her to regret being with him, it would kill him.

But what Colby was suggesting was even crazier.

"Can you, Colby?" he shot back. "You're suggesting that we share her. Can you handle the shit that's gonna come down from the rest of the town?"

"If I have to. With the people I love by my side, I can face anything. But it's not solely my decision. What do you say, Faith? Do you want to hitch your wagon to two stallions who will devote themselves to loving you forever? Who'll be your family?"

Faith turned and threw her arms around Colby's neck, sealing her lips over his in a brief but passionate kiss. As she pulled away, she laid her palm against the side of his face and kissed his cheek. She then turned toward Ben and straddled his lap. Nose to nose, she gazed at him with love and determination.

"I choose you, Ben. And Colby. I hope you believe in me enough to know the world is a big place and what I have with you two is worth fighting for. Will you choose us?"

"Ah, sweetness." He brushed his cheek against hers. "You gut me with one look. I don't want to be something you regret."

"But if we don't try, won't that be a bigger regret?"

Yes. It was. Simple as that.

How could he refuse a woman who had so much courage, it frightened him? Especially when the man standing behind her with a hopeful grin was just as fearless.

"Untie me," he said. "I need you in my arms."

"Does this mean you've seen the light, brother?"

"It means if I don't kiss this woman in the next second, I may just die."

Faith smiled. "You don't need your hands to kiss me, silly."

Maybe not, but he feared the worry in his chest wouldn't ease until he had her pressed against his every plain.

She didn't wait for Colby to take action as she stole Ben's breath with a kiss that only stoked his desperation for more. The moment he felt the pressure easing around his wrists, he shook off the rest of the rope and gathered her against his chest. Her taste, her essence stole inside him and filled the empty ache he had carried throughout the last week.

And Faith was just as hungry, wrapping her legs around his waist and holding on as if she'd drown without him.

When his lungs began to burn, he came up for air. "How do you do it? One moment, I feel as if you've taken me out at the knees, then the next, as if I can move mountains?"

She nuzzled her cheek against his. "I feel the same way about you. Helpless and empowered all at the same time. I love you, Ben."

He pulled back to cup the side of her beautiful face. Beneath his rough palm, her skin was like satin. "I love you too. So much so, it makes me dizzy."

Though her lips curled up ever so slightly, the light in her eyes turned up as bright as a shooting star, and was just as magical, as the blue depths sparkled. Then her gaze shifted to the man to their side who watched them with all of the happiness Ben felt inside reflected in his smile.

Faith held out her hand to Colby, who took it as he stepped closer. She took each of their hands and snuggled them against the cushion of her breasts.

"I can't believe we're really going to do this," Colby said with a shake of his head. "This is so cool."

"I wouldn't say cool, but it is pretty damn special," Ben said. "So what now, sweetness?"

"Well…" She licked her lips and glanced up at them from under her lashes in a way that sent a curl of heat through his blood. "I want you two to take me home, strip us naked, and hold me. Hold me for a really long time."

"I like the sound of that," Colby agreed.

"Trey may have something to say about calling it a day this early, but I think if I told him it was a family emergency, he'll understand." Ben stood, but didn't release his hold on Faith, keeping her locked in his embrace.

With his best friend by his side and the woman they loved in his arms, he swore he felt as if the sun and stars all aligned, and everything was right in the world.

He looked at Colby and smiled. "You heard our woman. Let's head home."

Epilogue

"I CAN'T BELIEVE I'm freaking out like this. Why am I freaking out?" Faith asked the completely rhetorical question as her fingers curled around the frame of the passenger-side mirror of Ben's truck.

Only a couple dozen feet away from them was the entrance to Stuart's Steakhouse, but the door might have been deep behind the gates of Mordor and just as heavily protected, given the level of anxiety wrapped around her like a thick length of chain.

"We don't have to do this," Ben reminded her and slid a comforting arm around her waist. "I'm fine with grabbing takeout from the teriyaki place."

"But I really want a steak." She bit her lip and shook her head. "This is crazy."

Beyond crazy. Certifiable. After a long day of hauling all of her things from her former apartment to the ranch, hunger hit her hard and she had begun to imagine the grazing cattle as flame grilled, seasoned with salt and pepper and surrounded by loaded baked potatoes. Since they were all too tired to do anything more than open a can of soup and throw it on the stove, a nice dinner out at Stuart's had sounded perfect. That was until they stepped out of the truck and every pair of eyes of those seated by the windows had turned to gawk at them through the panes of glass.

This was their first outing as a trio since deciding to give their unusual relationship an honest go a few weeks prior. With all of their time devoted to deciding where they were going to live, setting up house, and having lots of cozy sexy times, going out into town as a group hadn't even been on the radar.

But now there they were. The three of them. Together on what was essentially a date. And the actuality of walking into the restaurant to who knew what type of reaction had Faith's feet rooted to the asphalt.

Holy hell, was this stupid. She was hungry, Stuart's had food, and she was with the two people she loved most in the world. Two men who supported her one hundred percent. If she said, "Nope, we're outta here," she knew they'd say okay, settle her back in the truck, and take her anywhere she wanted to go.

It was that support that gave her the courage to loop her arms around theirs and take that first step forward. "I'm starving. Let's eat."

"You're the boss, sweetness," Ben said with a wink, and settled his hand over hers.

As they walked toward the door, she snuck a glance at both men and saw a matching set of pinched lips. Ben might talk a good game, but she sensed they were both just as nervous as she was, which meant she was going to do her damnedest to be brave.

Colby held open the door, and Ben's guiding hand was warm against her back. Just as she expected, the noise level in the restaurant died as they entered and waited by the hostess stand.

"Table for three?" the young girl asked with obvious interest in her eyes as her gaze bounced between them.

"Yes, ma'am," Ben answered.

She picked up three menus and gestured for them to follow. "Right this way, please."

With each table they passed, Faith's heart beat faster and faster as the diners followed their progression across the room. She nodded and smiled as Ben and Colby issued greetings to those they knew. In return, they received a bunch of wide-eyed stares and mumbled responses that made her want to laugh. What were these people expecting? That they'd forgo their manners because they were out together? Or drop to the floor and get down and dirty? It hadn't been the three of them who had forgotten what it meant to be polite and kind to each other.

As they approached their table, Ben went around to pull out the chair on the other side. "Sit here, Faith. There's a draft over there and I know how you tend to get chilly."

"Thank you," she said with a smile and sat down. Colby took her napkin, unfurled it with a snap, and draped it across her lap.

Behind her she heard a woman whisper to her companion, "Why didn't you pull out my chair?"

"Because we're married. You can seat yourself," he replied.

Faith couldn't stop herself and laughed as she reached for her men's hands and gave them a squeeze. They smiled back, and all of her nervousness melted away. Who cared what anyone else thought about them? She was the luckiest woman in the world to have such wonderful men to call her own.

After the hostess left them to look over the menu, Ben nodded in the direction of the door. "Faith, honey, your dad just walked in."

And *boom*. All of her anxiety returned tenfold as she whipped her head around to face the entrance.

Not a word had been spoken between them since she had walked out of her childhood home. Not a voicemail, text, nothing. And every day she felt the distance grow, widening to a point that she was afraid it would never to be breached.

Deep lines bracketed her father's mouth, and the shadows beneath his eyes indicated he hadn't had an easy time of it of late, which for some reason she found comforting. He appeared tired, worn, and much older than she realized. When he wore his big smile and bounced from job to job, it was easy to forget he had made the leap to over the fifty-year mark.

When she had left, it had been her every intention to wait for her father to make the first move, but seeing him staring off into space as he waited for the hostess to return, she couldn't keep in her seat. The possibility he might be even slightly miserable about their rift gave her hope that maybe he was ready to reconcile.

Before she realized she had moved, she was up and crossing the dining room toward the man who had been the first in her life to set the example of how a true gentleman was supposed to behave.

"Dad," she called out as she neared.

George's gaze shot in her direction. His eyes widened, and for a second he tensed as if to take a step closer, but he rocked back on his heels, looking away as he swallowed hard and his fingers tightened around the brim of his hat.

Was he really going to just stand there? Act as if she didn't exist? Did she need to start crying? Shout? Throw herself at his feet and beg him to see reason?

Of course, she was going to do none of those things. The choice she had made had been the right one for her, but she was willing to hold out an olive branch. Her father had to be the one to willingly take it.

"I miss you," she said. Quietly. Truthfully. Hoping the break in her voice and the tears stinging her eyes were enough to move her father just a bit.

He swallowed again, and his lips pinched together. He rotated the hat in his hands around and around as the blue of his eyes began to shimmer.

Just when she thought her lungs would burst from holding her breath for so long, he blinked and whispered, "I miss you, too."

The air whooshed past her lips and her posture wilted. A step forward. A tiny step, but still progression. Could she keep up the momentum?

She gestured behind her. "We just sat down. Would you like to join us?" She drew in another breath. "Please."

He glanced to where she indicated and the corner of his lips ticked. "Are you, are you with your...fellas?"

Another breath in and slowly out. "I am."

His gaze took another journey around the room, and he appeared as if he too were trying to slow his racing heart and stay in control. "I guess—I guess that would be fine. If they won't mind."

"No. They won't. It'll be perfect."

She held out her hand and for the longest time her father stared at her upturned palm. A near-hysterical giggle tickled her lips. It wasn't as if her fingers would grow claws and lash out at him, but it was almost as if he were afraid she would do just that.

When he finally reached out and clasped her hand, his grip was firm, almost desperate, and his smile was tight, as if he were afraid that if he spoke, the delicate truce between them might shatter.

She led them back to the table, and Ben and Colby stood as they approached.

"Take my seat, Mr. O'Leary," Colby said. "I know you'll want to sit by Faith."

Again, Ben held out her chair for her and soon they were all settled around the table with the waitress by their side asking if they were ready to order. Having eaten there many times, they were all quick to decide, and a minute later, the four of them were on their own.

Colby looked at her from across the table and motioned with his brows in a silent request if she wanted to start a conversation or should he. A glance to her left confirmed Ben was in the same boat, his lips twisting with uncertainty of who would be the first to break the ice.

Finally, it was her father who heaved a large sigh and sat back in his chair. "So. Which one of you is gonna make an honest woman of my Faith? Or am I gonna have to carve all of your initials into the cradle I'll be making for my future grandchildren?"

"Dad," she burst out laughing. That was her pops she remembered. "We haven't thought things through that far."

He waved his hand at her. "From what I've heard around town, you all are pretty smitten. It'll come soon. And just so you all understand, I'm expecting the first born to be named George." He narrowed his gaze on the men. "Boy or girl."

"Agreed," Colby said with a chuckle.

Ben nodded. "Will do, sir."

"Good." Her father settled his napkin onto his lap. "I don't know about you all, but I'm about ready to go back into that kitchen and snatch the first thing I can get my hands on. I'm starving."

Did the lights get a little brighter? The air a little fresher? It was as if the clouds parted after a storm and a ray of sunshine beamed down to engulf her in its warmth.

Above the din of the diners eating and conversing, she overheard a woman say behind her with jealousy coloring her tone,

"Can you believe her? There's Faith O'Leary and all of her men. Sitting there just as right as rain."

That's right. Her smile widened as she looked at the three most important men in her life. And she wouldn't have it any other way.

SPECIAL OFFER!

Thank you so much for purchasing *To Have Faith*. Did you enjoy Ben, Faith, and Colby's story? Are you ready for more?

As you know, word of mouth via reviews are the main way readers find new authors. To show my appreciation to my readers, post your review of *To Have Faith* on your favorite book website and email me with the link at Anna@AnnaAlexander .net. In return, I'll send you a PDF copy of the next book in the Sprawling A series, *Sweet Kisses*, for free! Yes. Free!

Again, thank you so much, and I look forward to hearing from you all soon.

ABOUT ANNA ALEXANDER

Award winning author Anna Alexander is the author of the Heroes of Saturn and the Sprawling A Ranch series. With Hugh Jackman's abs and Christopher Reeve's blue eyes as inspiration, she loves spinning tales of superheroes finding love. Anna also loves to give back and has served on the board for the Greater Seattle Romance Writers of America as chapter president and on the committee for the Emerald City Writers Conference.

Sign up to receive news about Anna's latest releases at
http://eepurl.com/Q0tsz

Anna welcomes comments from readers.

Website
http://annaalexander.net/

Facebook
www.facebook.com/pages/Anna-Alexander/282170065189471

Twitter
twitter.com/AnnaWriter

Newsletter
http://eepurl.com/Q0tsz

Also by Anna Alexander

Men of the Sprawling A Ranch Series

The Cowboy Way

The Marlboro Man

To Have Faith

Heroes of Saturn Series

Hero Revealed

Hero Unleashed

Hero Unmasked

Hero Rising

Cavern Series

A Night at The Cavern

Only at The Cavern

Elite Metal Series

Bound by Steele

Adamantium's Roar